"When was the last time you played on a swing?"

Amanda laughed in spite of herself. "I don't know. Longer ago than I care to think about."

Before she could protest, Ian pulled the swing backward, lifting her feet off the ground. Her stomach gave a sharp jump at the sudden motion, and she tightened her hands on the chains, letting out a little yelp.

Joyful anticipation rose within her as the swing arched backward once more and Ian's hands came firmly in contact with her back, sending her skyward. When the swing hit a point so high it bounced on the chains, Ian gripped her waist as she came back down.

"Whoa!" Ian slipped his arm around her, lost his balanced and pulled her off the swing. The two of them tumbled to the ground.

Amanda froze, realizing what an intimate position they were in. Ian smelled wonderful, looked even better and she didn't want to let go or ge

Dear Reader,

Did you ever wish you could outrun your troubles and start your life over in a brand-new place with brand-new people? Sort of a "do over" as Mitch and Phil said in the movie *City Slickers*. That is precisely what Amanda Kelly decides to do when a tragic accident turns her life upside down. She leaves Colorado, tucks herself away in her granny's log cabin in the woods of east Tennessee and loses herself in her work as an R.N. at the local nursing home. It doesn't take long for her to become attached to one of her residents—Zebadiah Bonner. At eighty-seven, Zeb's mind is still sharp, his sense of humor fully intact. But most of all, Zeb is a romantic at heart, and he's determined to see his grandson, Ian, find the right woman. Zeb's pretty sure that woman is Amanda. Now, if he can just get her and Ian to see things his way, he might have a chance to become a great-grandfather.

Ian is haunted by his own ghosts, and while he finds himself falling for Amanda, he's not so sure she's the woman for him. Still, he longs to get to know her better. Why is she hiding in the hills of Tennessee? And what will it take to draw her away from her self-imposed sentence of seclusion? Amanda is captivated by Ian's sexy Southern drawl and the fact that he's a man with a big heart. But his way of thinking has her running scared. Come with me, dear reader, on the journey that Ian and Amanda take. I hope you'll find it pleasant, and that you'll smile a little at the creative license I've taken in writing of the activities in the lives of the senior residents of Shade Tree Manor. Both the nursing home and the town of Boone's Crossing are purely figments of my imagination.

I love hearing from my readers. You can e-mail me at BrendaMott@hotmail.com. Please reference the book on the subject line. Thank you, and happy reading!

Brenda Mott

The New Baby
Brenda Mott

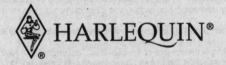

HARLEQUIN®

TORONTO • NEW YORK • LONDON
AMSTERDAM • PARIS • SYDNEY • HAMBURG
STOCKHOLM • ATHENS • TOKYO • MILAN • MADRID
PRAGUE • WARSAW • BUDAPEST • AUCKLAND

ISBN 0-373-71211-1

THE NEW BABY

Copyright © 2004 by Brenda Mott.

All rights reserved. Except for use in any review, the reproduction or utilization of this work in whole or in part in any form by any electronic, mechanical or other means, now known or hereafter invented, including xerography, photocopying and recording, or in any information storage or retrieval system, is forbidden without the written permission of the publisher, Harlequin Enterprises Limited, 225 Duncan Mill Road, Don Mills, Ontario, Canada M3B 3K9.

All characters in this book have no existence outside the imagination of the author and have no relation whatsoever to anyone bearing the same name or names. They are not even distantly inspired by any individual known or unknown to the author, and all incidents are pure invention.

This edition published by arrangement with Harlequin Books S.A.

® and TM are trademarks of the publisher. Trademarks indicated with ® are registered in the United States Patent and Trademark Office, the Canadian Trade Marks Office and in other countries.

www.eHarlequin.com

Printed in U.S.A.

This book is dedicated to my dad,
who is my brainstorming partner and
knight in shining armor. And to my mom, who calls me her
rodeo queen and believes I can do anything. I love you.

With special acknowledgment
to the health care professionals, law enforcement officials
and women who have been in Amanda's shoes
who all gave generously of their time to answer
my many questions. Any errors are my own.

Books by Brenda Mott

HARLEQUIN SUPERROMANCE
1037—SARAH'S LEGACY
1127—COWGIRL, SAY YES

Don't miss any of our special offers. Write to us at the
following address for information on our newest releases.

Harlequin Reader Service
U.S.: 3010 Walden Ave., P.O. Box 1325, Buffalo, NY 14269
Canadian: P.O. Box 609, Fort Erie, Ont. L2A 5X3

PROLOGUE

AMANDA KELLY AWOKE in excruciating pain. Overhead, bright lights invaded her vision even before her eyelids fluttered open, creating a dizzying pattern of flashing dots. She blinked and tried to focus as the sounds of the hospital emergency room flooded her ears.

"What's her BP?"

"BR 90 over 50, pulse 140…"

The rapid-fire words slipped through her mind like water. She tried to move, but her arms were too heavy. Weighted down. Her neck…her head…anchored in place. Panic seized her as she struggled with the oxygen mask fitted over her face. She wanted it off.

The voices assaulted her once more. Clearer this time.

"Start a large bore IV. We've got to get some blood right away."

"Eighteen gauge started—we're waiting on blood bank."

"We can't wait for type and cross, give her some O."

Beneath her, the gurney moved like a go-cart, making her stomach churn, increasing the dizziness. Strange faces were above her, examining her.

''She's pregnant? Shit! Get an obstetrician in here now!''

''Hang in there, Amanda. We're going to take good care of you.''

''Has anyone contacted her family?''

She tried to speak. Couldn't. Her mind was wrapped in cotton.

Her eyes, so heavy. She closed them.

Amanda awoke later, with no concept of how much time had passed. The hospital room seemed cold, sterile—too white, like the lights that had flooded her senses earlier. A monitor bleeped beside the bed. Clear plastic tubing snaked from her wrist to the IV drip above her.

Amanda swallowed as her sister's face came into focus. Tear-streaked, pinched with pain. Lips trembling.

''Amanda.'' Nikki reached for her hand.

''Nikki?'' Amanda's heart leaped then plunged as anxiety seized her. The memories came back in a rush.

A mountain road.

The young girl, standing on the gravel shoulder, her tire flat.

In her mind, Amanda pulled over to offer help. The use of her cell phone. She recalled reaching for the seat belt that cradled her rounded stomach, undoing the buckle. Then the squeal of tires and the gunshot-like sound of the SUV slamming into her Chevy Blazer from behind.

Dread now pushed all other thoughts from her mind as she reached instinctively to slide her hand over her stomach. Her throat closed and tears burned the back of her eyes. Her belly, once round, full with child, was now deflated like an empty balloon.

Her throat constricted as she choked on a sob. "No-o."

The devastation on her sister's face was enough to confirm what she already knew. She squeezed her eyes closed as Nikki gripped her hand. Willing it to not be true.

But the baby was gone.

The baby she'd carried as surrogate for her sister.

CHAPTER ONE

THE MOUNTAINS OF TENNESSEE weren't as tall and rugged as Colorado's Rocky Mountains, but they were equally beautiful in Amanda's eyes. Their beauty represented all she sought for her move—change, a fresh start, an entirely new world.

In the three months since the accident, she'd become someone she no longer knew. She needed to find herself. And the small town of Boone's Crossing in east Tennessee was the perfect place to do just that.

Granny Satterfield's log house had been in the family for three generations, though no one had lived there in a long while. It rested in a hollow, or "holler" as the locals pronounced it, six miles from town, surrounded by dogwood, hickory and oak trees. Knee-high grass and irises in vivid shades of lavender and deep violet choked the yard, front and back, tangled vines climbed over the lawn ornaments Granny had always treasured. Alongside the house ran a creek, close enough to the bedroom window for the relaxing sound of trickling water to lull Amanda to sleep each night. Even so, dark dreams plagued her. Drove her into nightmares so vivid, she'd wake up in a cold sweat, fear making her heart race in what quickly turned into a panic attack.

Sometimes she dreamt of the baby she'd never had

a chance to hold. And other times, she saw her sister, Nikki, and her brother-in-law, Cody, wandering aimlessly down a long, dark hallway, searching for something they'd never find. Once, she even dreamed of Caitlin Kramer, the young girl who'd had the flat tire that night. From what Amanda had read in the local paper, Caitlin had been a top-notch equestrian with high hopes of making the Olympic show jumping team. But the injuries she'd sustained had ground her dreams into dust.

Nikki, Cody, Caitlin…and how many others? How many people, herself included, had been affected by the chain reaction set off when one drunk had decided to climb behind the wheel? The thought made her crazy.

THE RINGING PHONE pulled Amanda from her half awake, half asleep state of mind. Throwing back the covers, she stood, then hurried to the kitchen and lifted the cordless receiver from its base. "Hello?"

"Hi." Nikki's voice came across the line sounding a little fuzzy, which probably meant she was using her free cell phone minutes. Not that she'd had any reason to worry about long-distance rates lately. Shamefully, Amanda had been avoiding her sister, ignoring her messages on the answering machine, still hurt by the harsh parting words they'd exchanged when she left Colorado.

"Nikki." The wall clock told her it was four-thirty in Deer Creek. "What are you doing up so early?"

"Trying to catch you at home."

She rubbed the ache that hammered between her eyes. "If you're calling to tell me what a horrible sister I am, I already know. I'm so sorry I haven't called you sooner.''

''Well, you ought to be. I was beginning to worry.'' Nikki's concerned tone bordered on big-sister bossiness, leaving Amanda torn between laughing out loud and bursting into tears.

Though she'd telephoned Nikki briefly upon arriving in Boone's Crossing, she'd only called to let her sister know she'd gotten there safely and that she'd found a position as Assistant Director of Nurses at the nursing home in town. Nikki would've worried about her, no matter what sort of hurtful words stood between them. Their conversation had been stiff and brief as the two of them sidestepped one another's feelings.

Now Amanda felt awful for not being in touch. She missed Nikki far more than she'd believed possible. ''I'm sorry,'' she repeated. The silence stretched between them while she scrambled for the right words. *How are you?* seemed shallow, since Nikki had not been fine in a long while. And, *What's going on with you?* fell short for the same reason.

''Are you okay?'' Nikki asked.

''I should be the one asking you that.'' Amanda took a deep breath and decided to dive right in. ''I'm fine, if you mean physically. But mentally…no. I can't stop thinking about you and Cody…'' She fought to keep her voice from trembling. ''…and little Anna.'' *Can't stop being afraid every time I drive on a highway.* This was exactly why she'd avoided her sister. She'd hoped time and distance would begin to put things right between them. Instead, it felt as though nothing had changed.

"We're getting by," Nikki said.

But from her tone, Amanda knew different. Cody had responded to the loss of the baby by channeling his hurt into anger, striking out at everyone around him. Herself, Nikki, even his best friend Mark, who ironically had once been Amanda's fiancé. But that was a whole other can of worms. One she didn't want to open ever again.

She and Nikki had stood by one another, awkward, confused, each hurting in her own way. Who was the real victim here? And how did they put the pieces of their lives back together?

Seeing a therapist hadn't helped much, not for any of them. And neither had any of Amanda's attempts to make things better. She'd wanted to repay Nikki and Cody for the expenses they'd incurred during the surrogacy procedure—expenses that had eaten up their entire savings, leaving Amanda with the feeling that she'd robbed them of their last chance for a child of their own. Nikki had responded to her offer with offense and sadness. *How could you think the money mattered?* Cody had become even more angry. *You can't buy back our daughter, Amanda!*

"Come on," Amanda prodded. "I know you better than that. Remember, you're talking to the kid who used to find your diary no matter where you tried to hide it."

Nikki's sob wrenched her heart, and Amanda cursed under her breath, wishing she hadn't pushed the issue. That she hadn't been such a coward and run over fifteen hundred miles to get away from the pain that chased her anyway.

"We're not getting along," Nikki said. "I thought

for a while the counseling was working, but now I feel like we're right back to square one.''

Amanda let her feet slide out from under her, sinking down to sit on the cool linoleum, her back pressed against the cupboard where Granny Satterfield had always kept a jar of lemon drops. They'd been Granny's cure for whatever ailed you. Amanda longed for the days when life was so simple. When she was five and Nikki was eight, and the two of them climbed Granny's trees and rode their pony double, talking about what they'd be when they were all grown up.

"Come home," Amanda said. The idea was spontaneous, flying from her lips before she could stop it.

"What?" Nikki gave a dry laugh. "You're the one who needs to come home, Amanda. We haven't lived in Tennessee since we were in elementary school."

Amanda squeezed her eyes shut. "I know," she whispered. "But it's so peaceful here, and the people are really friendly. I'm not going to lie to you and tell you that coming here has solved everything for me, because it hasn't." Again, frustrated anger rose inside of her. She'd been perfectly satisfied with her life before the accident—well on her way to having everything she'd dreamed of. She was certain Mark would change his mind about not wanting kids once he'd seen the baby, and that the two of them would marry as planned and have children of their own. "But I do think being here is going to help me heal." *Eventually.*

"It's not the same here without you," Nikki said. "There's no one to go to lunch with, or shopping." Her voice came out thick. She sniffed. "No one to talk to."

Amanda swallowed over the obstruction in her own throat. "You've got friends there who love you, hon."

"Yeah, but not like you. No one else has ever loved me so unconditionally."

Her heart clenched as Amanda struggled not to cry. She'd hated watching Nikki suffer through repeated miscarriages, the result of an incompetent cervix, and had been more than willing to carry Nikki and Cody's biological child when the subject of surrogacy had come up. Nikki's words echoed in her memory— *Now that's what I call sisterly love. Amanda, you are the most caring, giving, person.* They'd hugged each other and cried, but those tears had been happy ones.

The tears she now heard in her sister's voice were anything but, and she felt like hell for leaving Nikki behind. How could she explain that she'd had no choice? That she'd felt as if her last thread of sanity had been torn in two?

"I can't come back right now," Amanda said. *Maybe never.*

"But you loved your job," Nikki prodded. "I know it was tough to try and go back after—"

Amanda cut her off. "I have a job I like here." She knew Nikki meant well, but the accident had created a cesspool of pain, anger, fear and remorse Amanda could not wade out of, no matter how hard she tried. And she absolutely could not bring herself to face her job as an RN in the maternity ward at the Deer Creek County Hospital. Being around the babies, the expectant mothers, was more than she could bear.

"Not one you love with a passion," Nikki countered. "Is it really so rewarding, taking care of old people? Watching your patients die on a regular basis?''

Amanda fought her irritation, knowing her sister didn't mean for her words to be hurtful. "Yes, it is rewarding. In a different way.''

"Yeah, well, maybe so. But the way you took off reminds me too much of Mom.''

"I'm not chasing shadows, Nikki.''

"I don't want you to become like her—a nomad.''

For as long as Amanda could remember, their mother had moved them from town to town, state to state, holding down various jobs. Always thinking the next place would be exactly what she'd been looking for—whatever that was. "I don't plan to. Boone's Crossing was about the only place we ever had roots, thanks to Granny. Why don't you take a week or two and come down?" she asked again. "School will be out in a few days.'' How Nikki managed to cope with teaching a room full of kindergartners after the emotional upheaval she'd suffered, Amanda didn't know. She personally couldn't have done it.

"I don't know.'' Nikki sighed, and Amanda could picture her jabbing her fingers through her honey-brown bangs, then twisting them around her fingers. It was a habit Granny Satterfield had never been able to break her of.

"Maybe putting some distance between you and Cody would help,'' Amanda coaxed. She swallowed hard, forcing the words out. "He doesn't mean the things he said. It's just the cop in him.'' No matter if Cody had meant them or not, her brother-in-law's harsh words had cut deeply.

How could you be so stupid, Amanda? So irrespon-

*sible. Stopping on a dark highway like that, for
God's sake!*

And Nikki, torn between her husband and her sister.
*Cody, that's not fair. Amanda, maybe you'd better
leave for now.*

She'd left all right. Taken off for Boone's Crossing
without much of a second thought.

"I'm not so sure of that," Nikki said quietly, and
Amanda wasn't sure if she referred to the fact that
some distance would help or that Cody hadn't meant
what he said. "*Some* distance, huh?" she added dryly.
"You don't think fifteen hundred miles would be
overdoing it?"

Amanda chewed her bottom lip. "You're the only
one who can answer that, sis. But the invitation's
open. Any time." She forced a note of humor into her
voice. "You know where Granny kept the spare key.
It's still there."

Nikki made a sound that could've been a sob or a
laugh. "Not that she ever bothered to lock the door
anyway."

"You let me know," Amanda said. "Promise?"

"I'll think about it. And don't go so long without
answering my phone calls, do you hear me? I can still
kick your butt, you know."

"You can try," Amanda teased. "I love you, sis."

"Love you, too."

Amanda hung up, but made no move to rise from
the floor. Somehow, she found comfort sitting here,
looking at Granny's kitchen on a child's level. Her
earliest recollection of this room had been when she
was around four years old, though she'd stayed at
Granny's even as a baby. The last time she'd set foot

in here while Granny was alive, she'd been in middle school. But once Amanda had reached high school, other interests had taken the place of her summer trips to Tennessee, and then there had been college, nursing school:....

She felt ashamed that she'd only managed to visit Granny once as an adult, and that had been at the hospital. Though she'd seen her a few times prior to that, when Granny had come to Colorado to "stay a spell," it wasn't the same as coming here to the log house. To Boone's Crossing, where gospel music and old-fashioned manners were still an integral part of life, giving Amanda the feeling of being wrapped in a warm, handmade blanket.

Too bad Granny wasn't here now, to offer words of wisdom. Still, she recalled one thing her grandmother had always said. No matter the ups and downs a person faced day to day, life was far too short to waste one single, precious minute. Putting Granny Satterfield's house in livable order had kept Amanda's mind and hands busy, and her position at Shade Tree Manor filled her days and gave her purpose.

Yet, no matter what she'd said to Nikki, she did not feel whole. Instead, she seemed to follow a mechanical pattern of waking, going to work, coming home to an empty house and repeating the routine the next day. But she hadn't lied about the satisfaction taking care of senior-aged residents gave her. They were the bright spot in her day, and with that thought, Amanda pushed herself up off the floor, put the phone back in place and headed for the bathroom.

She showered, dressed, and twisted her hair into a serviceable knot on the back of her head. In a matter of minutes, she arrived at Shade Tree Manor. Starting her second week on the job, she felt safe and comfortable among both the staff and residents, and as she walked through the door, her co-workers greeted her. One of the LPNs, who she'd taken an immediate liking to on their first meeting, rolled her eyes as Amanda approached the nurses' station.

"Boy, am I glad to see you." Reed-thin and six feet tall with wavy black hair, Roberta Baker hid a tender heart beneath a faux display of gruffness. She worked the night shift and showed a devotion to the residents Amanda liked to see in her nurses.

Amanda tucked her purse under the counter, and turned to face her. "I take it you're ready to go home."

"Honey, let me tell you." Roberta blew out a puff of air that sent her bangs flying. "Albert's at it again, thinking he's Daniel Boone. I caught him in the hallway, not once, but twice—" she held up two fingers for emphasis "—wearing nothing but his skivvies and a raccoon skin hat. I think we've finally gotten him to go to sleep, but I'm telling you what's the truth—y'all better keep an eye on him."

Amanda smothered a chuckle. She loved the melodious way Roberta spoke, with her thick southern accent. She hailed from Kentucky, Boone's Crossing being just a short drive from both Kentucky and Virginia. While it was sad that Albert's mind had been seized by dementia, Amanda got a kick out of the way Roberta described his antics. Apparently, the seventy-five-year-old gentleman was good for some unique forms of entertainment, though Amanda had yet to witness one personally.

"We'll watch him," she promised as Roberta gathered her purse and prepared to leave.

A short while later, after making sure one of the LPNs was keeping close tabs on Albert, Amanda headed through the day room on her way to the employee lounge. She could do with a quick cup of coffee. The day room was all but empty. Two residents watched a morning news program, another was working at a jigsaw puzzle.

It was the resident sitting in a wheelchair at a card table in the far corner who caught her eye. At eighty-seven, Zebadiah Bonner had a sharper mind than a lot of people twenty years his junior. And he'd been a friend of Granny's, though Amanda hadn't remembered him. He'd come to Shade Tree Manor just a few days prior to Amanda's arrival, following three weeks in the county hospital with a broken hip. Now on the slow road to recovery, starting with a regime of physical therapy, Zeb was generally in high spirits. His injury had done nothing to quell his feistiness.

He was playing chess by himself. It was the unique set of game pieces that had initially captured Amanda's attention the first time she'd met Zeb. Handpainted, they were figures from the Wild West; cowboys on rearing horses, saloon girls, covered wagons. A gift from his grandson, the chess set was Zeb's pride and joy. But he refused to play with anyone. Instead, he moved both sets of chess pieces on his own, making the game go the way he wanted.

"Good morning, Zeb." Amanda stood beside the old man's wheelchair, her hand on his shoulder. "How are we doing today?"

He cocked his head and gave her a toothless smile.

Zebadiah also refused to wear his dentures most of the time. "I don't know about you," he said, "but I'm finer than frog's hair, now that a pretty blonde is in the room." He winked, then turned his attention back to the chessboard, focused on his next move.

"Still playing alone, I see." Amanda gave his shoulder an affectionate squeeze.

"Darned right. Ain't gonna play with nobody else, especially Charlie." He looked up at her once more, his blue eyes bright beneath the ball cap he always wore. "He cheats you know."

"So you've told me." She gave his shoulder a final pat. "Well, I'm off for a cup of coffee. See you later."

"You wouldn't happen to have a bottle of Southern Comfort tucked away in that employee's lounge, now would you, honey?" Zeb arched one brow, eyes twinkling. It was a game he'd played with her since day one. Craving in jest the drink he'd given up long ago.

Amanda played along. "Nice try." She pointed her finger in mock reprimand. "Behave yourself, now, or I'll tell Charlie you've invited him out here to be your opponent."

"Oh, don't you do that." Zeb shook his head, raising his hands in surrender. "I promise I'll be good."

Amanda laughed, then headed for the lounge. By the time she'd grabbed a cup of coffee and started back across the day room toward her office, Zeb was no longer alone.

Her chest gave a little hitch at the sight of the man seated near his elbow. She'd guess his age to be either side of thirty. His long legs, clad in faded jeans, stretched out in front of him, the toes of his work boots peeking out from beneath the table. Like Zeb, he wore a ball cap with a farm product insignia on the front. The blue denim of his shirt looked worn to the point of comfort, and his hair showed beneath the cap just enough for her to see it was a warm shade of brown. But it was his eyes that had her heart doing a funny little blip. Deep, chocolate-brown with thick, dark lashes, they studied her as though he were intent on reading her mind.

No one should look that sexy in a work shirt and John Deere cap.

Amanda forced herself to look away. "Hey, Zeb, did you find yourself a chess partner after all?" With a will of their own, her eyes darted back to focus on Zeb's companion.

A deep chuckle rumbled in the man's chest, and when he grinned, dimples creased his cheeks. "Not me. Papaw's too much competition for my liking." His southern drawl slid over her like melted butter. His statement was accompanied by a wink, not flirtatious, but one that left her feeling as though the two of them shared a secret.

"This here's my grandson Ian," Zeb said. "The one who gave me this." He indicated the chess set with a wave of his hand. "Ian, meet Miss Kelly, my favorite nurse. She's Olivia Satterfield's granddaughter. Y'all were too far apart in age to play together back then, or you might remember her."

Ian half rose from the chair to briefly grip her hand. His palm curled around hers, warm, callused. The hand of a working man. "Ian Bonner," he said. "Pleased to meet you, Miss Kelly. I'm sorry I *don't* remember you."

"Amanda." She tried not to stare. But his eyes…

good Lord, talk about tall, dark and handsome.
"Amanda Kelly. And it's nice to meet you, too, Ian."

"He brought contraband." Zeb spoke in a stage whisper, one hand shielding the side of his mouth. With the other, he hooked his thumb in the direction of a box of doughnuts on a corner of the card table.

"So I see." Amanda pursed her lips and squirmed as she noticed Ian's gaze lingering on her. "But since you're not on a restricted diet," she went on, "I suppose we can let a box of doughnuts slip by this once."

"If you're gonna eat 'em, you'll have to put your teeth in, Papaw," Ian ribbed. Then he flipped open the lid and held the box up in offering. "Would you like one?"

The tempting scent of chocolate and powdered sugar wafted over her, but she barely gave a second thought to the proffered treats. Ian Bonner was far more distracting than bakery goodies, which meant she needed to get back to work.

"No thanks. If I eat a doughnut, I'll end up wearing it on my hiney."

Zeb guffawed, then gave her an approving look. "Nothing wrong with your hiney," he teased. "I doubt a doughnut or two would hurt it."

Embarrassment filled her as Amanda realized what her comment had evoked. Ian shifted his eyes to her hips, then looked back up at her and hid a smile with obvious effort. The expression on his face made her blush even more. "You're a masher, Zeb," she said. "Admit it." She shook her finger at him once more. "And don't forget you need to take those doughnuts to your room. No food or drink allowed in the day room."

"Spoilsport," Zeb said. Then to Ian, "C'mon, son. I've got a bottle of Jack Daniel's hidden in my closet that'll go real nice with these doughnuts."

"I thought that was moonshine." Amanda's lips twitched.

"Nope. That I hid under my bed." Zeb began to put away his chess set, placing the pieces inside the hinged compartment of the rosewood-and-mahogany playing board.

"It's a shame to interrupt your game," Ian teased. But his smile was for Amanda, and she felt her face warm all over again.

"No problem." Zeb closed the board. "I was losin' anyway."

IAN HATED TO LEAVE Papaw. It didn't seem right, having him here in the nursing home when the old man had spent the better part of his life in the hills, hunting, fishing, running his small tobacco farm. But a fall from his mule had put him in the hospital with a broken hip, and Shade Tree Manor was the best place for him to recover.

"I've got to go now, Papaw," Ian said, rising from the chair next to his grandpa's bed. "I'll be by again soon." He tried to visit Papaw as often as possible, but for the last week or so, things at the welding shop had kept him busy enough that he'd only managed to come by twice.

Papaw waved a gnarled hand in farewell, already absorbed in watching his favorite game show. Ian smiled, noting a dab of chocolate stuck to the corner of his grandpa's bottom lip. He tossed a paper napkin in Papaw's lap, then crumpled up the bag that had held two cartons of chocolate milk and stuffed it into the trash can. "See ya." He gave the old man a quick hug, then walked out into the hall to the open reception area.

There she was again. The nurse that had left his stomach doing funny things that had nothing to do with too much chocolate. *Amanda Kelly.* He liked the way her name sounded inside his mind. She hadn't noticed him the last time he'd been here, but he'd sure noticed her. And when she'd walked up to Papaw's card table this morning, he'd had a hard time keeping his eyes where they belonged. He might not have recalled seeing her years ago, but her shapely curves, pretty green eyes and blond hair definitely had his attention now.

Today she wore a pale-green blouse with her white pantsuit uniform. The blouse brought out the color in her eyes, and Ian wondered how close she was in age to his own thirty-two years. From Papaw's earlier comment, he concluded she must be somewhat younger, certainly not older. She had her back to him at the moment, and though her jacket hid a good deal of her figure, he was sure Papaw was right. There was nothing wrong with the way she was shaped. Nothing at all.

She stood inside the nurses' station, bent over the computer with another woman who sat at the keyboard. They talked and Amanda nodded, then picked up a stack of papers and made her way into the reception area. She glanced up at him and smiled, then averted her gaze and walked on by. He started to say something, anything that would make her stop and talk to him, but before he got the chance, one of the sheets of paper she carried slid out of her grasp and fluttered to the tile floor.

He would've picked it up for her, had he reached her sooner. As it was, he was but a couple of steps shy of doing so when the glass doors of the front entrance swung open and a young man and woman hurried into the building. Ian recognized the guy as Danny Taylor, who worked at the auto parts store in town. Danny's wife, barely more than a girl, carried a baby in her arms, wrapped in a pink afghan. Laughing and talking, neither of them paid attention to where they walked, and as Amanda bent to retrieve the paper from the floor, Danny nearly bumped into her.

"Look out, Danny." His wife balanced the baby in the crook of one arm, and clutched his sleeve with her free hand, tugging him sideways.

"Excuse me, ma'am." Danny gave Amanda an apologetic smile as she straightened, paper in hand.

"No problem." Her lips curved in response, but her face went ghastly pale, and Ian wondered if she'd stood up too fast after bending over to reach what she'd dropped.

Her eyes locked on the baby, and the look of sadness and longing he saw there gave him a chill. Amanda's expression closely mirrored one he knew he'd worn more than once.

How many times had he searched the faces of babies so many years ago, looking for familiarity in their features? And later, in the scout troop he occasionally supervised. Most recently, wondering where his son might be today, he caught himself watching the faces of teenagers he saw around town. The pizza delivery boy, the kid who pumped gas at the BP station…

No matter how futile the effort, Ian couldn't stop looking.

Amanda wore that same haunted expression as she stared briefly at the baby, then turned away and quickly tried to hide what her face so clearly said she'd felt. She saw Ian watching her, and waved her fingers in a see-you-later gesture, then headed down the hall and ducked into an office, closing the door behind her. Ian mumbled a greeting to Danny and his child-wife as they passed by, his thoughts whirling. Outside, he climbed into his pickup and cranked the engine, leaning his elbow on the open window as he backed out of the parking space.

Had Amanda given up a baby when she was young? He shook off the thought, telling himself it was ridiculous to assume things about a woman he didn't even know. Her reaction could've been due to any number of things. Maybe she had a half-grown kid at home and longed for the days when the child had been an infant. His cousins often complained how quickly their little ones grew up. Or maybe she wanted a baby and didn't yet have one.

Or maybe he was nuts, thinking and worrying over a stranger and what her life might involve. But he couldn't help it. The sorrow he'd seen in Amanda had hit him right in the stomach. And the way she'd tried to hide her emotions before anyone noticed left him wanting to go back inside the building and ask her what was wrong. Tell her he'd sit and listen if she needed an ear to bend or a shoulder to lean on. Because he'd been there.

He'd felt pain as deep as that in Amanda's eyes on a cloudy day sixteen years ago.

A day when he'd signed his newborn son away to a pair of total strangers.

CHAPTER TWO

IAN PULLED OFF HIS welding gloves and laid them on the workbench next to the horse trailer he'd been working on for the better part of the afternoon. Bought at a bargain, it needed new feeder racks, tack compartment dividers and metal hooks for halters and ropes. The customer who owned it was a regular, always finding something or other for Ian to weld or repair.

Hot and tired, he set his hood on the welder and removed his welding sleeves. Despite the day's accomplishments, he still felt an empty hunger no amount of hard work ever seemed to erase. He hadn't been able to get Amanda Kelly off his mind these last few days, no matter how many customers came to his shop to chat and bring him things to do.

He thought back to the conversation he'd had with Papaw the other morning while they ate the doughnuts he'd brought.

"I couldn't help but notice the way you looked at Miss Kelly," Papaw said. His sharp blue eyes had studied Ian.

"Sure, and who wouldn't?" Ian couldn't help grinning. Papaw still had an eye for the ladies, and probably would until the day they laid him to rest. "She's a good-looking woman."

"Won't get no argument from me on that," Papaw said. "But I reckon I saw more to the way you watched her than that."

"What do you mean?"

The old man grunted. "You know what." He shook one finger at Ian. "You're a workaholic, boy. When was the last time you took a woman out?"

"On a date?"

"No, on a fishing trip." Zeb gave him a playful punch in the arm, his aim as good as it ever was. "'Course I mean on a date."

Ian shrugged. "I don't know." He pondered the question. "Last Valentine's Day, when Billy Ray's sister Sheryl was in town?"

"That's just what I'm saying." Papaw shook his head in a gesture of hopelessness. "You need to get out more."

"I can't ask Amanda out," Ian protested. "She doesn't even know me."

"Can't never did anything. Go on and ask her. I'd do it myself, if I were ten years younger."

Ian laughed and Papaw gave him a sly grin, made wider than normal by his dentures. Then he grew serious. "How're you ever gonna make a family of your own if you're alone all the time?"

How indeed? The thought ate at him now as Ian closed the shop door, locked it and headed for the barn. Banjo, Papaw's buckskin mule, brayed at him from the connected paddock, wanting a treat. Ian gave him some sweet feed, then walked up the hill to the house he'd called home for the better part of his life. The worn porch steps creaked as he climbed them, and Cuddles, the Rottweiler he'd had since she was a pup, rose from her place near the steps and wagged her stubby tail. He patted her and fed her from a sack of dog food he kept on the enclosed back porch before going inside the house.

The kitchen was way too quiet without Papaw here. He'd lived with Ian ever since Mamaw passed away a year ago. But then he broke his hip, and all that had ended. At least for a while. From the fridge, Ian grabbed a can of beer, popping the top as he walked into the living room. Maybe his grandpa was right. He really didn't have much of a social life, and couldn't remember the last time a woman who wasn't a relative had entered this house.

The men on the Bonner side of the family seemed to outlive their women more often than not. His mom had succumbed to cancer long ago, and his dad now lived in Virginia, close to three of his own sisters and their grandkids. With Ian an only child, Matthew Bonner had probably given up on ever having grandchildren of his own. Ian often wondered if his dad regretted having taken part in convincing him to give up his son all those years ago.

Sinking into his favorite chair, he propped his booted feet on the ottoman and looked around, trying to view the room the way a stranger might see it. What would Amanda Kelly think of this place if he were to invite her over? The living room was clean but cluttered, the windows bare of curtains. With neighbors no closer than a mile away, and the house sitting up on a hill some distance off the road, there was no need to worry anyone would look in. Like most other homes outside Boone's Crossing, the place was surrounded by woods, with a grove of trees in the yard, the pasture spreading out beyond.

Ian closed his eyes and pictured walking up the front steps with Amanda, inviting her in for a cold drink. Probably sweet tea or Coke. She didn't look like a woman who drank beer. Maybe wine. Not his thing. But then what did he know? As Papaw had pointed out, he didn't make much time for dating, and overall, women were a mystery to him.

Still, he'd managed to do his share of tomcatting in his younger days, which had gotten him in trouble to begin with. His high school sweetheart, Jolene Bradford, had taken his heart, his class ring and his virginity, all in short order. Getting Jolene pregnant during their sophomore year hadn't been the smartest thing he'd ever done. Giving up their baby boy had seemed a step in the right direction toward growing up and making responsible decisions. Or at least, it did at the time.

But as the years went by, the regret of not knowing what had become of his own child had worn on him. He'd lost himself in work, starting with after-school jobs and helping Papaw at the welding shop and with putting up the tobacco they used to raise. One day seemed to fold into the next, one year into another, until he now owned the shop and Papaw was in the nursing home.

What did he really have to show for his life? He'd always thought he'd have a family by now. A couple of kids and a wife to come home to…even if coming home only required walking up the hill. Though he had searched time and again, he'd never found his son, and the pain of that stayed with him.

Shaking off the melancholy thoughts, Ian let his mind wander back to Amanda. Maybe he ought to come right out and ask her on a date. He could take her to supper or something. Dancing maybe. *Nope.* He shook his head. He hadn't danced in so long, he'd likely make a fool of himself by stepping on her toes. It would have to be supper. Someplace nice but not too romantic. *Dinner.* That's what she'd probably call it. Just thinking about her western accent made him smile. It was hard to understand at times, but he liked the sound of it—the way the words rolled off her tongue. Though they barely knew each other, he hoped she'd accept his invitation, if for no other reason than the fact that their grandparents had been friends.

Would a woman like Amanda find a lifestyle like his worthy? She was a nurse, probably used to fancy things and men who worked white-collar jobs.

"You're getting way ahead of yourself, Bonner," he muttered out loud. But there wasn't any harm in getting to know her. He could hear Papaw's voice inside his head, as sure as if he were sitting right there beside him.

Can't never did anything, son.

Papaw was right.

At the door, Cuddles scratched and whined to come in. Rising from his chair, Ian abandoned his half-empty beer to open the screen for her. "Some watchdog you are," he said, as she bounded inside and rolled over on the braided throw rug. Her paws in the air, she begged for a tummy rub. Ian laughed and scratched her belly. "Big baby."

Maybe Amanda liked dogs.

Maybe he'd find out, the next time he visited Papaw.

TO IAN'S DISAPPOINTMENT, Amanda wasn't working at Shade Tree Manor when he stopped by there Wednesday morning. But Papaw told him she lived at her granny's cabin, and that Saturday was also her day off. He'd therefore planned to drive out to the old Satterfield place as soon as he finished a few odd jobs at the shop. Instead, he found himself in charge of the group of kids he'd volunteered to look after on a once-a-month basis. The Cumberland Cubs, a scout troop of a dozen boys under the age of twelve.

He shouldn't have answered the phone.

Oh, he liked taking the boys camping well enough. But last Saturday had been his weekend with the Cubs, and he hadn't planned to act as scout leader this weekend, too. Yet he never seemed to be able to say no to someone in need.

He now stood, dressed in jeans, a long-sleeved khaki shirt and hiking boots, next to a commercial-sized van that belonged to the head scoutmaster—his best friend, Neil.

"I sure appreciate this, buddy," Neil said after giving the troop one more round of last minute instructions. "Having Peggy and the girls down with this cruddy spring flu, and my other two scout leaders sick, I didn't know who else to call. And I hated to disappoint the boys. They love camping out at 'Livia Satterfield's old place."

"The Satterfield place?" Ian's ears perked. "That's where you were planning to take them?" They rotated locations on their monthly overnight outings.

Neil looked at him as if he'd grown an extra eye. "Yeah. You know we generally go there at least every other month." Olivia Satterfield had loved the woods almost as much as she loved kids, and she'd let the Cubs camp on the back of her ten acres anytime they wanted. But Ian had assumed that was all in the past, now that Amanda lived there.

"I know, but—is the new owner okay with it?"

Neil shrugged. "Olivia left the place to her daughter, Bridget. And when I talked to her after the funeral, Bridget said 'Livia wrote it up in the will that the Cubs were to keep camping there for as long as the place remains in the family. I thought I'd told you that?"

"If you did, I didn't hear you," Ian said, trying not to smile. *Perfect.* "I guess we'll find out if her granddaughter feels the same way."

"Won't matter. Like I said, it's in the will." Neil cupped his hands around his mouth. "Okay, troop, let's load up! Pronto!"

The boys piled into the minivan, and Ian climbed behind the wheel, feeling like a kid himself. A kid with a crush.

"Hey, Ian." One of the youngsters leaned over the seat and tapped him on the shoulder. "Thanks for taking us camping."

His conscience gave a mental blush. He shouldn't be happy they were headed for Amanda's place just so he could see her. He loved kids, and the Cubs came first. The purpose of this camping trip was to be sure they had a good time.

"You're more than welcome, Jeffrey." Ian wondered how it would feel to drive a van full of children of his own. Maybe he'd find out someday. If he could ever find someone to be their mother.

He waited while the boys settled in place with all doors shut. "Is everybody buckled up?"

"Yeah!" they chorused.

"And is everyone ready to have some fun?"

"Yeah!" Their voices were louder this time, full of enthusiasm.

Ian's lips twitched. He was already having a good time. "And is everybody ready to kiss some girls?"

"No!"

"Yuck."

"I'm not going if we have to do that."

He let out a hearty laugh. "Okay, no girl kissin'. How about catching frogs?"

"Yeah!"

A grin plastered on his face, Ian waved at Neil and drove away.

AMANDA SANK INTO the steaming tub of bubbles. From the headphones of her portable CD player, the sounds of nature helped her relax, as did the scent of the aromatherapy candles lining the vanity. Closing her eyes, she dozed and awoke a short time later. The headphones were silent but she could hear the faint chatter of birds. Laughing at herself, Amanda sat up straight in the tub. She had all the nature sounds she wanted right outside her window.

Discarding the headphones, she leaned forward and turned on the hot water to bring the tub's temperature up to a comfort level once more. Then she rose and flipped open the latch on the window. Hands slick, she pushed upward on the sliding pane of frosted glass and very nearly lost her balance. Creaky with lack of use, the window stuck a moment, then slid abruptly to a wide-open position. Through the screen, she heard the running creek, and the birds, louder now, singing in the trees…

And the voices of children.

Kids? Out here? Frowning, Amanda turned off the water and peered over the edge of the windowsill. She didn't see anyone. Her nearest neighbors lived some distance down the road in either direction. So where were the sounds coming from? Head cocked, she strained to listen. For a moment, she heard nothing and wondered if she'd imagined the whole thing. Then a burst of laughter rang through the air, followed by a shout and a man's voice.

Hastily, Amanda closed the curtains and climbed from the tub. She dried off haphazardly with an oversized bath towel, doused the candles, then wrapped herself in a terry-cloth robe. Who on earth was out in the woods behind her house? Belting the robe at her waist, Amanda stepped into the kitchen and let out a startled gasp.

A boy, who looked about nine or ten, stood in front of her sink. Chubby with sandy hair and freckles, he stared at her, eyes wide, candy-stained mouth open. A plastic cup of water slipped out of his grasp, landing on the floor to pool across the linoleum.

"Who are you?" Amanda clutched the bathrobe against her damp skin. "And what are you doing in my kitchen?"

The poor kid clamped his mouth shut, then tried to form a sentence. "I—I…" He looked down at the water spreading around his feet, then back up at her. "You're not Miss Rachel."

He referred to the woman who'd been Granny Satterfield's dear friend, and who had kept an eye on Granny's house for the past two years. Sixty-five, Rachel Fultz lived down the road on the way to town.

"No. I'm Amanda Kelly. This used to be my Granny Satterfield's place."

"I'm Troy Stoakes," he said. He bent over to pick up the plastic cup and Amanda belatedly realized he was wearing some sort of scout uniform.

Boy Scouts were supposed to be honorable, dependable, good kids, so surely this one meant no harm in entering her house. But the fact that he'd walked in without knocking was a bit unusual, even for small-town etiquette.

"If you've got a towel, I'll clean this up."

"It's okay," Amanda said, still confused. She reached for the roll of paper towels hanging near the stove. "Troy, why are you in my kitchen?"

Now it was the boy's turn to look confused. "I know Miss 'Livia died, but I thought Miss Rachel was taking care of the house. Miss 'Livia always let us come in for a drink or a cookie, and Miss Rachel said it was still okay to come in here for water." He took the wad of paper towels from her and proceeded to clean up the spill. "I can't drink from the creek outside. My ma says it'll give me jagardia."

Amanda pursed her lips in a smile. "You mean Giardia." She knelt beside him and helped mop up the water.

Troy paused in his task long enough to point at the

cupboard beside the sink. "Miss Rachel keeps cups for us in there."

"I see." She hadn't thought much about the plastic cups, since quite a few of Granny's things still remained in the house and in the toolshed outside. And while the utilities had been turned off until Amanda's arrival, the old hand pump at the sink worked without electricity, fed by a natural underground spring. "But I still don't understand what you're doing here at my granny's place." She frowned, remembering the sound of laughter she'd heard through the bathroom window. She gave a nod in the direction of the woods. "Are there Boy Scouts out there?"

Troy stood, paper towels dripping in his hand, and Amanda pulled the trash can out from under the sink for him. "Uh-huh. We're sleeping in the woods behind your house." He tossed the soggy towels into the container. "We camp out several times a year, and this is one of our favorite spots." He smiled at her, revealing a row of teeth darkened by what must be black licorice. "We're the Cumberland Cubs."

"Oh." Amanda bit her bottom lip. This boy was sweet. "Where's your scoutmaster?"

"He's out back. His name's Aain." Carefully, Troy refilled the plastic cup, took a big gulp of water, then set the cup in the sink. "Can I go now?"

Amanda shrugged. "Sure."

"Bye." He pushed open the screen, then paused and looked back at her. "I'm sorry I made you yell, ma'am."

"That's all right."

Amanda put the trash can back under the sink as the kid hurried away, letting the screen door slam behind him. She walked over and shut the door as well, making a mental note to lock it from now on. In-grained habits faded far too easily out here in Granny's beloved woods, where the only thief Amanda could remember had been a raccoon after the eggs in Granny's henhouse. She flipped the latch in place and went to her room to get dressed, deciding she'd better have a talk with Troy's scout leader.

Aain? What sort of name was that?

She hung her bathrobe on a hook behind the door, and slid into her underwear and jeans as light dawned inside her mind. Troy had a thick, southern accent. He hadn't said "Aain." He'd said *Ian.* And he'd also said they'd come to camp here on Granny's property.

Her property now, since her mother had no interest in the place. Did he mean Ian Bonner?

Fully dressed, Amanda slipped on her tennis shoes and hurried out the back door, picturing Ian, with his dark brown eyes and sexy drawl. Sleeping in the woods, practically in her backyard. She told herself it might not be him. Maybe it was another Ian. But who-ever it was, he'd brought kids. And that made her a bit uncomfortable.

How dare he do so without asking? While she'd be more than happy to honor Granny's wishes, she still felt the man owed her the courtesy of making sure she didn't mind before simply descending on her with an entire troop of scouts.

Knowing she should be wearing boots in case there were snakes, Amanda strode across the backyard to-ward the woods, her footsteps quiet in the tennis shoes. Quiet enough that she managed to come close to the man who sat on a fallen log in a clearing just behind the house without him noticing her. It was Bonner. He was watching the boys pitching tents and unpacking supplies.

"You're doing fine, men." He chuckled. "I'd help you, but you know the rules. So tell me—what does a Cumberland Cub do before turning to his leader for help?"

"Ask a team member!" More than one boy shouted.

"And try, and try again," another added.

"That's right." Ian raised one fist in the air in a gesture of triumph and encouragement. "So keep at it."

But the look on his face told her how much he wanted to dive in and help the kids, in spite of what he'd said. At last, he noticed her, and Amanda's heartbeat rose, then dived as he turned to face her. She did her best to ignore what she felt, watching Ian. She had no business being attracted to him or any other man, seeing as how she wasn't ready to begin a relationship with anyone right now. She wasn't even sure she could ever take a step past casual friendship again. Dating led to intimacy and that led to heartbreak. She'd had enough of that being engaged to Mark.

The accident had robbed her of everything, had put her thoughts into a whole new perspective. She'd once loved working in the maternity ward, taking care of countless newborns. Precious little things, swaddled in teddy-bear blankets. Wearing teensy-weensy booties, their skin so soft and sweet-smelling. She'd dreamed of one day having a child of her own.

Then Anna had been killed, and now Amanda no

longer wanted what she'd once held dear. A husband…a family.

It would be a cold day in hell before she ever allowed herself to be pregnant again.

CHAPTER THREE

TELLING HERSELF SHE WAS being ridiculous, thinking way too far ahead, Amanda walked calmly toward Ian. After all, she didn't even know him. And while she was pretty sure he'd looked at her the other day as though he liked what he saw, that hardly meant he was going to jump up and propose. She knew it was her past experience, coupled with the accident, that made her overly cautious. She and Mark hadn't made certain things clear right up-front when they'd begun dating. Things like the fact that she had wanted children and he didn't. They'd argued heatedly over the matter. Her decision to act as surrogate for Nikki had been the final blow to their already shaky relationship.

Mark had been long gone from her life when the accident happened. But the entire set of circumstances had driven the point firmly home for Amanda. Never again would she go into a relationship with blinders on.

"Hi, there." Amanda halted.

Ian rose from the fallen log. "Hey, Amanda. It's nice to see you again."

She pursed her lips and gave the group of scouts a pointed glance. "I didn't know I had company." She knew it wasn't realistic to think she could hide from children and babies forever, and as Ian smiled at her, her initial irritation slowly began to melt.

"We knocked," he said, as though that explained everything and excused his act of trespassing. "I didn't think you were home."

She started to explain that she'd been wearing headphones and hadn't heard him, then decided she'd rather not have Ian Bonner picturing her in the bathtub. "You must have a different set of rules here in the South." Amanda folded her arms and gestured with one hand. "Out west trespassing is against the law, and finding the owner not at home doesn't give free license to come on in. We call that burglary." She fought a losing battle with her annoyance. Who could stay mad at a guy with such a soft, sexy voice?

Ian saw right through her. His lips curved. "You're absolutely right. But here in Tennessee, if it's among neighbors, we call it borrowin'." He grimaced. "I didn't know Troy went inside your house until after the fact. We've got our canteens and some bottled water, but he always gets a kick out of using the kitchen pump."

Amanda softened. "Well, maybe I'm giving you a hard time." She nodded toward the group of kids. "Troy told me Granny let the boys camp here frequently."

"She did." Ian nodded, but he still looked properly chastised. "And I was given the impression your mom okayed it as well. Something about it being in your granny's will? But with you staying here, I guess it was mighty rude of me to assume everything was settled. I apologize."

Leave it to her mother to fail to give her the finer

details of Granny's will. Bridget had barely hung around long enough to attend the funeral before heading out once more to her latest "hometown."

"It's all right," Amanda said.

"I do have a defense, however, even if it is a weak one." Ian's dark eyes lightened with amusement.

"Oh?"

"I'm only a part-time scoutmaster. The regular guy had to stay home at the last minute with his sick wife and kids. Spring flu's going around."

"Then you better get your flu shot," Amanda said in her best nurse's voice.

He laughed, and the sound relaxed her. He was easy to talk to, like someone you'd known a long time. She supposed there was nothing wrong with making friends in Boone's Crossing.

"You don't mind if we stay then?"

"No." She told herself she could handle having the boys around, but probably not often and not for long. "But I'd appreciate more notice next time."

He studied her. "Really, if it's a problem, we can make this our last outing here."

Suddenly, Amanda felt like the bad guy. "It's just that I came out here—to Granny's place—for some privacy and a little quiet time."

"A vacation?"

She shook her head. "You might say I'm working through some personal issues."

"Oh." His tone told her he was curious, but not nosy enough to push. "So, I take it this is the first time you've been here in quite a while?"

"That's right." Regret filled her all over again that she hadn't come to Tennessee to spend time with

Granny more often. Why was it that only hindsight was twenty-twenty? "I was just a kid the last time I stayed in Boone's Crossing. Well, other than when I came here for Granny's funeral."

"Ah—then you probably have no idea what you've been missing out on." Ian sat down once more on the fallen log, scooting over to make room for her.

"What's that?" Amanda asked as she sat beside him.

"BJ's Barbecue. Established in 1995. It's the best this side of the Mississippi." He shifted his weight in such a way that his shirtsleeve touched her bare skin.

Amanda resisted the urge to move—whether closer to him or farther away, she wasn't sure. "Really? I guess I'll have to try it sometime." As soon as the words were out of her mouth, she realized how her comment sounded. Like she was fishing for him to ask her out. On the other hand, he could've been doing the same, bringing up the subject in the first place. Feeling jittery once more, Amanda subtly shifted farther away from him. "Although I'm not sure when I might have time," she amended.

"Busy schedule?" he asked. His dark eyes held a look of disappointment.

Or was that only wishful thinking on her part? Like it or not, she was deeply attracted to Ian. "Most of the time, yes. I rarely take two days off in a row. But I don't mind. My residents mean a lot to me."

"That's nice," Ian said, his tone softening. "I know Papaw sure thinks the world of you."

Amanda smiled. "Ditto. I know it's not right to play favorites, but Zeb holds a special place in my heart. I feel like I've known him a long time, even though I don't remember him as a child."

"He has that effect on just about everyone he meets." Ian laced his fingers together and let his hands dangle between his knees, elbows propped on his thighs. "I sure miss having him at the house."

"I didn't realize he'd lived with you." Amanda tried to hide the surprise in her voice. Most people would go to whatever lengths it took to avoid taking care of an elderly relative.

Ian nodded. "Yep. Right up until his mule bucked him off."

"Is that really how he broke his hip? I thought he was teasing me."

"No, he wasn't kidding." He looked straight at her, and she found it hard to pull her gaze away from his eyes. "Papaw's always fancied himself a cowboy. I've tried to tell him Roy Rogers never rode a mule."

She couldn't help but laugh. "No, but Festus did. On *Gunsmoke*."

"Yeah, that's right, he did." Ian watched the scouts, checking their progress of making camp. He was silent for a full minute.

Amanda knew she ought to leave. She started to rise, words of farewell on the tip of her tongue.

"Would you like to go to BJ's with me?" Ian cocked his head, studying her intently.

She froze in place and swallowed. "I don't know, Ian. I—"

"Hey!" One of the boys, a redhead wearing round, wire-rimmed glasses, shouted as he raced toward them. Troy Stoakes ran with him.

They halted near the log, exchanged gleeful looks,

then stared at Ian. "I thought you said there'd be no girl kissing on this camping trip." Troy's freckled nose wrinkled as he pursed his lips and grinned. "But you're sitting mighty close to her." He spoke in a singsong voice, waggling his forefinger at Amanda.

His buddy snickered. "Guess she's more fun than catchin' frogs." His face flushed as bright as his hair. He glanced at Amanda, then raced away, howling with laughter.

"And she looks pretty good in a pink bathrobe," Troy said, backing out of reach as Ian made a playful grab for him. He spun on his heel and took off after his friend, hooting and whooping.

"I'll get you both," Ian called, cupping his hands to his mouth. "Just wait until you're asleep tonight." He chuckled, lowering his hands to his knees. "God, I love kids."

Speechless, Amanda could only look at him.

He grinned, his dimples doing damage to her heart. "O-kay," he said, drawing the word out in two syllables. "I guess those boys are better at mind reading than they are at reading trail signs."

Amanda's face heated. "And here I thought only girls were that silly."

Ian rose from the log, offering her a hand. She took it, and let him help her to her feet. Again, she noted the work-rough texture of his palm and longing and regret filled her. Black memories swirled through her mind, threatening to darken the warm, sunny day and blot out the happy voices of the children in the nearby clearing. The familiar rush of adrenaline-driven anxiety filled her. She took a deep breath, focusing on a relaxation technique her therapist had taught her, and managed to shake off her panic.

"Thanks," she said, then realized she'd never finished answering Ian's question. "About BJ's—please don't take it personally, but I'm going to have to say no."

He held up one hand. "Hey, don't worry about it." He studied her a moment, then gave her a good-natured smile that made it all the harder to walk away.

Awkward silence stretched between them. "I'm home for the rest of the day," Amanda said, gesturing toward the house. "If anyone gets a skinned knee or a bug bite or whatever, feel free to holler."

"A nurse on call right next to our campsite." Ian nodded, and his dimples appeared once more. "Beats the heck out of my first-aid kit."

"See you." Amanda lifted her hand in a wave, taking a step backward.

"Sure." He waved, too. "Enjoy your day off. I'll try to keep these hooligans at a dull roar."

She watched him walk away. He looked back only once, and it was almost enough to make her wish she'd said yes to his invitation.

Why? she asked herself as she headed toward the log house. *Why would you want to open yourself up to more pain?*

She had no answer. But then, that was why she'd moved to Tennessee. To sort things out slowly and give herself space until she finally discovered a long-term plan for living the rest of her life. At the moment, she had no idea where she was headed. The only thing she knew for sure was that right now there was no room in her journey for good-looking men with dark eyes, or silly fantasies about what might have been.

Maybe there never would be.

IAN COULDN'T BELIEVE he'd actually worked up the nerve to ask Amanda out. Sure, it was only for a barbecue sandwich, but he'd blown it at that. He was far more out of practice at this dating business than he'd thought possible. Papaw would give him hell if he found out.

Ian lay in his sleeping bag, hands laced behind his neck as he looked up at the stars. Nearby, he'd pitched a tent in case of rain. Actually, he'd probably crawl inside before too long and zip himself in to avoid the insects and the possibility of snakes paying him a visit. But he liked watching the night sky and the lightning bugs. Around him, the boys were settled in their own tents, mostly quiet. A few smothered chortles came here and there, but as long as they kept it down, he'd let them have their fun. After all, that's what being a kid and camping out with your buddies was all about.

Fun seemed to be a word that had slid further and further from his vocabulary as of late. Ian peered through the trees at the log cabin. He could see it pretty clearly in the light of the full moon. All of the windows appeared dark. But of course, he couldn't see those on the other side. He'd only been in the house a couple of times when Olivia Satterfield was alive, and he didn't really remember the layout. But it stood to reason the bedrooms were likely toward the back, which meant either Amanda was asleep, or she was in the living room in the front area of the house, out of his line of sight.

They'd parted rather awkwardly tonight. He hoped he hadn't made her too uncomfortable by asking her out on a date. Maybe she had a boyfriend back in Colorado, or even a husband for all he knew. She'd said she had come here to work through some personal issues. People separated all the time, trying to get their heads on straight and make things right. He hoped that wasn't the case with Amanda, because he wasn't ready to give up on her yet.

He liked her. It was easy to see she was warm and had a sense of humor, and she seemed to like kids, even though something was a little off in that area. No matter what she'd said, he could tell she wasn't overly thrilled with having the Cubs camped out here in her woods. She'd simply been too nice to say no. He'd overlooked the fact because he didn't have the heart to disappoint his troop. But he wondered what lay behind her hesitancy. He was pretty sure it wasn't just a matter of privacy.

With a sigh, Ian slid from his sleeping bag, still clad in his jeans and shirt. He never completely undressed when camping with the kids. There was always the chance of an emergency, and he didn't like the thought of being caught in his boxers, barefooted. He'd left his socks on, and now turned his hiking boots upside down and tapped them against a rock to make sure no crawly creatures had decided to take up residence inside them. Feeling the need for a short walk, he slipped the boots on and laced them up, then headed down the path toward Amanda's.

For whatever reason, he felt compelled to take another look at the house where she lay sleeping. To think about her awhile longer, and see if he couldn't come up with a way to get to know her better, other than hanging around Papaw at the nursing home.

The sound of crying reached him as he neared the yard. Pausing, he listened and heard nothing. His ears must be playing tricks on him. But there it was again. Quiet sobs, coming from the creek bank. Ian hesitated, wondering if he should leave well enough alone, turn around, head back to camp, and mind his own business. But he couldn't. It always pained him to hear a woman cry.

Though he could hear Amanda, he could not see her. The clouds had blown across the sky, covering the moon. But as he took a step, they shifted once more on the high breeze, and he spotted her sitting on the bank of the stream. Her back was to him, and her blond hair cascaded nearly to her waist. It was the first time he'd seen it down, rather than in a bun or ponytail. Legs pulled up to her chin, arms wrapped around her knees, Amanda had her head down, crying as if her heart had been shattered.

Torn once more between leaving her to her privacy and the urge to soothe her, Ian walked quietly up behind her. "It can't be all that bad."

Amanda swung around and let out a yelp. She clambered to her feet, which were bare, and swiped at her cheeks with both hands. "My God, you scared the life out of me." Emotions in control, she stood staring at him, her expression caught between anger and embarrassment. She reminded him of an overgrown kid, in the faded jeans and pale yellow blouse she'd had on earlier, her feet and arms creamy white as though they hadn't seen much sun lately.

"Sorry," Ian said. "I didn't mean to scare you."

"What are you doing?" A look of concern laced with suspicion flashed in her eyes. Her gaze darted toward the house as though measuring the distance.

Surely she didn't think he was going to pounce on her like some sex-starved maniac?

The sex-starved maniac that he actually was. He held his hands up in surrender. "Don't shoot, I'm unarmed."

She only looked at him. "I thought we'd said our goodbyes earlier." She shifted her weight from one foot to the other, her expression changing. "It's not one of the boys, is it? Is someone sick or hurt?"

"No." Ian shook his head. "Everyone's fine. I couldn't sleep, and I heard you crying. I thought I'd make sure you were all right." He studied her. "You are, aren't you?"

She sniffed and tucked her hair behind one ear. "I'm okay." She shrugged. "Just a little homesick, I guess." But her eyes betrayed her, telling him there was more to it than that. She looked at him like she wanted—needed—someone to talk to.

He nodded. "Yeah, Papaw said you'd come out here all the way from Colorado."

"I did."

"Mind if I ask what brought you here?"

"My car," she said dryly, then winced. "Sorry." Her smile was wooden. "Just a little humor to lighten the moment. I apologize for treating you like an intruder."

"No problem." He lifted a shoulder. "I guess in a way, I have been, what with me and the boys barging in on you."

"Well, I suppose that hardly makes you Jack the Ripper."

"Not even close." He smiled, wishing he could get her to relax and laugh again. He'd liked the way she joked around with Papaw, and he wondered if she realized how different she was outside the walls of Shade Tree Manor.

Realizing there *was* such difference made him all the more curious. "So, since we're both wide awake, want to talk a little bit? It's always nice getting to know your neighbors."

Again, a look passed over her face as though she did want to talk, yet was still hesitant. With seeming reluctance, she nodded. "Okay." Then as though unwilling to be rude, added, "Would you like something to drink? A Coke? I could bring it out on the porch so you don't have to leave the boys." She glanced in the direction of the trees. "Or is the porch even too far away?"

"No," he said. "They're fine. We've got the tents set up in the clearing. Right where you and I were talking earlier."

"Okay, then." She turned and walked across the thick grass, sidestepping the lawn ornament he'd made for Olivia Satterfield a long time ago.

He'd nearly forgotten about it. Composed of welded scrap iron, the whimsical billy goat with flowing beard had its head down in a perpetual grazing position.

"Tacky thing, isn't it?" Amanda said. "I guess I ought to have it removed along with the others." She waved her hand at an assortment of ceramic statues. "It would make things easier for the boy who mows my lawn."

Ian hid a grin. "It might at that." He looked around. The grass wasn't knee-deep anymore, the way it had been after Olivia's passing, but it was still a few inches tall. He knew that Rachel Fultz had kept an eye on the house for the past couple of years, but apparently her neighborly duties hadn't included caring for the yard.

"I can't believe how fast the grass grows out here," Amanda went on, climbing the porch steps. "I had it mowed less than a week ago."

"It's the humidity," he said. He paused at the bottom of the steps. "I'll wait here. Just in case." He motioned toward the woods and his scout troop.

"Okay. I'll be right back." She hurried inside and returned with two cans of Coke. She handed one to him, then sat on the edge of the porch rail. Her body posture seemed tense, and somehow vulnerable, as though she wanted to trust him but still wasn't completely sure she could. Something about Amanda compelled him to reach out to her.

He settled on the steps, where he could keep an eye out for his boys. A protective feeling rose inside of him, the way it often did, with sudden gusto. He never saw it coming. It was simply there. One minute he'd be minding his own business, walking along with the Cumberland Cubs, or maybe passing by a group of kids at the little mall in the next town. And there it would be. The need to watch over and protect. The way a father would.

How many kids ran around out there in the world, unsupervised, with nobody to care for them? The thought made him furious, and he prayed on a regular basis that his own son had gotten better than that in the way of parents.

"Ian?" Amanda spoke his name as if she'd repeated it.

"Sorry." He took a sip of his pop. "Just woolgathering. Guess I'm more tired than I'd thought."

"We don't have to do this," she said. Her features closed over once more, as though she were blocking out her emotions, ready to backpedal on spending social time with him. "I mean if you'd rather take the Coke with you…"

"No." He shook his head, not willing to let her pull away so quickly, just when he was getting to know her a little better. "I like talking to you. It's nice to have someone around that's above the age of ten and only has two legs."

"Excuse me?"

"My dog." He pursed his lips, teasing Amanda, enjoying it. "She's over the age of ten, in dog years anyway. But friends of the four-legged variety don't say much."

Amanda laughed softly, the sound dropping over him like a rush of warm air. "What kind of dog is she?"

"Rottweiler."

"A Rottie? Oo-oh." She shivered.

"No, she's not mean." Ian twirled the Coke can. "As a matter of fact, she's a big old baby. Three years old and a hundred and five pounds. And all she wants is to have anyone and everyone rub her belly."

"Now that's my kind of dog. Granny used to have a bloodhound that was the same way."

"Yeah." He nodded. "She might not talk, but she's a good listener. Guess it's true what they say about dogs being man's best friend. Or woman's." He raised his can in a toast to Amanda, then took a swallow.

"Animals *are* good for telling your secrets to." She gazed into the distance, her eyes not focused on anything in particular. "There's a little gray squirrel that comes up here on the porch sometimes. I call him Skippy. He loves croutons, and I feed him and talk to him."

Ian sobered, his humor fading as he watched her. The wistful expression in her eyes moved him. It was similar to what he'd seen reflected in his own mirror, and instantly he thought about what had happened the other day at the nursing home, and how it had made him feel. Like he could relate to Amanda in some way.

"It's nice of you to let the boys stay here."

"Like I said, I don't mind once in a while."

He hesitated, still studying her, and told himself to tread with care. He didn't want to scare her away or seem overly pushy. "Do you like kids?"

"Sure." Her answer came out a little too quickly. "Why do you ask? Am I being too mean in not inviting your scout troop over more often?"

"No, not at all. I just…" He let the words trail away. Maybe he was getting too personal. Scratch the "maybe." He was being nosy and he mentally chastised himself for behaving rudely. It wasn't like him, which only showed him that Amanda had him rattled. "Forget it. I didn't mean to pry."

"No—what were you going to say?" Amanda persisted. "What did you notice?"

He focused on the look in her eyes. Her expression had shifted, changed, enough for him to see that whether Amanda realized it or not, she was reaching out to him. His curiosity overcame what was left of his hesitation. He lifted a shoulder. "The other day at the nursing home—when you saw the baby that young couple brought in." He halted, at a loss for words. He was making a mess out of this, when all he'd meant to do was reach out to her. "Is there something about kids that bothers you?" he asked.

Amanda's face paled in the moonlight. "You're very observant," she said quietly. "I'm surprised you noticed my reaction."

Immediately, he felt like an oaf. "Forgive me. It was rude of me to bring it up. I didn't ask you to be nosy, it's just that—"

She cut him off. "Speaking of children, maybe you'd better go check on your scouts."

He grimaced, then panicked as Amanda's lower lashes suddenly glistened with unshed tears. She held them back, her jaw set, her body tense. *Lord, he'd made her cry.*

His decision was instant, one he wouldn't later be able to explain.

"Amanda, the reason I asked was because I thought we might have something in common." He hurried on before she could interrupt. "Something that hurts so deeply it cuts like a knife." He clenched his fist and brought it up against his heart. "Right here."

She said nothing, but the expression on her face softened.

"They say it's sometimes easier to talk to a stranger about your troubles than a friend," he went on. *He* took a deep breath and went for broke, knowing this wasn't just about her anymore. He needed someone to talk to. Someone who might truly understand. "I have a son out there, Amanda. Not in the woods. Not in my scout troop.''

She stared at him, her mouth partially open as if she thought he was crazy.

He probably was. "I have a son," he repeated, "who I gave up a long time ago. A boy I can't get off my mind, no matter how much time passes. And I can tell you right now that hiding doesn't help. And sometimes talking to your family doesn't either, because they're too close to the matter. But talking to *someone* sure beats the hell out of the alternative." He stood. "I am rightly sorry for intruding on your privacy. I'll have the kids packed up and out of here first thing in the morning." Coke in hand, he turned to go.

"Ian." She spoke his name quietly, but her voice snagged him as if she'd shouted. "What's the alternative?"

He kept his back to her, briefly squeezing his eyes shut. "Getting lost in your own sorrow. Drinking." He turned to face her once more. "Working sixteen-hour days. There's a dozen different poisons." He shrugged. "You can name your own. I've tried most of them." He held her gaze. "I hate seeing people in pain. And I think something's eating you up, Amanda. Something that brought you clear out here from Colorado. Don't forget there are folks to talk to if you need them." Again, he started to leave.

"Ian."

He halted. Held his breath. "Yeah?"

"I love barbecue."

He looked at her, certain his ears were playing tricks on him. "You do?"

"Yes. It's my favorite."

He nodded. "Good. Pick you up at five-thirty, to-morrow evening?"

"I work until four. Better make it six."

"Six it is."

He headed for the woods, no longer worried about snakes. The one that had kept a choke hold on his emotions had uncoiled about three lengths.

He glanced back over his shoulder, but Amanda was gone.

CHAPTER FOUR

BJ's BARBECUE STOOD surrounded by a thicket of trees in the west end of Boone's Crossing. From a smokestack in the roof of the rustic building housing the restaurant, wispy gray tendrils feathered upward, carrying with them enticing aromas of hickory and barbecued meat. Amanda inhaled as she accepted Ian's outstretched hand and climbed down from his four-wheel drive pickup. She closed her eyes in pure bliss. "Mm-mmm. If the food tastes half as good as it smells, I'm already sold."

"You won't be disappointed," he said.

She looked at him and smiled in an effort to calm her nerves. She'd come close to calling Ian's welding shop and telling him she'd changed her mind about going out with him. But then she'd remembered the way his eyes had looked when he'd told her about the son he'd given up, and she'd put the phone down. Maybe he was right. Maybe it was nice to have someone to reach out to. Someone to talk to who wasn't personally involved. She hadn't had a date in over a year, and told herself to quit being silly. Tonight's outing was all in friendship.

So why had she taken such care with her appearance, going through one outfit after another in rapid succession, until she'd finally decided on black jeans and her favorite peach blouse? She'd curled her hair and put on some makeup. With her feet in a pair of sandals, toenails painted a tame coral, she'd felt comfortable—until Ian had pulled up in her driveway. Instantly, her stomach had been seized by a case of the jitters that had calmed only marginally on the drive to BJ's.

Dressed in blue jeans, a maroon western shirt and cowboy boots, Ian looked twice as yummy and tempting as anything she expected to find on the menu. He had on a black ball cap, but he'd taken it off earlier to swat a wasp that had found its way inside the truck. Amanda couldn't shake the picture from her mind of his light-brown hair that waved slightly and made her want to touch. The combined scents of herbal shampoo and a cologne that reminded her of outdoors and new leather had left her hormones in an uproar.

Ignoring the way her pulse jumped at his touch, she held Ian's hand just long enough to move away from the truck. She walked with him through the crowded parking lot toward the log building. Her shoes crunched against cedar chips, strewn between the asphalt and sidewalk. Rocking chairs lined the wrap-around porch, several occupied by people waiting for a table or enjoying a chat with friends after their meal. Hanging baskets held pansies and petunias in shades of pink, white, red and yellow, and a lifelike mannequin near the entrance clad in bib overalls, a flannel shirt and straw hat gripped a chalkboard menu in its hands, advertising the special. *All you care to eat barbecue ribs—$7.99,* Amanda silently read.

Her mouth watered all over again, until she focused once more on Ian as he held the door open for her.

No way was she going to order something that would leave her with sauce on her face, hands, and likely down the front of her blouse as well.

The inside of the restaurant proved to be as charming as the outside, with tables covered in bright gingham cloth, antique lanterns hanging from the ceiling and rough-hewn log walls. The place was packed, and several people waved or spoke to Ian. After giving his name to the hostess, he led Amanda back out to the porch, where they waited in the rockers until the hostess greeted them and showed them to a table in a corner of the nonsmoking section. She took their order for soft drinks and left menus.

Amanda spotted an offer of barbecued pork on a bun, served with coleslaw and curly fries. "I think I'll have number three," she said, tapping the menu with one finger.

Ian gave her a mock frown. "Are you sure? That's not much of a supper."

"It's fine." Again, she pictured herself with sticky fingers and messy chin.

"Well, I'm not shy," he said, in tune with her thoughts. "I'm having ribs."

The waitress returned with their drinks, and Amanda ordered the barbecue sandwich, then sipped her cherry cola. Ian ordered the ribs in a soft drawl that left goose bumps tickling her arms. She could listen to his voice all night and never grow tired of it. Starting guiltily out of her daydream, she realized he'd spoken to her.

"Someone's trying to get your attention," he said, indicating with a nod directed behind her and to her left.

Amanda turned to look, then smiled and waved at the towheaded boy who sat at a nearby table. "That's Delbert Brock. His cousin, Gavin, mows my lawn. Delbert came with him last time and took a liking to that little squirrel I told you about. He got the biggest kick out of feeding him peanuts." Not until the words were out of her mouth did she realize exactly what they implied. She'd enjoyed having the boys around, unconsciously mothering them with cold drinks and extra sunscreen, and had to admit that their presence wasn't all that different than having Ian's scouts in her woods.

Kids were kids, and she loved them every bit as much as Ian did. But the thought of having some of her own left her cold with fear. Maybe it was easier to deal with Delbert and Gavin than it was Ian's scouts, because they were closer to being grown. Gavin was old enough to drive, hauling his mower and yard tools around in a truck, and Delbert looked about fourteen or fifteen.

Two young men, past the point of needing to be coddled.

Amanda gave Ian a half smile. "Guess your scout troop might like to meet Skippy next time, too, huh?"

He looked at her intently. "We don't want to wear out our welcome. It's okay to value your privacy, Amanda." Briefly, he reached out and folded his hand over hers where it rested on the table.

The gesture was enough to send her heart racing, and she was glad when the waitress brought their order, giving her something to do with her own hands besides squeeze Ian's in return. She got a kick out of watching him savor his food. He put away his share of the pork ribs and still somehow managed to eat them without making a mess, neatly wiping his fingers on the napkin in his lap.

"Your legs must be hollow," Amanda teased. "I think I've gained five pounds just watching you eat."

To her amusement, his face flushed beneath his tan and he swiped the napkin across his mouth before answering. "I told you the food here was something you don't want to miss out on. It's enough to make me forget my manners and make a pig of myself—no pun intended."

Amanda laughed and began to relax. "It's beyond good," she agreed, polishing off the last of her curly fries. "I'm going to have to walk home to wear off the calories." The barbecue sandwich she'd eaten had been twice as big as she'd expected, served on a bun so large there was no way to hold it and still maintain good table manners. She'd ended up eating it with her fork.

"I still agree with Papaw," Ian said, his lips curving enough to make the dimples appear in his cheeks. "You don't have to worry about calories, but if you'd like to take a walk after we eat, I know a good place to go."

"All right, you're on." What could a walk hurt? She wasn't so much worried about getting a workout as she was about finding a way to make this date end on a casual note, and exercise might be just the ticket.

A short time later, Ian drove them back toward town, turning down a side street near the nursing home. The road dead-ended and a park stretched out before them, playground equipment still visible in the fading evening light. The place was empty, save for a couple with three children at the pond feeding the ducks, and two kids on the slide. A stray dog nosed its way around the trash container near a picnic table, then trotted off on some unknown mission.

"This is nice," Amanda said, watching the family with wistful envy. She tore her gaze away from them with effort. "I've been here a few times on my lunch break."

"The place is usually packed around lunchtime after Sunday church services," Ian said. "Lots of folks picnic here. It's also popular with the teenagers for parking on Saturday nights."

His dark eyes held her gaze long enough for Amanda's thoughts to travel down a path best left unexplored. Briefly, she wondered if he'd brought her here hoping to indulge in a bit of what the high-school kids came for, but before she could dwell on the thought, Ian opened the truck door and climbed out.

She started to exit the pickup as well, but he hurried around to help her down as he had previously. "Come on. I've got something to show you."

"Oh?" Curiosity played with her emotions as Amanda chastised herself for her silly suspicions. If the man wanted to take advantage of her, he'd had plenty of opportunity the other night in the dark cover of the woods surrounding Granny's cabin.

They walked toward the center of the park, stopping halfway between the picnic tables and playground equipment. A gazebo Amanda had admired on her last trip here stood, still under construction, encircled by bright orange mesh fencing.

"My cousin and I built this," Ian said.

"Really?" She looked at him, surprised. "I thought you were a welder."

"I am. But I'm sort of a jack-of-all-trades. We should have the gazebo finished by this coming weekend."

"Just in time for 'Good Neighbor Days.'" Her co-workers had been talking about the upcoming annual pre-summer celebration and town picnic, held the first Saturday of June.

"That's right." Ian nodded. "Are you going to come?"

Amanda hesitated. Too much of a good thing—in this case, being around Ian—might prove not to be such a good thing after all. And besides, she'd come to Boone's Crossing to hide, to heal, not to socialize. "I don't know." She avoided his gaze. "I'll have to see what's going on."

"Well, I hope you can make it. I plan to bring Papaw, but I'll probably have to wheel him over in his chair. My pickup sits too high off the ground for him to get in with his hip and all."

"I'm sure Zeb will enjoy the outing." She looked at the gazebo once more, with its intricate woodwork. "You and your cousin did a good job. I'm impressed."

"Thanks. I'll tell her you said so."

"Her?" Amanda raised her eyebrows.

"Yep. Samantha Jo was always handy with a hammer and nails." He grinned. "She raises a few eyebrows around here with the good ol' boys."

Amanda laughed. "I'm impressed. Your family seems to be multitalented. Zeb told me he used to run your welding shop with you."

"More like the other way around. He and Dad had the shop when I was a kid. Papaw taught me everything I know when it comes to building or fixing things." He gestured toward the playground equipment. "I built those monkey bars for the kids to climb on. Welded each piece together to make it extra strong. Safe. And I did the ladder for the slide, and the frame and all for the swing set."

"Wow." She'd had no idea he was so skilled, and had somehow pictured him welding something of a more generic, shop-related nature. "Are those wooden seats?"

"Yeah. Come on, I'll show you."

She followed him to the swing set and stopped in front of it. The frame was made of heavy steel piping, but the swings themselves were indeed old-fashioned-looking wood, suspended from chains. Amanda ran her hand over the surface of one of the brightly painted red-and-blue seats. "It's so smooth."

"No splinters that way," he said. "And the chains are small enough to hold, but big enough not to pinch any little fingers."

"The nurse in me gives you an A-plus for safety," she said, with a thumbs-up gesture.

He laughed. "Sounds more like a teacher."

Sudden melancholy gripped her. "My sister teaches kindergarten," she said. "Back in Colorado."

"Yeah?" He nodded approval. "Seems like you've got a well-rounded family. Any other siblings?"

"Nope. Just me and Nikki. And you?"

"I'm an only child. Mom's gone—we lost her to breast cancer some years back—and Dad lives in Virginia."

"I'm sorry to hear about your mom," Amanda said. She focused on some distant point beyond the playground equipment. "Unfortunately, death doesn't discriminate."

"No, it doesn't. What about your folks? Do they live in Colorado?"

She faced him once more, curling her fingers around the chain on one of the swings. "My parents divorced when Nikki and I were too young to remember. I have no idea where my father is. Mom lived in Colorado for a while, when Nik and I were in high school, then she took off again."

"Again?"

"Yeah." She quirked her mouth. "She never stays in one place long. That's why Nikki and I spent our summers with Granny. She was our roots, the one home we knew would always be there. Mom drove us nuts growing up, always making us change schools. We'd barely make friends at one, then move on to another. So we made her promise to stay in one place while we finished high school, and that turned out to be Colorado. But as soon as we were both in college, she took off for Texas, and from there she went to Oklahoma and finally recently ended up in Montana."

"Wow. I've never been out of state, unless you count driving across the line into Kentucky or Virginia." He paused. "What made your mother want to move around so much, if you don't mind my asking?"

Amanda sighed and sank absentmindedly onto the swing. Gripping the chains in both hands, she pushed it with her foot enough to make it sway. "Mom's a dreamer. One time she moved us to Nashville, hoping to become a country star."

"No foolin'?"

She nodded. "Another time she decided to become a pilot. It only took one flying lesson before she realized that wasn't her cup of tea. She was always struggling to take care of us and see that we had everything we needed. Nikki and I did what we could to help out with after-school jobs. But each time Mom seemed to think things would be better in the next town, at the next job, and that her dream career was somewhere just out of her reach. Guess you can't fault her for trying."

"Nope." Ian's face took on a faraway expression. "It must've been rough for her, going it alone without your dad."

"It was." She wondered if he was thinking about his own son, and if he'd given the child up to make sure the boy had all he would need. How old had Ian been when he'd become a father? Probably not old enough to handle the responsibility. A sudden measure of irritation welled up inside her. "I can't fathom how some people can walk away from their children while others would give anything to have a baby of their own."

He turned his head sharply to look straight at her, and immediately she realized how her comment sounded. She'd been thinking of Nikki, and how much she'd wanted to be a mother. And of the many times they'd discussed heartbreaking stories heard on the news, in which some frightened teenager abandoned her baby in a Dumpster.

"Some folks don't walk away," Ian said, his tone thick with pain. "There are people who give up their child because it's the right thing to do."

"Oh, Ian, I didn't mean you." Amanda felt the color flood then drain from her face. "Really, I didn't." She swallowed, not wanting to get into an explanation behind her comment—one that would lead to personal issues. She had no desire to talk about the baby she'd lost. The pain was still sharp and fresh, eating her up inside.

"It's okay," he said. "Sorry if I sounded short. I know you were talking about your dad."

"Yes." Amanda nodded, letting him draw the wrong conclusion.

He was silent a moment. "Hey, how about I push you?" With obvious effort, he'd lightened his tone.

"Push me?"

"Yeah." He took hold of the chains, above where she gripped them. "When was the last time you played on a swing?"

She laughed in spite of herself. "I don't know. Longer ago than I care to think about."

"Well, then you're overdue for some fun."

Before Amanda could protest, he pulled the swing backward, lifting her feet off the ground. Her stomach gave a sharp jump at the sudden motion, and she tightened her hands on the chains, letting out a little yelp. Her hair lifted away from her face as Ian let go, giving her a push, sending her forward. She chuckled, feeling silly, and tucked her feet out of the way so they wouldn't drag. At five-five, she wasn't exactly tall, but she was still too big for the child-sized swing. Too big, but apparently not too old.

Joyful anticipation rose within her as the swing arced backward once more, and Ian's hands came firmly into contact with her back, sending her skyward. Higher and higher he pushed the swing, and Amanda clung to the chains, letting the silliness enfold her, leaning back to let her hair fly wildly away from her shoulders as he sent her sailing into the air over and over again. She shrieked with laughter when the swing hit a point so high it bounced on the chains, and Ian gripped her waist as she came back down, his hands steady.

But she'd been ready to thrust forward again, and the momentum of the swing, coupled with his holding on to her, sent her sliding backward instead.

"Whoa!" Ian slipped his arms around her, lost his balance and pulled her off the swing. The two of them tumbled to the ground, and he put out a protective hand to stop the swing from coming back to whack her in the head.

Amanda froze in place, fully realizing what an intimate position they'd ended up in, limbs entwined, their faces mere inches from one another. "I haven't done that in ages," she said, attempting to take her mind off the urge to stay right where she was. Ian smelled wonderful, looked even better, and felt so warm and solid, she didn't want to let go or get up. But she forced herself to do both.

She brushed off the knees of her jeans. "This reminds me of the tree swing Grandpa Satterfield made for Nikki and I when we were small."

Ian picked up the cap that had tumbled from his head, and put it back on. Amanda straightened, and tried not to notice the way he watched her.

He cleared his throat. "I never really heard Papaw talk about your grandpa."

"That's probably because Granny was a widow for

so long." Amanda pushed her hair away from her face with both hands, knowing she must look a mess. "I can barely remember him. The tree swing is one of the only memories I have."

But Ian wasn't thinking of swings anymore. The expression in his eyes said he wanted to kiss her, and Amanda took a step backward, making sure she didn't do something foolish like let him. Or worse still, kiss him first.

"Your hair looks fine," he said, stilling her motions with a gentle touch to her wrist. "I like it that way."

"What way?" she joked, in an effort to make light of how he made her feel. "Tangled like a bird's nest?"

"No." He reached up to gently pull a strand away from where it had snagged on one of her earrings. "Windblown. Natural. You look like you've been having fun."

She nearly choked. For one crazy second, she'd thought he was about to say she looked like she'd been having sex. *Get a hold of yourself!* Amanda knew it was only the fact that she hadn't been intimate with anyone for such a long time that had her thoughts running rampant. It had been one more sore spot between her and Mark, shortly before their breakup. He'd been against the surrogacy procedure for many reasons, but finding out that it meant abstaining from sexual relations until a pregnancy was confirmed had sent him over the edge. The subject had led to their final argument and ultimate parting.

The sobering thoughts brought her back to reality.

"Listen, Ian, I've had a wonderful time with you this evening. But I really need to get home."

"Sure," he said. "No problem. I had a nice time with you, too." He pressed his hand against the small of her back, walking her toward his truck.

The gesture was friendly and nothing more, as though he realized he'd overstepped the boundary she'd drawn. Still, Amanda couldn't stop the feelings his touch evoked, bringing back a reminder of the way his strong hands had pressed against her when he'd pushed her on the swing. Making her wish things were different, and that there could be more than friendship between them. With difficulty, she reminded herself she wasn't ready for anything more, and that she'd better listen to her head, even if it would have been much more enjoyable to follow her heart.

The heart that told her Ian was everything she'd ever wanted in a man. Warm, funny, sexy, compassionate. She'd seen the pain in his eyes when he'd spoken of his son, and knew he hadn't made the decision to give up his child lightly. She'd safely bet her last nickel Ian Bonner would make the best father and husband a woman could ask for.

It figured she would find the perfect man now, when she was no longer looking.

IAN HEADED FOR Shade Tree Manor as soon as he'd dropped Amanda off at her place. It was that, or face going home to an empty house with only Cuddles to greet him. There, he might be tempted to sit in the living room and think about how hard it had been to keep his distance from Amanda. It would be easy to dwell on the way she'd made him feel, and take things a step further by pondering what he might do to make her feel the same way about him.

It was obvious Amanda had no interest in getting serious. Which shouldn't matter, since he barely knew her. But somehow it did matter. He wanted to get to know her better, and planned to see what he could do about that, even if she didn't want to take things past casual dating. He had time. He wasn't in a rush to find Mrs. Right. Never had been before now anyway, so what difference did it make if he spent some time with Amanda?

Wondering what issues she was dealing with that had made her come to Boone's Crossing, Ian strode across the parking lot and into the building. He called out a greeting to the nurses at the front desk, already missing Amanda's presence. Papaw was watching an old western on cable TV when Ian entered his room.

"Hey, Papaw. How's it going?"

Zeb gave him a toothless smile. "Fine and dandy." He reached out to clasp Ian's hand in an affectionate greeting. His blue eyes twinkled. "So how'd it go? Tell me all the juicy details about your date with Miss Kelly." He leaned forward in his wheelchair. "Well, not all of 'em, just the G-rated ones." He cackled and punched Ian in the arm.

"You old codger." Ian tapped the bill of Papaw's hat. "It wasn't anything like that and you know it."

"Aw, can't a guy have some fun? I know you're a gentleman, least you'd better be." He shook a warning finger, then ducked his head toward Ian's again. "Speaking of women, you oughta see the little number who came in this morning."

Ian clamped his lips together in an effort to hide a grin. Papaw took his womanizing seriously. "Oh?"

"Mm-hmm." Zeb licked his bottom lip. "Got a little touch of Alzheimer's but she's a pretty thing. Eyes as blue as anything, and she's only seventy-two.''

"Is that right?" Ian lost his battle and chuckled. "Now, Papaw, how do you know how old she is? Women never tell their age.''

"No, but if you're smart you can find a way to figure it out.'' Papaw nodded wisely. "And speaking of which, the nurses were talking about birthdays, and I heard one of 'em say Miss Kelly is twenty-seven. Still young enough to give your daddy those grandkids he's missing out on.''

"We're just friends, Papaw.''

"Uh-huh.'' Zeb gave him a wink. "That's the way it gets started. You watch and see if I'm not right. I'm bettin' the two of you'll be going steady by the time the fireworks light the air this Fourth of July.'' He jabbed Ian in the ribs. "Maybe you'll start a few fireworks of your own.''

Ian laughed. "Papaw, you're too much.''

"I'm serious. You ain't getting any younger. Before you know it, you'll be rooming here with me at Shade Tree.''

"I don't think so.''

"Don't just think, boy. Do. *Do* something to make things happen the way you want 'em to.''

"I took her out to supper. What more do you want?'' Ian sank into the chair near the foot of the bed, feeling sullen. How was it Papaw always managed to sense his deepest emotions? He'd wanted to kiss Amanda at the park, but it didn't take a brain surgeon to see she didn't want the same thing.

"It's a start, son, but you've got to do more than that. You need to charm her. Dad-gum it, don't tell me I'm gonna have to hold your hand and give you instructions on courtin'."

"Aw, go on." Ian stretched his legs out and laced his fingers across his stomach. "You've set your sights on that new pretty lady, and now you're the matchmaking wizard—is that right?" He enjoyed sparring with Papaw. It kept him from thinking the serious thoughts Zeb evoked in regards to Amanda.

Zeb lowered his voice to a whisper, the way he did on the rare occasion when he chose to swear. "Wizard my ass. I'm the Grand Poo-bah, and don't you forget it. Now listen up."

Ian sat obediently in the chair, hanging on Zeb's every word simply to humor him. Surprised a few moments later to find he was no longer laughing at Papaw's scheme. As a matter of fact, what Zeb said made perfect sense and just might work. At any rate, it wouldn't hurt to try. So long as Amanda never found out that he'd gotten a refresher course in the art of pursuing a woman from a man who was damn near as old as the town he called home.

"You keep me posted," Zeb later said, as Ian prepared to leave.

"Good night, Papaw." Ian buzzed a kiss against his grandpa's cheek.

With a chuckle, he headed for the parking lot.

CHAPTER FIVE

AMANDA AWOKE from a dead sleep to the sound of shattering glass. Heart racing, she bolted upright, prepared to grab her pepper spray. It took a moment for her to realize the culprit of the break-in was not an intruder, but a tree branch.

Lightning crackled across the sky, illuminating the bedroom and the broken maple branch, thrust half in, half out of her window through the ruined screen. Wind rustled across the leaves, accompanied by splatters of rain. "Ah, geeze." Amanda threw back the covers and slipped her feet into her tennis shoes, wary of the broken glass. With the lamp on, she could now see shards of it scattered over the carpet. The rain continued to hammer its way in, drenching the carpet and the rocking chair beneath the window.

Amanda tugged the chair into the center of the room out of harm's way, then hurried to the kitchen where cardboard boxes left over from her move were neatly broken down and folded, awaiting a trip to the recycling center. Glad she'd procrastinated in taking them, she gathered a box, duct tape and a stack of hand towels from the utility closet and ran back to the bedroom. She tossed her supplies on the bed, knowing she'd first have to move the tree branch before she could patch the window.

After putting on a hooded jacket, she raced outside. By the time she'd pulled the branch away and haphazardly repaired the window from inside, she was completely soaked. Leaving her coat on the edge of the bathtub to dry, Amanda slipped out of her sodden nightgown and towel-dried her hair. As she cleaned up the broken glass and laid towels down to absorb water from the carpet, she looked at the clock and groaned— 3:30 a.m. And she was now wide awake. Grumbling, she continued plucking stray shards from the carpet and managed to nick her finger on one. The only bandage strips she had were those of cartoon characters, ones she'd kept on hand for her little patients when she'd worked at the hospital in Deer Creek. She rummaged through her purse and found one with pictures of Snoopy on it. It would have to do.

With the room finally in order, she got back into bed with a book, hoping to relax and fall asleep once more. But her mind whirled with memories of the previous day and the way Ian had pushed her on the swing. Giving up all hope of sleep by the time the clock rolled to five, Amanda showered, dressed and went outside to assess the damage left by the storm. Broken branches from the maple lay scattered over the yard, and the creek beside the house had swollen to angry proportions, but the shattered window and torn screen seemed to be the extent of the damage done. Her car had escaped the fallen limbs by mere inches, but twigs and leaves were scattered next to the grill and front tires.

The toolshed next to the house, its wood weathered gray with age, had once served as a garage. It was still crammed with whatever junk Granny Satterfield had collected over the years. It had been no surprise to Amanda when she'd discovered her mother had never bothered to sort through it, even though she and Nikki had offered to help shortly after Granny's funeral. She'd have to clean it out soon. It would be best to have her car under shelter, and going through Granny's things would give her something more constructive to do with her free time than dwell on thoughts of Ian.

But as she drove to the nursing home, her mind refused to cooperate, and when she saw his truck in the parking lot, her stomach did a funny little flip. She didn't see him or Zeb in the day room as she went for her morning cup of coffee. Unable to resist, Amanda strode down the hallway to Zeb's room and paused in front of the open door.

Zeb was in his wheelchair, a colorful patchwork quilt draped across his lap. Ian was in a chair next to the television. "Good morning." He greeted her, both his words and the expression on his face telling her he, too, hadn't forgotten the fun they'd had yesterday.

"Hello, Ian. Morning, Zeb." She moved into the room. "How's every little thing today?"

"If I was any happier, I'd be twins," Zeb replied. He had his teeth in, and he held up an apple-and-cinnamon pastry laden with frosting. "The boy's spoiling me again." His eyes twinkled. "Though I think the only sweet he's really interested in is you."

"Papaw!" Ian shot his grandpa an incredulous look, then turned toward Amanda. "He speaks his mind, what little is left of it."

"Humph." Zeb tapped one finger against his temple. "I've forgotten more than you'll ever know."

Amanda ignored the rush of warmth Zeb's words had caused. "You keep feeding him like that, and we're going to have to get him a bigger wheelchair." She gave Zeb a wink, then patted his birdlike shoulder. "Well, I'd better get busy. Just thought I'd say hello."

"Cute Band-Aid," Ian teased, nodding at the hand she'd lain on Zeb's sleeve.

Amanda quirked her mouth. "It was the best I could do on short notice."

"What happened?" His dark eyes studied hers, making her all the more self-conscious.

"The storm put a tree branch through my window." She wiggled her index finger. "I don't recommend cleaning up broken glass at three-thirty in the morning. I think I was more asleep than awake."

"Broke your window, did it?" Zeb spoke casually. "Guess you'll need to have it repaired."

"Do you know a good glass man?" As soon as the question was out, Amanda mentally chastised herself. Ian had said he was a jack-of-all-trades. Would he think she was hinting for his help?

Was she?

"Did it damage the window frame?" Ian asked.

She shook her head. "Just the glass and the screen." She held her hands up to demonstrate. "The pane is about this big. It's one of those old-fashioned windows that slide up and down."

"I've got an uncle over in London who owns a glass shop," Ian said.

"Kentucky, not England," Zeb added.

Amanda smiled. "Great. Is he listed in the phone book?"

Zeb made a noise as though clearing his throat, then exchanged a quick glance with Ian.

"He is," Ian said, "but it's hard to get an appointment sometimes. He's partners with his brother, and they cover a wide area of Kentucky and a lot of Tennessee as well. If you'd like, I can come over and measure the window frame, and pick up the glass. Wouldn't be hard to install it."

Zeb gave a nod of satisfaction, and Ian briefly narrowed his eyes at his grandpa before looking at Amanda once more.

"I wouldn't want to put you to any trouble," Amanda said. But at the same time, she didn't want to insult him by turning down his kind offer.

"No trouble at all," Ian said. "I can run over and measure it as soon as the storm lets up."

"Are you sure?" Amanda groped for a final save.

"The boy said it's no trouble," Zeb insisted. Then he gave her a wink. "I wouldn't turn down free help if I were you. Don't you have enough moving expenses already?"

"I swear!" Ian glared at Zeb. "Did you lose your manners along with your teeth?"

But the look of affection in his eyes took the sting out of his words. Again, Amanda was moved by how much Ian cared for his grandfather.

Zeb waved Ian's comment aside. "I'm not trying to be rude, son, just practical. You weren't going to charge her for your help, were you?"

"Oh, I couldn't—"

"Of course not, I—"

She and Ian spoke at the same time, and Amanda

smiled as he gave her a go-ahead gesture. "I couldn't ask you to work without paying you."

"There's no need. You can buy the glass, but my labor's free." He returned her smile. "I don't charge friends for my time."

What could she say to that? And she certainly didn't want to hurt Zeb's feelings either. "Perfect. I won't be home until after four, though. If you need to go inside the house, the key's hidden in a Mason jar under the lilac hedge closest to the shed." Normally, she wouldn't be so quick to divulge the location of Granny's spare key, but somehow she knew she could trust Ian.

With her key and her house, but not with her heart.

Her pulse raced once more as he looked at her and nodded. "I'll take care of it as soon as this storm blows over."

"No hurry," she said. "Thank you." Waving so-long to Zeb and see-you-later to Ian, Amanda hastily left the room.

THOUGH THE STORM HAD lasted the better part of the day, the sun now made a halfhearted attempt to break through the clouds as Amanda drove home. Anticipation had her looking for Ian's truck as she turned onto Oak Hollow Road and neared her driveway. The truck was there all right, and she wondered again if she'd been wrong to accept his help.

She hated to seem ungrateful, and she knew that was the way things were done here in Boone's Crossing—neighbor helping neighbor. Yet she didn't want to give him the wrong idea—that she was out to find a man. She shook her head. Of course Ian didn't think that. She'd made it clear that friendship was all she wanted.

Turning her thoughts in a more sensible direction, she parked in front of the toolshed and spotted Ian in her open bedroom window. He waved as Amanda climbed from her car and once more surveyed the damage the wind had done to Granny's poor maple. It was the tree where the swing had been long ago, and it made Amanda sad to see the maple getting old, some of its branches already dead. It had been a dead branch, plus part of a green one, that had broken out the window, leaving twigs, leaves and pieces of bark scattered helter-skelter over the lawn amid Granny's yard ornaments.

"Made quite a mess, didn't it?" Ian spoke from behind her, and Amanda turned to see that he'd come out the back door.

"I'll say. How's the window coming?"

"Fine. I've got all the broken glass out of the frame." He gestured and Amanda spotted the ruined screen leaning up against the house. "Thought I'd get the window in first, in case it decides to rain again. Then I'll put in a new screen."

"Sounds like a plan." She walked with him, back into the house, and laid her purse and car keys on the kitchen counter.

With Ian in her bedroom, Amanda carried a change of clothes to the bathroom down the hall and slipped out of her nurse's uniform, suddenly uncomfortable with his close proximity. Deciding it was best to put a little space between herself and him, she donned a pair of shorts, a T-shirt and tennis shoes and went back outside. Armed with a plastic lawn-and-leaf bag, she began the task of cleaning up the debris. Ian had moved the larger branches over by the shed. She had no idea what she'd do with them. She supposed she'd have to have them hauled off. Maybe Gavin could do it the next time he came to mow the lawn.

She ignored her inner voice that reminded her Ian had a pickup truck, too. Another excuse to spend time with him was not something she needed to pursue.

"I can help you clean up the rest of that if you want."

Amanda turned to find Ian standing behind her once more, holding the extracted window frame. Lost in thought, she hadn't heard him come out the door. She blushed, feeling as though he'd read her mind. "Thanks." She kept her reply deliberately vague.

"Do you mind if I use your toolshed?" He nodded in the direction of the locked door. "I need someplace to lay this flat, and putty and replace the glass."

"Sure, if you can find some room. I'll get the key." She ducked inside the house and retrieved the key from a peg near the back door. As she unlocked the shed, she glanced over her shoulder at Ian. "You'll have to excuse the mess. Granny's stuff is still in here."

"No problem."

He followed her through the door. The musty odor of a room too long closed wafted over them. "Maybe I can get the windows open," Amanda said. "Let a little air in here for you while you work." She grimaced. "That is, if we can find you some working space."

The shed was full to near capacity; boxes and odds and ends of things were stuffed or stacked everywhere.

She saw an old bed frame and a broken rocking horse that Amanda remembered riding as a child. A workbench lined one wall, a window above it. But boxes had been stacked on top of the bench, blocking most of the light. Amanda reached to move one.

"Let me help you with that." Ian leaned the frame he carried against the open door, then hurried over to lift the box from Amanda's grasp.

She reached for another and as she did, hit her shin on something under the workbench. "Ouch." She bent to rub her leg, glaring at the offending object. "There's junk all over the place, isn't…" She let the words trail away as Ian pulled another box off the stack, letting more light filter through the dusty window. Light that revealed what she'd banged her shin on.

Sucking in her breath, Amanda bent and took hold of the object. She ran her hands lovingly across the smooth surface, then tugged the cradle out from under the workbench. A lump rose in her throat as she knelt beside it. Made of cherry wood, it had been handcrafted by her Grandpa Satterfield. He'd carved baby animals into the headboard and footboard—bunnies, squirrels, ducklings—and sanded the entire surface until it was smooth to the touch. Then he'd varnished the wood and presented it to Granny when she'd had their first and only child—Amanda's mother.

And later, Granny had rocked Nikki and then Amanda in it when she looked after them while Bridget ran around the countryside, chasing whatever she felt was more important than staying home with her babies.

Amanda had forgotten all about the cradle. Or

rather, she'd recently blocked the memory from her mind. Somewhere, she had photos of herself as an infant, tucked inside of it, a three-year-old Nikki proudly rocking her little sister back and forth while she smiled for the camera. Years ago, she'd thought she'd one day rock her own children in that cradle, knowing Granny would always keep it in the family. Granny had told her and Nikki that the cradle would be waiting for them to grow up and use it for their babies. And that she hoped they'd carry on the tradition of passing it down to one of their daughters or sons.

When Nikki's friends had thrown a baby shower for her, with Amanda the co-guest of honor, they'd talked about bassinets and rocking chairs, and Nikki had brought up the subject of the cherry-wood cradle. Nikki had said she would ask their mother if it was still at Granny's, and the shower guests had ooh-ed and ahh-ed over what a wonderfully sweet and traditional idea it was for Granny Satterfield to have come up with.

And hours later, Amanda had left Nikki's house, never dreaming fate would rip everything apart in a matter of minutes.

Suddenly, the stale air in the toolshed seemed hot and cloying. Amanda couldn't breathe. Couldn't move. Panic seized her, sending the familiar rush of adrenaline, coupled with sick, hopeless fear, in a surge that reached every extremity of her body. She began to tremble, not fully aware she was crying until a drop of moisture hit her hand where she gripped the cradle's edge.

Ian touched her shoulder. "Amanda? What is it— what's wrong?" He crouched down beside her.

The compassion in his eyes was enough to undo her. Choking back a sob, she turned away and covered her mouth with one hand. Beneath it, she bit her lip, willing herself to gain control. Willing her breathing to slow to normal. She couldn't break down in front of Ian. She barely knew him.

"Amanda," he repeated. This time he gently took hold of her, both hands on her shoulders, encouraging her to look at him.

She stood, leaning against him as he rose to his feet, and suddenly she was in his arms. Sobs she couldn't contain, no matter how hard she tried, wracked her body.

Ian rubbed gentle circles on her back. "It's okay," he soothed. Softly, he kissed the top of her head, then moved his hand up to massage the base of her neck as she tucked her head against his shoulder. "Whatever's bothering you, I'll listen." He slipped his arm around her waist. "Here. Let's get you outside for some fresh air."

He led her through the doorway, out by the lilac hedges where shade canopied the lawn. Bees droned about, their hypnotic buzzing filling Amanda's mind. She sank onto the wooden bench that rested against the toolshed wall.

Nikki's words from that day in the hospital came back to her with clarity.

The baby didn't make it.

And the expression on her face—so sad, so hopeless.

It was a little girl.

Any baby would've been a huge blessing to Nikki, boy or girl. But Amanda knew, deep down, that her sister longed for a daughter more than anything in this world. Nothing could fix or change the loss she'd experienced, and guilt still weighed Amanda down like a slab of iron. Along with it came fear. She was afraid to ever get pregnant again, afraid to try having a baby of her own. What if something were to happen? What if something were to go wrong yet again? The questions whirled through her mind on a regular basis.

Would they ever stop?

Swiping at the tears on her cheeks, she looked up at Ian. "I'm sorry. I don't know what came over me."

He sat down next to her. "There's no need to apologize. Something obviously upset you." Quietly, he waited, his eyes full of questions.

Amanda started to continue with her lie. To brush away his observation with some inane reason for her behavior. But she couldn't. The need to talk to someone overwhelmed her. "I lost a baby a few months ago," she said.

She saw the compassion in Ian's expression, and she struggled to hang on to her control.

"I'm so sorry." He put his hand on her shoulder once more.

She'd heard so many empty words of sympathy—at the hospital, at Anna's funeral—and none of them could change a thing. No amount of kindness or compassion could bring back Nikki's little girl. But Ian meant well, just as everyone else had.

"Is that why you came here?" he asked.

She nodded. "I thought I could run from the pain. But it's not really helping."

He was silent a moment. "Is the—uh—father still in the picture?" he asked.

Startled, she met his gaze. "I wouldn't have gone out with you if I was involved with someone."

He shrugged. "I just thought—well, maybe that you were separated or something."

Amanda shook her head. "No. I was engaged once, but that was over long ago."

"I see."

But she knew he didn't. He probably thought she was some loose woman, engaged to one man, then pregnant by another, and now going out with him. "It's not what you think." She shouldn't have said anything to Ian in the first place. What had happened to her, to Nikki and Cody, was highly personal.

"I wasn't thinking anything," Ian said, giving her shoulder a little rub before lowering his hand to his lap. "Amanda, I would never judge you. Lots of folks make babies without being married." His smile was sad, and she knew he was thinking of his own past, and a child that had been his flesh and blood. Ian had told her he'd given the boy up years ago. How many years? Was he grown now? Did he look like Ian?

Anna would never have a chance to grow. To walk, talk and learn.

Amanda bit back the hurt that threatened to choke her. "Well, not me," she said in reply to Ian's comment. "With or without marriage, I don't ever want to have another baby."

CHAPTER SIX

IAN FELT AS THOUGH Amanda had dashed a bucket of ice water in his face. *She didn't want kids.* How could he have been so foolish as to assume she would, simply because she was so good with them? He scrambled for a response. "Maybe you'll feel differently once the hurt isn't so fresh."

But she shook her head again, adamant. "No, I won't." Pain etched her face, and it tore him up. "It's just not fair. I ate all the right foods, took my prenatal vitamins..." Her voice quivered and she cleared her throat, her eyes still shiny with tears. "I don't understand why it had to happen."

Ian resisted the urge to take her into his arms once more. "There's no logical answer," he said. "But don't blame yourself, Amanda. Sometimes things just happen." Lord knows, his own guilt had weighed him down until he'd practically broken beneath it.

Surprise registered on Amanda's face, as though she hadn't thought he would so easily pick up on the guilt behind her words and in the look in her eyes. "The rational side of me knows that," she said. "But I still don't think I'll ever feel normal again."

"You will," he said. "It takes time. A few months isn't near enough." Even sixteen years hadn't been enough for him. While his son hadn't died, Ian had lost him as completely as if he had. His pain had lessened, but never completely disappeared.

"No, it isn't." Amanda gave him a sad half smile. "Sorry to get all emotional on you. We can go back inside and clear the workbench off now. I'm okay."

"I'll do it," he said. "Why don't you stay out here. Get some more air." It would give her some privacy, some time with her thoughts. And allow him to sort out his thoughts as well.

"All right. If you're sure you don't mind. I'll get back to work on cleaning up the yard."

"And I'll get busy on that window, before it decides to rain again." Reluctantly, he left her and entered the toolshed once more. He knew she wasn't about to stop thinking of the baby she'd lost.

No more than he could stop thinking about what Amanda had said. Knowing she didn't want children still left him reeling. He liked her a lot, and was more than a little attracted to her. He'd even begun to think that Papaw was right. That it was time for him to seriously look for a woman to marry and raise a family with. The more he was around Amanda, the more he'd begun to hope she might be the one. Physical attraction aside, she was definitely a woman he'd longed to get to know better, which had been exactly what Papaw had advised him to do last night.

"Find ways to be around her as often as you can, son," Papaw had said when they'd talked after Ian's date with Amanda. "Before you know it, nature will take its course."

Zeb's simple wisdom had left Ian with a warm and hopeful feeling. When the opportunity to repair her window had arisen, he'd decided to take Papaw's advice. He'd thought to then spend the evening with Amanda. Maybe take her out for supper again. Or even better, he'd hoped she'd invite him to eat with her here at her house. He'd pictured the two of them sitting on her porch in the dark once more, watching the lightning bugs. But this time, he would steal a kiss.

He'd felt like a boy in love.

But now, Amanda had dashed his hopes to the ground with one single statement.

He looked at the cradle beside the workbench and let his breath out on a disgusted sigh. Why was it he always found flaws in the women he dated? None of them ever turned out to be someone he'd want to spend the rest of his life with. While he hadn't exactly been in a hurry to find that special someone, in the back of his mind it was what he wanted. As he'd grown older, he'd found it easy to picture himself with two or three kids. That way they wouldn't have to grow up lonely the way he had, with no brothers or sisters to play with. This time, when he had a child, he'd do things right.

If Amanda didn't want children, then there was simply no place for their relationship to go, and the disappointment of that weighed on him like a ton of steel. It seemed pointless to waste his time with her, if the two of them had polar opposite views on the subject of children. Yet he felt sorry for the loss of her baby, and he couldn't douse his feelings just like that. He'd been attracted to Amanda from the get-go, and he loved the way she took such care with Papaw and her other residents. How could someone so nurturing not want to be a mother?

Knowing it really wasn't any of his business, Ian

finished the task of clearing the workbench, then got busy replacing the window glass. He told himself to quit thinking about Amanda. To finish the project, say his goodbyes, and leave it at that.

But by the time the window and screen were replaced, his stomach was growling, and one look at Amanda was enough to undo his resolve. She wore denim shorts and a light blue T-shirt, and a ladybug had snagged itself in her ponytail. The speckled red bug made her look cute and innocent, and he didn't want to turn his back on her. There was no reason he couldn't at least remain friendly.

"Are you hungry?" Amanda asked.

His stomach growled again, making it impossible to deny the fact. He gave her a sheepish grin. "Guess I am. I usually don't pay much attention to anything when I'm busy." He patted his stomach. "But my belly is quick to remind me if I skip a meal."

"Did you do that?" she asked, her tone exactly one of a scolding nurse.

Ian took a step closer, unable to resist. "You know, you're mighty cute when you're in nurse mode. And I like your taste in hair doodads." He reached out and plucked the ladybug from her ponytail.

The hint of a smile tugged her lips. "Well, I guess wearing a live bug is original anyway." She let the ladybug crawl from his hand to hers, then carefully freed it by placing it on the leaves of a lilac bush.

When she brushed her hair out of her eyes, Ian resisted the urge to still the movement of her hands. Amanda had a natural beauty that went beyond what most women could only achieve with makeup. He loved her earthiness and her sensitivity toward all living things. Why, oh why, could she not want a baby?

"Would you like to go out to BJ's again?" he asked, knowing he shouldn't. Dating was not on the path toward a more casual relationship.

"Thanks, but I'm pretty tired." She gestured toward the house. "I thought I'd whip us up something simple, if that's okay with you."

He let a grin escape, unable to tamp down the hopeful feeling that rose inside of him. "I never turn down a home-cooked meal."

"Believe me, it won't be anything fancy." She glanced over her shoulder at him as he followed her through the back door to the kitchen. "I don't spend a lot of time cooking."

Ian struggled with the way his heart twisted as he watched Amanda move around the room. He wanted to dive right in and help her prepare the meal, even if he wasn't the best of cooks either. The longing to know what it would feel like to share such an everyday chore with her—a woman he cared about—pulled at him.

Instead, he washed his hands at the kitchen sink, then watched Amanda as she went about preparing their meal of grilled cheese sandwiches, macaroni salad and slices of cucumber marinated in peppered vinegar water and onions. He took the jug of sweet tea out of the fridge upon her instructions, and poured tall glasses over ice. They fixed their plates buffet-style, and carried them to the porch.

He found himself unable to get Papaw's words out of his head. *Before you know it, nature will take its course....*

And equally unable to shake his own fantasy of kissing her.

Maybe he wasn't completely ready to give up on her yet. "So, did you decide if you're going to the picnic this weekend? You can come along with me and Papaw if you'd like." *Don't even go there,* his inner voice warned. *She's not the right woman, so why prolong your misery?*

Amanda hesitated. "I don't know. I came to Granny's to be alone. To sort out my thoughts."

"I can understand that. But what's the fun in being alone all the time? Come on. You'll have a good time and no one will bite you." Except maybe him. He wouldn't mind nibbling Amanda's sweet-smelling skin.

She pursed her lips in final thought, then nodded. "All right. I guess I'll come."

Relief flooded through him, and he hurried to say something before his musings got him in trouble. "Good. Papaw will enjoy your company. He likes the outdoors, and misses his farm. I know it bothers him more than he's letting on that he can't get around and do things the way he used to. Being outside helps a little."

"Then I guess when I see Zeb tomorrow, I'll tell him he and I have got a date." The smile she gave him was enough to make Ian rethink his earlier decision.

Could he really bring himself to look at Amanda as nothing more than a friend? Being around her was bound to be hard on his heart, and easing away from her would be a difficult task. But cutting her out of his life abruptly now that he'd begun to get to know her would be even harder.

"You'll make his day," Ian said. He took a bite from his cheese sandwich, watching Amanda eat. As she chewed one small bit of food at a time with delicate, ladylike manners, all he could think about was tasting her lips.

Not exactly on the list of things friends did together.

Ian turned his attention back to his meal, before he let his true thoughts become obvious. Before he gave in to temptation, took Amanda into his arms, and showed her a more enjoyable way to savor the outdoors than having a picnic.

SATURDAY DAWNED warm and sunny, and by the time Amanda helped Ian get Zeb situated under a shade tree near the gazebo, the temperature was already hovering near eighty.

"This is nice," Zeb said. He patted Amanda's hand. "Thanks for bringing me along on your date with my grandson." He gave her a wink.

"You know my date is with you, Zeb," Amanda said, winking back. She caught Ian's gaze over Zeb's shoulder.

He smiled, making her wish things could be different in her life. That she'd met Ian years ago.

"I'll drink to that." Zeb raised his bottled water in toast. "It's not every day a pretty woman wants to go out with an old man with no hair and even less teeth." Then he leaned forward and spoke in a stage whisper. "Don't tell anyone you put vodka in this here bottle."

Amanda laughed. "Your secret's safe with me." She fitted his lap with the quilt he loved so much. He'd refused to leave it behind, even though the warm summer day seemed a bit much for such a heavy throw. "Now, what would you like to eat?"

Good Neighbor Days were already in full swing, the barbecue grills fired up, picnic tables lined end to end, covered with checkered plastic cloths and crowded with colorful containers of food. Amanda fixed a plate for Zeb and noticed that some of the kids from Ian's scout troop were there. She waved to Troy Stoakes—the boy who'd been in her kitchen—which made his redheaded friend whisper and giggle once again.

It both saddened her and warmed her heart to watch the children play in the park. She loved kids so much, and wished Ian was right. That she'd get over her fears of having a child of her own after some time had passed. But she didn't think all the time in the world could ever help her move past what had happened to Anna.

Both Ian and Zeb seemed to know just about everyone at the picnic, so it wasn't any surprise that the two soon became engrossed in talking to a number of their friends and neighbors, leaving Amanda alone with her thoughts. She really ought to make this the last time she and Ian socialized. Her window was fixed, and she could be polite to him at the nursing home, but that was where she needed to draw the line, before she got herself in trouble. The man was too good-looking to resist for long.

"Excuse me. Are you Amanda Kelly?" The words pulled her attention to the woman who'd walked up beside her. She wore shorts and a tank top, her long legs tan and fit, as though she frequently worked out.

"Yes, I am." Amanda scooted over to make room for her on the gazebo seat.

"Ian told me you were new to town. I'm his cousin, Samantha Jo Turner." The woman pushed her sunglasses up into her mass of curly, dark hair and offered her hand. "Folks call me Sami."

Amanda shook her hand, not at all surprised by Sami's firm grip. No wonder she looked so fit, being a carpenter. "Nice to meet you. I hear you and Ian built this gazebo."

"That's right." They chatted a moment. "Say, you didn't happen to see a kid running around here wearing a Tim McGraw T-shirt, did you? He's sort of chubby—has sandy hair and freckles. He hangs out with a skinny little redheaded boy?"

"You mean Troy Stoakes? The kid from Ian's scout troop?"

"That's him. His mother's looking for him. I asked Ian, but he hadn't seen him and neither had Neil—the head scoutmaster."

"I did a little while ago," Amanda said. "He was with his friend." She motioned toward the monkey bars. "They were running and playing over there by the playground equipment."

"I imagine they didn't go far, then. He and Jacob live for fried chicken and hot dogs."

But minutes later, another woman approached. "I'm sorry to interrupt," she said, "but I still can't find Troy anywhere." A worried frown creased her brow. "Sami, have you seen him yet?"

"No." Sami frowned, too.

"Well, I wonder where he could be?" The woman

put her hands on her hips and scanned the surrounding area.

"Maybe he got sidetracked playing," Amanda suggested. She looked around, but with so many kids and people, it was hard to single out one boy.

A little girl with brown pigtails, dressed in bib overall shorts, ran toward them and clambered up the gazebo steps. Breathless, she halted. "Mom, Sally says she saw Troy and Jacob playing out there." She pointed. "In the trees."

"Oh, Lordy." Mrs. Stoakes pressed one hand against her ample breast. "Please tell me your brother didn't wander off out there." She rolled her eyes. "Ever since he became a Cumberland Cub, I can't keep him out of the woods."

"Maybe a snake bit him." Troy's sister gritted her teeth and wrinkled her nose. She curled the index fingers of both hands into fangs and made a hissing sound at her mother.

"Tara, stop that!" Mrs. Stoakes impatiently waved her hands at her daughter.

"We'd better go look for him," Sami said, rising.

"I'll help." Amanda tossed her empty pop can in the trash barrel.

They made their way around the park, past the pond, calling Troy's name as they neared the trees. "Let's split up," Sami said. "Amanda, you go that way, Patricia, you head over there. And Tara, you keep searching around the park."

Amanda headed through the trees, still calling. Her pulse raced. She'd seen too many missing children posters, watched too much true crime on TV, not to worry. But Boone's Crossing was a small town. Surely

Troy and Jacob had simply wandered off and lost track of time. Trying not to think about the snakes Tara had mentioned, she kept walking. How far could a child go?

With a boy's boundless energy, Troy could be anywhere. She cupped her hands around her mouth. "Troy! Jacob! Where are you?"

From somewhere up ahead, she heard a voice. "Over here. Help me!"

Fear seized her, and Amanda picked up her pace, half running through the trees. "Troy?" she called again.

But it was Jacob, breathing hard, who appeared around a bend in a game trail that wound through the woods. His freckles stood out against his skin, his face flushed and sweaty. "That way," he gasped. "At the gravel pit." Frantically, he motioned with one hand. "Come on!"

Amanda ran, silently praying. "What happened?" she asked, keeping up with Jacob. "Is Troy hurt?"

Jacob shook his head, speaking between breaths as he ran. "No...but he's gonna fall...if we don't hurry."

Dear God! Was he about to fall into a gravel pit? She hadn't even remembered there was one in the area. "Fall where?"

But Jacob didn't have to answer. Instead, he pointed as they broke from the trees and halted in front of a chain-link fence.

Beyond the fence was the gravel pit. Down inside it stood a crane, and hanging precariously on to the boom of the monstrous machinery, like a rag doll flopping in the wind, was Troy.

CHAPTER SEVEN

"GO GET HELP—hurry!" Amanda waved Jacob away. "And have someone call 911." Without a second thought, she squeezed through a gap in the fence, slid down into the pit and began to climb. Up onto the crane's huge track, digging in with fingers and tennis-shoe-clad toes, onto the deck, then up the steel boom, telling herself she could do this. She'd never been afraid of heights, but right now Amanda was frightened out of her mind. Not for herself, but for Troy.

He'd made it about halfway up the top side of the boom—some thirty feet in the air—before he'd somehow gotten his ankle wedged in the bracing. She imagined he'd slipped, and she thanked God that he hadn't plunged to the gravel bed below.

"Hold on, Troy! I'm going to help you." Above her, he began to cry. "It's okay, honey. You're going to be fine. I promise." Breathing hard, Amanda continued her upward climb. Sweat stung her eyes and snaked its way down her back, giving her a creepy sensation. She exercised regularly, but it had been a long while since she'd done any serious hiking or rock climbing. She hoped she had the strength to keep Troy on the boom until help could arrive.

It felt like forever before she reached him. "See, I told you," she said, clinging to the bracing and trying to catch her breath. Forcing her voice to sound upbeat and positive, she said, "I'm here. Don't move."

Troy had grease on his arms, the back of one hand and the front of his shirt. "Miss Kelly." The tremor in his voice made the words come out on a squeak. "I'm so scared. I'm gonna fall!"

"No, you aren't. I promise." Carefully, Amanda worked her way around until she was positioned behind and slightly below Troy. This enabled her to actually sit on one of the steel cross members, lock her ankles around the bracing, and slip her arms around his waist. He made a "mm-mmph" sound, a sob stuck deep in his throat.

"It's okay. I've got you." She spoke in a soothing tone, breathing deeply, willing her heart to cease pounding. "Look up, Troy." She knew if she said, "Don't look down," he'd do just that. "Look at that pulley, sweetie. Focus on the pulley and how strong it is, just like all the parts of this crane. We're not going anywhere. I'll hold you tight until help comes."

"My ankle hurts somethin' awful," he said.

Amanda dared a glance down, already certain from the angle of his foot that it was broken. "Try not to think about it," she soothed. "Gosh, what an exciting story you'll have to tell all your friends." Not that she wanted to encourage him, or let him think what he'd done was a good thing. But right now, his life depended on her keeping him calm. She needed Troy to cling with all his might.

She figured he weighed a good seventy pounds— too much for her to hang on to if he panicked and slipped. "Now, mind you," she continued, "I'm not saying this was the best idea, to climb up here, but you will have quite a story to share, right?''

"I guess so," he mumbled. "I only wanted to know if I could see the park from up here." He whimpered again. "I want down."

"I know. And you're going to get down, just as soon as help arrives. Jacob went back to get someone. Heck, you'll probably have half a dozen firemen coming to your rescue any minute. So you see, there's nothing to worry about. Okay?"

"Okay." He trembled in her grasp. "My arms are gettin' tired."

"Think about something else." Desperate, ignoring the cramp in her right calf, Amanda kept talking. "Has your scout troop ever gone rock climbing?"

"No. But we've hiked up a few steep trails."

"Okay. Perfect. Pretend you're on a hike with Ian." The mere thought of him made her wish he was here right this second. "And you're scaling the steepest trail you've ever seen. But you've spotted a nest of baby bald eagles, and you want to stop and watch for a moment. Look up there at that pulley and pretend it's the nest."

"That's silly," Troy said. But she could tell the comment was pure bravado, an attempt to hide the tears that still choked his voice.

"Of course it is," she said. "But what's wrong with being silly once in a while, hmm? So look up there and picture the baby eagles. See how they open their mouths, begging their mother to feed them. What do baby eagles eat? Has your scout group learned about that?"

On and on she talked, gradually getting Troy to relax a little, keeping his mind occupied for what seemed like an eternity before she heard sirens in the distance. Best of all, she heard the sound of Ian's voice.

"Amanda! Hang on, I'm coming up."

She dared a quick glance down and saw him, looking better than any action movie hero as he made his way up the boom, his sturdy work boots seeking a foothold while his strong hands gripped the bracing. Quickly he climbed, and Amanda shook with relief when he took Troy from her grasp. She scooted out of the way, allowing Ian to move in and wrap his arm around Troy.

"Hang on to me with one hand, and the boom with the other," Ian instructed. "We'll go down slow."

"I can't," Troy said.

"His foot is stuck." Amanda inched downward. "But I think I can dislodge it."

"Be careful." Ian's gaze met hers for a split second, and the look of protective caring she saw there made her heart skip even faster.

She lowered herself to a position where she could take gentle hold of Troy's ankle and work it out of the bracing. His tennis shoe came off in the process, tumbling with heart-stopping speed to the ground. Amanda squeezed her eyes shut for a split second and imagined what might have happened if she and Ian hadn't gotten there in time.

Troy whimpered with pain, his ankle dangling, useless. "I'm scared," he said again.

"You're all right," Ian said. "Come on, buddy. You're a Cumberland Cub. You can do this. Use your hands and let me do the rest."

Ian climbed down and as Amanda made her way after him, she saw that a crowd of people had followed Ian and Jacob to the gravel pit. Some stood outside the chain-link fence, while others had ducked inside, ready to lend a hand.

Paramedics, firemen and police officers arrived in a matter of minutes, and a cheer broke from the crowd as Ian reached the ground with Troy safely in his arms. Patricia Stoakes rushed forward and cried while she scolded Troy and hugged him, then profusely thanked Amanda and Ian.

Amanda couldn't help but wonder where Troy's father was. Maybe he simply hadn't been able to make it to the picnic. The EMTs soon had Troy resting on a stretcher, the boy all smiles now that he was safely on the ground—admired from a distance by his fellow scouts.

Amanda patted his leg. "Wow. You get to ride in the ambulance. What a day, huh?"

He looked at her with ambivalence, and she knew what he was likely thinking. Now that he was on firm ground, he probably felt foolish for crying. She leaned forward and whispered in his ear. "I'll never breathe a word about you being scared. Cross my heart." Unobtrusively, she made the gesture, then bumped knuckles with Troy, who wore his big grin once more. Amanda stepped back out of the way, allowing the EMTs to load him into the ambulance along with his mother.

"That was a very brave and foolish thing you did, you know." Ian whispered the words into her ear as he slipped his arm around her waist.

Ignoring the tingling sensation that jolted through

her, she tilted her head to look up at him and spoke dryly. "You climbed up there, too."

He gave her a faux grimace as they ducked through the crowd and headed back toward the park. "I reckon you've got me there." He gave her a squeeze, his arm still wrapped around her. "But I almost had a stroke when I saw you and Troy up there on that boom."

"That makes two of us," she quipped.

"Did you know you cut yourself?" With his free hand, Ian took hold of her wrist and gently lifted her arm to eye level.

Amanda peered at the cut on her inner arm halfway between wrist and elbow. "I didn't even feel it." At the moment, all she was aware of was her blood racing in her veins, her body tucked hip to hip with Ian's.

"You've got a scrape on your leg, too."

"And me without my first-aid kit."

He shook his head and clucked his tongue. "A nurse with no first-aid kit. Now that's got to be a crime."

"I have one in my desk back at the nursing home. I'll walk with you to take Zeb home." She squirmed in Ian's grasp, mind racing as she sought a way to duck out of his embrace without making her effort obvious. Not that she really wanted to. Ian's arm felt warm and strong around her waist, and the urge to slip her own around him took hold of her and wouldn't let go. She had no choice but to use Zeb as a means of escape as she and Ian reached the park once more.

"Sorry to run off and leave you like that, Zeb. I had no idea things were going to get so exciting."

"I was in good hands." Zeb gestured at Sami Jo, who'd come back to the gazebo to stay with him.

"What exactly happened?" Sami asked. "We heard the sirens and Jacob hollering."

Amanda filled her in as she and Sami and Ian wheeled Zeb back to Shade Tree Manor. "I knew you were someone special." Zeb reached up to grasp her hand and gave it an affectionate squeeze and shake. "A regular Wonder Woman. Miss Kelly, will you marry me?"

Sami laughed as Amanda felt her face warm.

"No fair, Papaw," Ian said. "I saw her first." His voice said the comment was all in fun, but the look he gave her with those sexy, dark eyes left her light-headed.

"I only did what anyone else would've done," Amanda said, tearing her gaze away from Ian's.

"Pshaw." Sami waved her hand. "Most folks would've waited for help. Amanda, what you did was really something, and I know Patricia's going to be eternally grateful to you. And to you, too, cousin." She gave Ian a quick hug. "Maybe we'll have to add a hero's parade to the annual picnic."

"Aw, shucks, ma'am," he teased.

Sami shoved him. "I should've brought my video camera."

Back at the nursing home, Amanda had to explain all over again what had happened as her co-workers gathered around, chattering about the wailing sirens, fussing over Amanda's minor injuries. Ian left the group long enough to settle Zeb back in his room, and Amanda slipped away to her office, genuinely embarrassed by all the attention. She truly hadn't thought twice about helping Troy. For her, there had simply been no alternative.

Yet she had to admit having Ian climb up the crane's boom like some sexy hero in an action movie had been enough to send her fantasies into overdrive after Troy had gotten safely to the ground.

"Need some help?" Ian's voice drew her gaze to the doorway.

She shook her head. "I think I can handle it."

But Ian ignored her reply and stepped up behind her desk. He took her hand in his, and gently turned her wrist to expose the cut on her arm. "You're making me crazy, you know," he said, his voice low and deep. "Amanda, I already knew you were special, like Papaw said, but watching what you did today..." He let the words trail away, his eyes telling her what she already knew.

Ian Bonner was every bit as attracted to her as she was to him.

She opened her mouth to protest all over again, but her reply snagged in her throat as Ian slowly brought her hand to his lips and pressed a kiss to her palm. His mouth was soft and hot against her skin, and it took every ounce of her willpower to pull away from him.

"Ian—"

"Okay." He let go of her hand, but not before he let it slide through his grasp by lacing their fingers together. "I can take a hint." Then he raised his eyebrows, looking down at the open box of bandage strips on her desk. "No Snoopy?"

"Not this time." She tore open the wrapper of one.

"Let me." Ian took the bandage strip and placed it over the cut, his hands lingering, contradicting his statement about taking a hint.

From the doorway, Sami cleared her throat as Amanda caught sight of her from the corner of her eye. "Sorry to interrupt, but you two local heroes are wanted out in the day room." She crooked her thumb over her shoulder.

"By who?" Amanda turned, tucking her arm against her chest, rubbing the place where Ian's hands had been.

"Lonnie Gentry—*Grass Roots Gazette.*"

"You're kidding." Amanda let her jaw gape.

"Nope. Brought a photographer and everything."

Ian leaned over and whispered in her ear. "Looks like our fifteen minutes of fame is here." He gave her a wink, then held out his hand, palm up. "After you."

IAN COLLAPSED on the couch with a microwaved ham-and-cheese pocket and a Coke. The hot shower he'd taken moments ago had done little to ease the pain that throbbed in the small of his back, but he barely noticed. Since the picnic two days ago his thoughts had centered on Amanda, and even the twelve-hour shift he'd worked today had done nothing to change that. The image of her clinging to the top side of the crane's boom, her arms wrapped protectively around Troy, kept coming back to haunt him. His mind had gone numb with fear when he'd looked up and seen them.

Amanda could protest all she wanted, and make light of what she'd done. But the truth was, only some-one who truly cared about children would have risked her life the way Amanda had to rescue Troy. Hell, he'd been a little shaky himself when he'd climbed up after her, torn between the need to get Troy to safety and an equal desire to make sure Amanda didn't fall. Her slender arms had trembled like soggy French fries when she'd finally let go of Troy, and the look Ian had seen on her face made one thing clear. Her protective instincts were in high gear when Amanda had climbed that boom.

Yet, in spite of what he'd seen in her eyes, it didn't negate the fact that she'd flatly denied wanting children. He understood how deep her pain must run, having lost her baby, but he still had a feeling there was more to her situation than that. Though he knew it was none of his business, and that his initial determination to ease away from Amanda was the right course to take, his heart wasn't listening. He couldn't stop longing to hover over and protect her—to do anything within his power to help her heal.

Cuddles eased over to the couch and nudged his hand with her cold nose. Ian looked at the dog's soulful brown eyes, and fed her the last bite of his supper. "You're a good dog, Cuddles." Sudden inspiration struck. "Want to go for a ride?"

Her answer was an eager whine and a sprint to the front door, then back to the couch to make sure he meant what he'd said. Outside, it took her but a minute to figure out the ride they were about to take wasn't going to be in the pickup truck. Cuddles leapt onto the seat of Papaw's authentically restored doctor's buggy before Ian could so much as catch Banjo. Chuckling, he harnessed the mule, and moments later, set out down the road toward Amanda's house. She was sitting on the porch, feeding her little gray squirrel, when he guided Banjo up the driveway. The squirrel took one look at the approaching buggy and scurried up a nearby tree.

Amanda rose from her chair. "Well, my, my." She put her hands on her hips. "Don't you look like something right out of *Gunsmoke*."

He grinned at her. "I thought I'd unwind from my Monday by taking Cuddles for a spin. Wanna come along?"

Amanda descended the porch steps, and carefully held the back of her hand out for the Rottweiler's inspection. With a wriggle of her body, Cuddles gave the proffered hand a sniff and a lick. "You are a sweetie," Amanda cooed, rubbing the dog's ears with both hands as she cradled Cuddles's massive head in her palms. She looked up at Ian, hesitation in her expression. "I really shouldn't," she said.

"Aw, come on. Have you ever taken a buggy ride?"

"No."

"Then you don't know what you're missin'." He hopped down from the seat and extended his hand. "I'll have you back in short order."

Amanda gave Banjo a wary look. "Is this the mule that broke Zeb's hip?"

Ian restrained a smile. "It is, but he'll be on his best behavior. I promise."

She tucked her bottom lip beneath her teeth, still wary.

"I've got something to show you that I think you'll like," Ian cajoled.

"Really?" There was a note of piqued curiosity in her voice.

He nodded. "Yep."

"All right." She took his hand and let him help her onto the seat.

He swung up beside her and retrieved the reins, clucking to Banjo. As his shoulder brushed against Amanda's, Ian caught a whiff of her lemon-scented shampoo. She had her hair in a French braid, and wore jeans and a sleeveless lavender blouse that reminded him of the lilacs in her granny's backyard—flowers that bloomed and were quickly gone. Amanda seemed equally as sweet and elusive, and he wanted to put his arm around her and keep her there. Instead, he asked, "How was your day?"

They chatted as Banjo bobbed along, pulling the buggy. Hearing a car behind them, Ian eased the rig onto the shoulder of the road, returning the driver's wave as he passed. Amanda sat gripping the edge of the seat, knuckles white, her back stiff with apprehension. Her breath came in short, rapid gasps, the same way it had the day they'd found the cradle in her shed. What on earth was wrong?

Ian frowned. "It's okay, Amanda. Banjo won't spook."

Visibly, she swallowed, and relaxed her grip a little. "I wasn't sure."

But something in her tone made him wonder what else, besides suspicions of a mule who'd been known to buck, lay behind her unease. "He only threw Papaw because he has a stubborn streak and didn't want to mind that day."

"Banjo or Zeb?" Amanda quipped, but her humor seemed forced.

Ian crooked his mouth in a half smile. "They're both stubborn. But Banjo's not shy of traffic."

"So, exactly where are we going?" Her question seemed more a change of subject than anything else, but he let it slide.

"I have a favorite place where I like to unwind. I thought I'd show it to you."

"Sounds great." She draped one arm around Cuddles, her free hand still gripping the buggy seat.

Ian turned Banjo onto a side road, then down a narrow lane through the trees. A canopy of leafy branches arced above, songbirds twittering from their safe haven. The scent of rich, moist soil and perfumed wildflowers wafted over them as the buggy moved along, and Amanda breathed deeply before exhaling a sigh of pleasure.

"This countryside is gorgeous," she said. "I'd nearly forgotten how abundant the trees and foliage are out here."

"Isn't it like that in Colorado?"

She shook her head. "Not really. The mountains have lots of spruce, pine and aspen, but there's a great deal of open country, too, with rocks, sagebrush, scrub oak. As a matter of fact, eastern Colorado is all plains. Denver is flat as a pancake."

"I didn't realize that." Ian halted the buggy a few minutes later and set the brake. Securing the reins, he helped Amanda down. Cuddles jumped from the seat and trotted a few feet away, her curious nose to the ground. All was silent, save for nature's sounds, and Ian took in the scenery, seeing everything he'd previously taken for granted through Amanda's eyes. He led her to an outcropping of limestone a few yards from the trail. Carved into the rock were the initials

ZB + OL, faded and not as deeply defined as they'd once been.

Ian leaned his palm against the cool surface of the limestone and looked at Amanda. "Can you guess whose initials these are?"

"Zeb Bonner?" Amanda smiled. "And…"

"Opal Lambert. Mamaw."

"Your grandmother? That's so sweet." She pointed at the rock. "Zeb did this?"

He nodded. "Yep. On the day he proposed to her. Right here at this very spot. He carved those initials with a sixteen-penny nail. Mamaw kept it in her jewelry box for years."

Her smile widened. "No kidding? That is so romantic." She traced the ragged edges of the initials with one finger, almost reverently. "Every time I turn around, I like your grandfather more and more."

"Well, he likes you, too."

"He told me he was a widower. When did Opal pass away?"

"A year ago." Ian sobered. "You know, she was the only one who didn't want me to give my son up for adoption."

Amanda settled onto a fallen log, her expression earnest. "Tell me about him."

Ian sat beside her. "There's not a lot to tell. I got my girlfriend—Jolene—pregnant. We'd been dating about four months, which seemed like a hell of a long time to me back then. We were sixteen and I thought I was in love, for a little while." He plucked a stem of grass and twirled it around. "When we found out about the baby, it woke us up to a whole new reality. I didn't want to get married, even though it seemed the thing to do, and Jolene wasn't crazy about the idea either. She was no more ready for parenthood than I was. We got a lot of lecturing from our folks and our grandparents, too. Enough so that we came to the conclusion the best thing to do was put our son up for adoption."

"But your grandma didn't think so?"

He ran the strand of grass through his fingers. "Nope. Mamaw said she'd help Jolene and me raise the boy up, if that's what we wanted. But we didn't have a lot to offer as parents, being kids ourselves, which my dad was quick to remind me of. He made me feel like I'd committed a huge sin, one that was best swept under the carpet." He gave a dry laugh. "Now he wishes he had grandkids. Go figure."

"Did you see your son?"

"Oh, yeah." Familiar pain raked through the scars of Ian's wounds as he recalled staring in wonderment at his tiny baby boy through the glass of the hospital nursery. "I'll never forget his little face—his eyes. But they didn't let me hold him." He clenched his jaw. "It made me mad, but my folks thought I shouldn't get attached. As I got older, I started feeling like I'd done the wrong thing, giving up my own flesh and blood." He shook his head. "I don't know. I lie awake at night sometimes and wonder where he is…what his life is like."

"Have you tried to find him?"

"Time and again. The adoption was handled privately through a local attorney, the records sealed." He sighed. "I haven't had much to go on in the way of information. For a long while, I kept thinking I might actually run across him somewhere, somehow, out there on the streets. Or that one day, when he was old enough, he'd look me up.''

"Did you try the Internet? Some of the 'people find' sites?''

"Not lately.'' He tossed the blade of grass onto the ground. "I don't even know his name. Jolene refused to give him one. I wanted to, but she said we ought to leave that up to the couple who adopted him. I never met them either. About the only thing I've done is plug in the names of Jolene and her parents...some of their relatives.'' He shrugged, feeling the same old frustration that gripped him every time he'd tried and failed in his search. "Like I say, it's not much to go on.''

"I'm sorry.'' The look in Amanda's eyes told him her words were genuine.

Did she remember what he'd said to her the night he'd invited her to BJ's? About losing oneself in booze or work, or a dozen other things? It made him remember she'd been crying that night. He wanted to know about the baby she'd lost, yet to pressure her didn't feel right.

"Tell me about yourself, Amanda.'' He spoke softly, waiting to see if she'd open up to him.

Her jaw muscles flexed, and for a moment, he didn't think she was going to answer. "You're wondering about the baby, aren't you?'' she said at last.

He reached over and took her hand in his. "Only because I care about you.'' His pulse thundered. What he really wanted was for her to tell him she hadn't meant what she'd said when they'd found the cherry-wood cradle in her granny's toolshed a week ago.

I don't ever want to have another baby.

Amanda looked down at their clasped hands, then back up at him once more. "I was a surrogate mother," she said. "For my sister, Nikki. I lost the baby in a car accident."

The words struck him like a runaway train, and Ian's breath caught in his chest. *Dear God.*

Her eyes took on a faraway look. "I was coming home from Nikki's house. Our friends had a baby shower for us, and I stayed awhile after the guests left, to help—" She stopped, stumbling over the words. Took a deep breath. "To help put away the gifts Nikki had gotten at the shower, and arrange some things in the nursery. A nursery she and I had painted and decorated together."

Already, what she said broke his heart. What had he been thinking in pushing her for answers, making her relive such suffering? "Amanda…"

"No." She looked at him, and her eyes swam with unshed tears. "You asked, now let me finish."

He nodded, but inwardly cursed himself.

"By the time I left, it was getting dark," she went on, "and it had started to snow. Nikki lives out in the country, and I had to take a two-lane mountain highway to get home. I saw a young woman standing on the side of the road next to her car. She had a flat tire, and she wasn't wearing a jacket. She looked cold and scared. I felt sorry for her and wanted to help. I had a cell phone, so I pulled over and unbuckled my seat belt to get out of my Blazer. At that moment, everything seemed to happen in slow motion. I heard a sound I'll never forget—like a gunshot." A single tear slid down her cheek. "The next thing I knew, my truck was moving. I don't remember anything after that, but Nikki got the details from the police.

"A man in another SUV hit me. We think he was drunk, from what witnesses said. He knocked my Blazer into a ravine, and then skidded into the young woman I'd stopped to help—Caitlin Kramer. She was severely injured. My Blazer rolled three times before coming to rest upside down." She pressed her fingers against her lips. "I suffered an abruption, which means the placenta pulled away from the walls of my uterus. I nearly bled to death. And the drunk…" She shook her head and clenched her jaw. "He managed to get away. Can you believe that?"

"Amanda, I'm so sorry." Ian put his arm around her shoulders. "I truly am. And I didn't mean to pry and make you sad."

She shook her head. "You didn't. I think about the baby—Anna—all the time. I'll never get over losing her." Her green eyes locked on his. "The accident caused me to have panic attacks. Driving again was difficult." She gave a dry laugh. "I don't know how I ever managed to get here all the way from Colorado. Certain things just seem to trigger the attacks."

Like riding past traffic in a buggy pulled by an ornery mule. Ian felt awful. "I hate to see you going through that," he said gently. "Aren't there medications to control panic attacks?"

"Yes. But I don't like the way they make me feel, all woozy and out of it. My therapist in Colorado taught me some relaxation techniques to try instead." She looked at him, her eyes sad and serious. "Besides, there's no pill in the world that will ever make me forget what happened to Anna. So if you're looking for commitment and children, don't look at me, Ian. I'm not the woman for you.''

Ian's emotions churned inside of him like cream shook up in a jar. Amanda's blunt words seized him, and he knew she was right; that he should thank her for a nice evening and take her back home. But it wasn't as simple as that, because like it or not, he cared more about her than he'd realized until this very moment. She'd gone through the kind of hell no one should ever have to face.

And he'd thought it was hard to give a child up for adoption.

How complicated Amanda's feelings must be—how deep her pain must run—to lose a baby that was not her own, yet was hers in a way. Her strength bowled him over.

''I'm not so sure about that,'' he said in reply to her comment.

And unable to help himself, wanting to hold Amanda and ease her away from the sorrow that gripped her, he took her in his arms and kissed her.

CHAPTER EIGHT

IAN'S LIPS CLOSED OVER HERS, and Amanda's rational thoughts scattered like dandelion seeds on the wind. He kissed her as though he cared. Not as if he wanted to take advantage of a weak moment, and not like a man who expected a thing in return. He kissed her like a man she could count on. A man of his word. And God help her, she kissed him back.

Telling herself she was only human and that any woman with even a single hormone in her body would respond the same way, Amanda let her lips part as Ian gently slipped his tongue inside her mouth. With a precarious hold on her resolve, she moaned and slid her arms around his neck. He tasted sweet and hot and she wanted the kiss to last forever.

With reluctance, she pulled away from him, but not before sharing repeated kisses. Not before becoming intimate with every curve and contour of his mouth and tongue. With her wrists still looped behind his neck, Amanda opened her eyes and met Ian's gaze. He looked at her like a man whose appetite had barely been whetted. Desire plainly showed in the expression on his face, but at the same time, the look in his eyes held more than that. He watched her with an intensity of expression that came straight from the heart. He wanted *her,* not just a hot, willing body to hold, and the thought left her shaky.

"Ian," she whispered. "I'm not so sure this is a good idea."

"Then don't think," he said. Once more his lips claimed hers, and this time his kiss was slow and lingering. Gentle, yet consuming.

A little sigh quivered through Amanda and escaped as Ian tasted her, paused, and tasted her again. His hands roved in small circles against her back. "Amanda." Belatedly, he wavered, their foreheads touching, his mouth close to hers. "You're making me crazy. I keep telling myself we're all wrong for each other, but when I hold you like this…it feels right."

He brought his hand up to cradle her jaw. "You're a remarkable woman, Amanda. And I'm having a hard time keeping my hands to myself. More than that, I want to get to know you better. But I have to be honest." He hesitated. "I *am* looking for a woman to share my life with. To have children with. I'm not into playing games."

His words seared like a branding iron, even though she appreciated his honesty. "Neither am I. That's why I told you, I don't ever want to have another baby." She slid her arms away from his neck and, keeping in control, used her wrists to break his hold.

"Amanda, wait." Gently, he caught her arm, eyes pleading. "I don't want to hurt you. I would never, ever do that. That's why I'm trying to be up-front with you. If you're interested in dating me, I'm all for that. But we have to be realistic about this—which I think we are—and know where to draw the line." He shrugged. "I like you. I don't want to stop seeing you."

She pursed her lips. "I'm not a nun, Ian. And I hardly intend to spend the rest of my life in celibacy. But I'm also not ready for anything serious at the moment. I'm sorry if I let things get out of hand."

"You didn't." With one finger, he traced her brow. "I kissed you." Mixed emotions flickered in his eyes. "I don't intend to pressure you. I only needed to know where we stand."

Amanda rose to her feet. "And now you do. Maybe we'd better call it a day." Without waiting for a reply, she turned and headed for the buggy. Ian moved to help her, but she was already climbing onto the seat. Her skin burned where his hands had been, and her lips tingled—ached—traitorous in missing his touch. She wanted more than she was willing to give herself. Hurt burrowed its way inside of her. Why couldn't she shake the pain that had followed her to Tennessee? This was supposed to be a new start, a brand-new life.

She watched Ian from the corner of her eye as he ordered Cuddles up into the buggy, then climbed onto the seat—the dog between them—took up the reins, and released the brake. This was her own danged fault for letting herself have more than friendly feelings for him. For letting him kiss her. She needed to get a quick hold on her emotions before they leapt completely out of control.

"You didn't do anything wrong," she said quietly as they headed back down the tree-lined lane. "And I don't want you to think I don't want to be around you. If you can take me for who I am, then I have no problem in spending time with you, Ian."

"I would never want you to be anyone other than yourself." He gave her a little smile that broke her heart.

Clucking to Banjo, he turned the buggy toward the main road.

AMANDA'S PHONE RANG two days later as she came in the door from work. Sami Jo's voice greeted her over the line. "I hope I'm not interrupting your supper or anything," she said.

"Not at all." Amanda laid her mail on the counter and, tucking the cordless between her ear and shoulder, pulled off her shoes as she talked. "Actually, I worked a little late today. I just got in the door."

"Well, I won't keep you long. I'm calling to see if you'd like to go shopping Saturday? I thought we could go to the mall in Knoxville. Maybe grab some lunch—make it a girls' day out."

Amanda's heart gave a hitch. Countless times, she'd received a similar invitation from Nikki. They'd spent many a weekend window-shopping, and an indefinite number of hours sipping lattes in the bookstore, content in the quiet comfort of one another's presence.

Breaking from her reverie, Amanda forced a cheerful note into her voice. "I don't know. I've been keeping busy working and trying to get Granny's place in order. I was sort of planning on cleaning out the tool-shed this weekend. There never seem to be enough hours in the day."

"I hear you there," Sami said. "But you can't work all the time. Are you sure you can't break away for a little while?"

Amanda hesitated. A part of her wanted nothing

more than to hide out at Granny's cabin, licking her wounds. Yet she had to admit, she'd had fun at the picnic last weekend. And Sami Jo was so sweet, and had made her feel welcome there as a part of the town. Amanda didn't want to hurt her feelings. ''All right. Sounds good to me.'' *Why not?* It might be nice to get out and do something different. Take her mind off of everything, including Ian. They arranged a time, and Amanda hung up the phone feeling okay about her decision, even though she wished it were she and Nikki going shopping together. She missed her sister so much. Leaving Colorado had seemed like the best thing to do, but she hadn't anticipated how difficult it would be to be separated from Nikki by what felt like endless miles.

With that thought, Amanda picked up the phone. Nikki's voice warmed her inside when she answered the phone. They chatted, and Amanda told her she was going to the mall, hoping a little socializing might help. That getting out would be better than holing up in the cabin.

''Of course it will be,'' Nikki said. She sighed. ''I wish I was going with you, but I'm glad you're making friends. You have fun with Sami Jo. Have a hot pretzel for me.''

''I still wish you'd consider coming out here for a while,'' Amanda said.

''Well, maybe I'll give that some serious thought. I love you.''

''Love you, too, sis. Talk to you soon.'' She hung up the phone, feeling somewhat better.

SAMI PICKED HER UP at ten o'clock Saturday morning, and they headed toward Knoxville, chatting, while on the radio, Toby Keith and Willie Nelson crooned a story of whiskey, beer and horses. Inside the mall, they weaved their way through a plethora of fellow shoppers. Only now did Amanda realize how secluded her life had indeed become, living in Granny's beloved woods.

Nostalgia gripped her once more as she longed for Nikki's presence. Talking to her the other day had made Amanda miss her all the more. The scents of fresh-baked chocolate chip cookies and caramel corn swirled around them like unseen tendrils of smoke, and Amanda hurried to keep up with Sami's long-legged stride as she headed with purpose toward a shoe store.

"They've got the best deals here," Sami said, "and their shoes actually last."

Amanda browsed through the sandals on display. She ended up buying a straw-colored pair that would look cute with her favorite sundress. Shopping bags in hand, she and Sami headed out into the mall's walkway once more.

"Maybe these will keep me from getting swollen ankles." Sami indicated the comfortable-looking loafers she'd bought.

"What's wrong with your ankles?" Amanda asked.

"Nothing yet." Sami grinned. "But in a few months, that might be another story. No more climbing around, building gazebos for a while I'm afraid." She patted her lower abdomen. "I just found out I'm pregnant."

Amanda went light-headed, and whatever Sami said as she continued talking blurred into indiscernible white noise. She did her best to mumble words of congratulations. But she wasn't totally sure she'd spoken them out loud. Sami didn't seem to notice, for she took hold of Amanda's arm and steered her into another store. "Oh, I've got to stop here. Do you mind?"

Numb, Amanda followed her as they laced their way through various departments, Sami chattering all the while. She didn't fully realize where they were until the scents of baby lotion and powder wafted over her. She sucked in her breath, and her senses suffered overload as she took in the shelves and spindles, fully stocked with everything a new mother might need.

Little washcloths. Rubber ducks. Teething rings.

The floor seemed to sway beneath her feet. Her throat clogged. Her eyes burned. She took a step backward and banged into a crib on display. Moved forward and almost toppled a high chair.

"Amanda?" Sami Jo turned to look at her, brow wrinkled, mouth agape. "My gosh! What's the matter?"

Shaking her head, Amanda swallowed over the tight, hard knot in her throat. "I can't do this," she said. "I'm sorry."

Ignoring the odd looks some of the other shoppers gave her, she turned and hurried out of the store, clutching her shopping bag like a shield. Her breath came in rapid gasps, and she knew if she didn't stop it she would hyperventilate.

The sweet, phantom scent of powders and lotions continued to project in her mind, as she flashed back on memories of the tiny babies she'd held in the nursery when she worked at the hospital in Deer Creek. She could close her eyes and remember exactly how soft their little hands were. Each tiny finger so perfectly formed, with itty-bitty nails. And a grip strong and sure as they fisted those fingers around her own, which seemed huge and cumbersome in comparison.

Lively, crying babies with good, healthy lungs, bringing joy and laughter to proud parents who welcomed the sound as reassurance their child was healthy—safely born into this world. Their legs kicking, eyes squeezed shut in protest at the injustice of being thrust from the warm, nurturing environment of their mothers' wombs, into the reality of bright lights and strange noises.

Amanda collapsed onto a bench near a potted plant. Nearby, a fountain sprayed mist into the air, and children laughed and shouted and tossed pennies into the water. She absorbed it all as she sat waiting for Sami to catch up. Waiting for her breathing to return to normal, willing those baby scents to leave her memory once and for all.

She wanted to scream.

The injustice of Anna's death shook her. *Dear God, take it back!* Why couldn't He just turn the clock to one minute before she left Nikki's house that night after the baby shower? She closed her eyes, a familiar litany echoing inside her mind.

If only she'd stayed for the cup of herbal tea Nikki had offered.

If only she'd spent more time searching for the CD she'd wanted to listen to on the ride home, but couldn't find in the mishmash clutter in the back seat of her Blazer.

If only she'd driven past Caitlin Kramer and let her worry about her own damned tire.

Why, why, had things happened the way they did? How many times had she offered comfort to a patient who had lost a baby? Feeling helpless to do or say anything that would truly make things better. Trying to keep a professional distance. All the while, her heart breaking for the loss the woman and all those close to her suffered. Never dreaming it would happen to her.

"Amanda." Sami's voice pulled her back to the here and now. "My gosh, what is wrong, sweetie?" Sami laid a hand on her shoulder, then reached up to brush the hair from Amanda's eyes.

She felt like a fool. How on earth was she ever going to move past the grief that darkened her life if she couldn't even accept the news that a friend was pregnant? Couldn't even walk through the baby department of a store.

"I'm sorry," she said as her breathing slowly returned to normal. "I didn't mean to run out on you like that."

"It's okay." Sami smoothed her hair once more, her hand warm and firm. "Here, let's go someplace a little more quiet where we can talk. Come on." She hefted her purse onto one shoulder, still clutching her shopping bag, and took Amanda by the arm. Amanda followed, barely remembering to retrieve her own purchase from where she'd let it fall at her feet, feeling ridiculous as they walked down a hallway past the rest rooms and out a side exit to a grassy area near the parking lot. A wrought-iron bench stood in the shade of a tree, and Sami plunked down beside her as Amanda sank onto it. "Now," she said. "Tell me what's wrong, sugar. Something obviously upset you." Genuine concern lined her sun-browned face.

Amanda tried not to let her gaze rove to Sami's still-flat belly. Tried not to picture the way it would soon become round and full, the way hers had once been. She took a shaky breath, unable to bear repeating the details of her accident yet again, but also unwilling to brush Sami off with a made-up excuse. "I lost a baby a few months ago," she said. She gave Sami a brief explanation—that she'd been a surrogate for her sister and that an auto accident had caused her loss. She left out the details. It had been hard enough to tell Ian.

"Oh, Amanda." Sami clasped one hand to her mouth, then her breast. "I am so, so sorry. Lord, and me going on and on about the baby stuff." She shook her head in self-reprimand. "I can't tell you how sorry I am."

"It's okay," Amanda said. "You couldn't have known."

"I feel just awful." Sami reached out and gave her a hug. "Let me buy you lunch, hon. Not that that'll really help, but, well, I invited you shopping to have a good time. I didn't mean to spoil your day. My God." She continued to shake her head.

"Don't beat yourself up," Amanda said. Her appetite was gone, but she didn't want to hurt her new friend's feelings. "Lunch sounds nice."

Relief flooded Sami's features. "How about the Olive Garden? It's my favorite. And since I can only keep food down half the time—" She halted abruptly, and once more, her face went crimson. "Lord, no matter how big my foot is, I can still fit it in my mouth, can't I?"

"It's okay," Amanda repeated.

But as she and Sami got in the car and headed for

the restaurant, she wondered if any part of her life would ever truly be okay again.

BY THE TIME Sami dropped Amanda off at home, she felt emotionally drained. She'd picked at her lunch, making a pretense of eating so as not to make her friend feel any worse, but she was pretty sure Sami hadn't been fooled.

When suppertime rolled around, her appetite wasn't much better. She fixed a salad and carried it to the living room. As she sat on the couch, looking out the window, her thoughts turned to Ian. He'd been so sweet and understanding the other day. It tore at her conscience to think she might have hurt him in any way, but she'd felt compelled to be honest about her feelings. Hearing about his son had touched her deeply. Losing a baby was awful; giving one up couldn't be much better. She hoped he would somehow find his son, and as the thought came to her, she realized something.

She'd come to Granny's cabin to start over, but in a way, she knew she'd simply been running from her feelings. As Ian had said that night they'd first sat on her porch and talked, a person could easily use work as a means of escape, and that was basically what she'd been doing since her arrival in Tennessee. Working, or keeping busy around the cabin until she was tired enough to sleep. Following a similar pattern the next day and the one after that.

Surely there were additional constructive ways to spend her free time. Maybe she'd take up gardening— start doing her own yard work. She was perfectly capable of mowing the grass, and somewhere in the mess inside Granny's toolshed was an old push mower. She could get exercise and a manicured lawn in the bargain. She would have to make a real effort to get the shed cleaned out.

Not wanting to think about the cradle that was also still in the toolshed, Amanda focused on positive things. Making friends, like Sami, was another step in the right direction of getting on with her life. And of course, there'd been her dates with Ian—if that's what you could call them. She'd tried to keep her distance, to keep time spent with Ian on a casual note.

But her heart screamed, *Admit it!* They had been dates all right. Right down to the hot kisses she'd shared with him on their buggy ride. Her sensible side warned her to tread softly, to make sure her relationship with him didn't become more than she was ready for. As she sat thinking about Ian's quest to find his son, Amanda's inner voice began to whisper once more.

Help him.

Why not? It was possible she might come up with some new ideas, maybe an angle or direction he hadn't yet explored. She loved doing things for others—it was, after all, why she'd gone into nursing. But deep down, Amanda knew she had another motive. Spending time with Ian was part of it, if she were to be totally honest. But more than that, helping him might also ease her conscience.

A conscience that zinged her every time she remembered the emotional line she'd drawn between herself and Ian. Every time she recalled the look in his dark, riveting eyes when he'd kissed her, and the look on his face when she told him she never wanted to have children. If she could only help him find his son, then Ian would be happy and she wouldn't have to feel guilty about pushing him away.

With new energy, Amanda picked up her empty salad bowl and carried it to the kitchen.

IAN RUBBED the tired, grainy feeling from his eyes and turned off the computer. Amanda's question the other day, when they'd gone for a buggy ride, had prompted him to once again search the Internet for leads on finding his son. But as always, he'd run into nothing but dead ends. Without much to go on, the task seemed hopeless. He was reminded of why he'd taken a break from searching some time ago.

The adoption had been a private one, handled by a local attorney. Shortly after signing the adoption papers, Ian had torn up his copy in an effort to erase his past and the mistake he'd made in getting involved with Jolene in the first place. He'd lived to regret it. When he'd begun his search, at the age of twenty, he had been told by the attorney's paralegal that the adoption was sealed—it was confidential information Ian was not entitled to. Frustrated, he'd given up—for a while. Later, he'd discovered the attorney was no longer practicing in the area.

He couldn't remember the name of the adoptive parents, and after some time had passed, he could no longer recall that of the attorney. He'd written it down once—Breck...or Beck?—and thought about hiring a private detective. But with little more to go on than the attorney's name, the endeavor seemed a waste of time and money. Jolene herself hadn't been anymore forthcoming in sharing information with Ian. He was certain she remembered the names of the couple who'd adopted their baby, but she had refused to tell him and had moved away a short time later. Feeling defeated, he'd wadded up the paper with the attorney's name on it and thrown it in the trash.

Who knew where Jolene might be by now, and if she'd married she'd likely taken her husband's last name. A few of her relatives remained in the area, but they'd responded to Jolene's pregnancy by turning on Ian, as though he were solely responsible for her condition. More than one uncle or cousin had bluntly told him to stay the hell away, if he didn't want to wind up on the wrong end of a shotgun.

The fact that he didn't even know his own child's name bothered him to no end. The adoption papers had stated only "baby boy," and though the names of the adoptive parents had also been on the papers he signed, he'd never looked that closely at them. Now he wished he had. How was he ever supposed to find his son with so little to go on?

Pushing his chair away from the desk, Ian stood, put his cap on and went outside to feed Cuddles and Banjo. He'd visited Papaw that morning, then spent the day working in the shop before deciding to look on the Internet. His search had left him restless, and thoughts of his son led to thoughts of Amanda. As he turned on the garden hose to fill the stock tank, his mind continued to wander.

He still couldn't get over the depth of her loss. He'd heard of women acting as surrogate mothers, but he'd never thought much about it. Being so close to Amanda, caring so much about her, had opened his eyes to a situation that had, until now, seemed foreign.

No wonder she'd seemed resentful toward the subject of adoption. He never would've brought up the fact that he'd given up his son had he realized how deeply Amanda was hurting. He felt the need to make things better for her somehow. Of course, the pain she felt wasn't the kind she could move past in short order. There was nothing he could do about it, but he could at least be there for her. He hadn't seen her in almost a week, and it felt like forever.

The ringing phone drew his attention, and he sprinted for the shop. Breathless, hoping somehow it might be Amanda, he picked up the receiver. "Hello?"

"Hey, cuz." Sami's voice filled his ear. "What're you up to?"

"Nothing much. Just taking care of Banjo." Something in her tone gave him pause. "What's going on?"

Sami let her breath out on a long sigh. "Look, I shouldn't be blabbing other people's business, but I like Amanda and it's plain to see you care a lot about her, too."

Ian's stomach lurched. "Is something wrong?"

"I took her shopping today, and I'm afraid it ended up a disaster." She told him what had happened at the mall. "I hadn't even had the chance to tell you my news," she finished. "I just found out yesterday."

"Congratulations, Sami. I'm really happy for you and John." Ian's chest tightened with pleasure and pride in anticipation of having another little second cousin to spoil. But his happiness was fleeting as he imagined what Amanda had been through, and how she must have felt looking at all the baby stuff.

"Thanks, but I'm worried about Amanda."

"It's not your fault. You couldn't have known."

"That's what Amanda said, but I still feel just awful. I'd like to do something to make her feel better, but I have no idea what." She paused. "I thought about sending her flowers, but I'm afraid that might upset her more. You know—kind of like bringing it up all over again, especially if people sent her flowers when the baby died. But if you did... Well, what woman doesn't like getting flowers from a man?"

Ian shifted the phone to his other ear and leaned against the shop wall, feeling like a dolt for not having come up with the idea himself. "Guess I'm really rusty on this dating business," he said. "I should have thought of giving her flowers sooner. Don't tell Papaw or I'll catch hell."

Sami's rich-throated chuckle danced across the line. "My lips are sealed."

Ian hung up the phone, his emotions torn in two. His initial excitement at finding the perfect excuse to see Amanda again fell short in knowing she'd suffered, reliving painful memories. The urge to drive to her house immediately was one he had a hard time keeping in check. She likely needed some space. But Sami's suggestion was a good one.

What sort of flowers should he get? Roses? He'd heard somewhere that yellow roses stood for friendship, red for love. Neither one seemed quite appropriate. Should he get both? Maybe he ought to stick with white. Or pink. He had no clue what those colors stood for.

As he headed back outside, an idea came to him. Never mind getting a bouquet from the florist. He'd do one better than that. He'd bring her something that would last and make Amanda think of him every time she looked around her backyard. Something that would also give him reason to spend the day with her. Or at least part of it.

The sound of overflowing water belatedly reached his ears, and Ian rushed to shut off the hose. The tank wasn't the only thing running over. His heart felt as if it, too, were going to overflow or maybe even burst with the contained feelings he harbored for Amanda. He realized he was doing little more than self-inflicting punishment by continuing to hang around her. Wanting something he couldn't have. But deep down inside, he couldn't help but hope that continuing to act on Papaw's advice would pay off. That nature would indeed take its course in turning Amanda's feelings for him into something more than friendship.

He'd let himself fall too far already.

All he could do now was hang on for the ride.

CHAPTER NINE

AMANDA SPENT the better part of Monday morning on the telephone in her office, going over various issues with the doctors who treated her residents. By the time she'd finished, a new arrival, Lily Crenshaw, had been admitted, and Amanda went to Lily's room to meet her and see to her initial care. Lily had been brought in after a long bout with the flu that had left her dehydrated. She'd spent some time in the hospital, only to go home and take a turn for the worse. With her family unable to provide the care she required, she'd come to Shade Tree Manor.

"Hello, there, Lily." Amanda spoke as she entered the room where Roberta was in the process of starting an IV. She introduced herself. "How are you feeling?"

"I've been better." Tiny in stature, the woman had birdlike arms and legs. She lay propped against a pillow, her pale silver hair spread out around her. "Never felt so weak in my life."

"Poor little thing doesn't hardly have a vein to get this thing started," Roberta said, indicating the IV she'd hung. "I think you'd best do it." She gave Lily's hand an affectionate pat.

"Let's see here." Amanda spoke soothingly to Lily, distracting her with chitchat while she inserted the Hep-lock, capped it off, and wrapped Lily's hand and wrist with gauze to keep the IV in place. "There you are, hon. That'll get you feeling better in no time."

Pale blue eyes narrowed, Lily focused intently on Amanda's face. "I've seen you before," she said. "At Good Neighbor Days, with Matthew Bonner's boy."

"Ian?" Amanda smiled, reminding herself this was a small town.

"That's right." Lily nodded. "Saw your picture with him in the paper, too. Local heroes, huh?"

"Well, I don't know about that." Amanda's face warmed. Everyone in town had made a huge fuss when the story of her and Ian rescuing Troy from atop the crane had made the front page of the local paper. Amanda had done her best to downplay the insinuation that the two of them were a couple.

Lily frowned. "I thought Ian was going with Jolene Kennedy."

"That was a long time ago, sweetie," Roberta spoke up. "And her name was Jolene Bradford, not Kennedy. We were in the same French class, and Lord how I envied her for snagging Ian Bonner." She gave Amanda a wry grin. "Sorry. But he really was something."

He still is. Amanda did her best not to let her feelings show. She focused on Lily.

Lily's wrinkled brow puckered in further confusion. "Are you sure Jolene's not with him anymore? She's kin, you know."

"No, honey." Roberta shook her head and exchanged a sympathetic glance with Amanda. "That was way back in high school."

It pained Amanda to see her patients so frail, their minds sometimes addled.

Lily held up one gnarled finger. "Well, you tell Ian I said hello, next time you see him."

"I promise." Amanda gave Lily's arm a pat. "You let us know if you need anything, all right?"

Leaving Lily in Roberta's capable hands, she made her way down the hall, unable to get the woman's words out of her mind. Maybe it wouldn't hurt to mention what Lily had said about Jolene to Ian the next time she saw him.

But when he came to visit Zeb on Wednesday, Amanda was too busy to do little more than wave hello to Ian. Moments later, one of her residents pitched a fit for reasons unknown, throwing herself from her wheelchair. She managed to hit her head in the process, and Amanda had held a square of gauze to the wound until the paramedics arrived. The cut required stitches, and the woman had been carted off to the emergency room. Then Albert decided to venture once again into the imaginary world in which he was Daniel Boone. Dressed in his pajamas and his worn coonskin cap, he staved off two orderlies and a nurse with a broomstick before Amanda was able to help bring him under control.

By the time she had a spare minute, Ian had already left. It was after lunch, and exhausted, Amanda opted for a quick sandwich in the break room before returning to her duties. She stayed an hour past her shift, and when she got home, changed into shorts and a T-shirt.

The sound of a vehicle pulling into her driveway caught her attention, and a quick peek through the window told her it was Ian's truck. Immediately, her mood picked up. She briefly checked her hair in the mirror before slipping into her shoes. Her French braid had come partially undone. Oh well. It would have to do.

She stepped out onto the porch. "Hey, there. What brings you way out here?"

"I brought you something." Ian walked around to the passenger side of his pickup and opened the door. Leaning in, he withdrew something from off the floorboard.

Amanda let out a little gasp as he straightened and turned her way, two of the most beautiful potted rosebushes she'd ever seen in his hands. "Oh my gosh. Those are gorgeous." She hustled down the steps and met him halfway as he headed up the walk.

Fist-sized blooms of blush-trimmed peach and magenta shot through with ivory, stood out among the greenery of the rose plants. Wary of the thorns, Amanda reached out to gently grasp the stem of one flower. Closing her eyes, she leaned forward and inhaled the fragrance. It reminded her of air sweetened by rain. She opened her eyes and found Ian watching her.

A smile tugged the corners of his mouth. "You like them, then?"

"Do I ever." She reached to take one of the potted bushes from him. "But you shouldn't have done that."

"I wanted to." A look of concern replaced his smile. "They were partly Sami's idea. She feels really bad about what happened the other day, and so do I. Are you okay?"

Amanda's stomach hitched briefly, and she pursed her lips in an effort not to let thoughts of the incident at the mall interfere with this moment. Ian's concern touched her deeply, as did Sami's.

"Yes, I am," she said. "There's no need for Sami to feel bad. Really." She managed a smile. "She's sweet. I like her a lot."

"She feels the same way about you." He reached out and brushed his fingers lightly over her cheek. "I care, too, you know. I'd do anything to see that pretty smile of yours on a regular basis."

Unable to help it, Amanda let her smile widen. "Thank you." Her heart raced. "Like" barely began to describe the way she felt about Ian. Pushing her feelings aside, she indicated the rosebushes. "Want to help me plant them?"

"You bet. That's why I'm here."

"All right then. I'll get a trowel." From the windowsill of the shed, Amanda retrieved the hand tools she'd recently used to prune and shape Granny's irises. She loved flowers, but hadn't done any gardening since she was a kid, when Granny had shown her the basics. She'd have to work on honing her skills, and her new hobby had even more appeal now that Ian factored into the deal.

Ian took the trowel. "I'll dig. No sense in you getting dirt under your fingernails."

"Like that would really ruin my manicure," Amanda joked. She kept her nails at a short, serviceable length and rarely wore polish.

"Maybe not," he teased, "but we can't have a nurse with dirty fingernails." He indicated the rosebushes. "Where do you want 'em?"

"How about on either side of the steps? That ought to look nice."

"You're the boss." He knelt and began to dig.

Using both the trowel and his hands, he scooped the moist soil out of the way to make a place for planting. Amanda crouched beside him, tamping the dirt down once the rosebush had been put in the ground. A short time later, both bushes were in place, the flowers cheerful and inviting. A welcoming splash of color to anyone who might ascend the porch steps.

"Perfect." Amanda stood back to admire them.

"They do look nice." Ian nodded. "Now for the rest."

"The rest?" She frowned.

"Yep." He headed for the truck once more. "You didn't think I only brought two, did you?"

"Ian!" Amanda let her jaw gape as she watched him pull two more rosebushes—one ivory, one bright yellow—from his truck. He handed them to her and retrieved a third pair; deep red, and a shade that hovered between pink and lilac.

He pushed the pickup's door shut with his foot, and chuckled as Amanda gave him a mock look of reprimand. "That's it, I promise."

"Really, you shouldn't have gone to this much trouble."

"It's no trouble. I thought you liked them."

"I do. That's not the point."

"Then what is?" Ian leaned closer, his dark-chocolate eyes full of mischief.

Amanda couldn't decide which smelled better—his cologne or the roses. Deciding it had to be him, she scrambled for a coherent reply. "I-uh." *Confound it, she'd already forgotten the question.* "You shouldn't be spending money on me. Let me pay you for them."

"No way," he said, his face mere inches from hers. "I can't think of anything or anyone I'd rather spend it on."

Clutching the roses as a defensive shield, Amanda managed to take a deep breath and a step backward. "Well, you still shouldn't have." She looked at the flowers. "But they are gorgeous."

"And so are you." Closing the distance between them once more, Ian dodged the roses and brushed a kiss across her lips.

Just one, she told herself as she kissed him back. *And then I'll stop.*

But kissing Ian was a lot like eating potato chips. Stopping at one wasn't easy. Only the fact that she was dangerously close to smashing the rosebushes between them brought Amanda to her senses. "Um—I guess we'd better find a place for these."

"Guess so." But the look in Ian's eyes told her he'd rather do other things besides plant flowers.

Amanda chose a spot on the freshly mowed lawn in front of the porch. The area offered plenty of morning sunshine. As she and Ian took turns digging and planting, she suddenly remembered what she'd wanted to ask him earlier.

"Ian, was Jolene's last name Bradford?"

Startled, he looked up at her. "Yeah. Where did that come from?"

"One of my residents, Lily Crenshaw, mentioned her the other day. She said she was related to Jolene, but she also seemed a bit confused. She called her

Jolene Kennedy. Anyway, Lily seemed to think you and Jolene were still dating."

Ian paused in the middle of tamping dirt around the base of a rose plant. "I'm not dating anyone." He met her gaze. "I mean, anyone other than you. Jolene has been long gone from my life for some years now."

"I know that." Amanda felt her face warm. "I wasn't fishing to see if you're dating other women. That's your business." But she couldn't stop the burning flash of jealousy his words created. "My point is, Lily was confused time-wise, thinking you and Jolene were still in high school. So I'm not sure if she was also confused about Jolene's last name, or if she might be right." She pursed her lips. "I thought it might be worth looking into."

Hope flickered in Ian's eyes, and Amanda felt a stir of excitement. If only she could truly help him find his son. On the other hand, she didn't want to set him up for disappointment by giving him a lead that might be false. "Maybe I shouldn't have said anything."

"No. You were right to tell me," Ian said. "It couldn't hurt to try. Chances are, Jolene is married with a new last name."

"How old would your son be now?" Amanda asked, unable to get the boy off her mind.

"Sixteen."

"Wow." The realization of all the lost years hit her dead center. Ian had missed out on his son's entire childhood. Yet even though the kid was grown, she imagined Ian still thought of him as his little boy— his baby.

Ian finished tamping the soil and held the trowel out to Amanda. She took it and began to dig the next hole.

"If Lily's right about Jolene's name, I wonder how she knew?" He frowned. "You said Lily Crenshaw, right?"

Amanda nodded. "Do you know her?"

"Papaw does."

"There you go. Maybe you ought to ask him about it." She chipped away at the soil to dislodge a walnut-sized rock stuck in the ground. "Either way, it might be worth running the name on the Internet. You know, I was planning to talk to you about that."

"Oh?"

"I'd like to help you search for your son. If you'd like some help, that is."

"That's mighty thoughtful of you. But I don't know what all we can try that I haven't already done, other than what we just talked about—searching for a Jolene Kennedy."

"Well, you never know." With the rock out of the way, she widened the hole. "Like they say, two heads are better than one."

They worked in silence for the next few minutes. Pushing thoughts of lost children from her mind, Amanda relaxed and focused on the moment. The sweet scent of the roses mingled with that of the rich potting soil and red clay dirt to create a pleasant combination of earth and living things. Working with Ian in the fading evening sun made her feel more alive than she had in months, and she was glad he'd brought the roses. She wished she could somehow prolong the moment.

A short time later, Amanda stood back to admire her and Ian's handiwork. "Wow. They sure brighten up the yard." She smiled. "But look at us. We're a mess.'' She held her hands away from her body. Dirt clung to her palms and fingertips, and bits of grass stuck to her bare knees. "Guess I should do my yard work in jeans, not shorts.''

Ian, too, was sprinkled with grass clippings and soil caked his hands and fingernails. "Nothing wrong with good, honest, hard work.'' He stepped up beside her. "And I happen to like your shorts.'' He looked down at her legs, which could use a tan, and Amanda shifted self-consciously.

"Thanks.'' She chuckled. "You've got dirt on your nose.''

"Do I?'' He wrinkled it, and closing one eye, tilted his chin in a comical effort to see. Then he looked back at her. "Know what?''

"What?''

"You've got dirt on yours, too.'' He reached out and swiped at the tip of her nose with one finger, leaving behind a smudge of potting soil.

Amanda ducked, and laughing, touched Ian's cheek. "Oops. You've got dirt on your cheek. And your chin.''

"Oh, you wanna play that way, do you?'' His dimples creased his cheeks as he swooped closer, and Amanda dodged, barely avoiding his grasp. The two of them scurried around the yard, laughing, chasing one another like a couple of kids. But it was Ian who called an all-out war when he paused near the water spigot.

"Oh no.'' Amanda held up her hands, palms out. "Don't you dare.''

"Hey, we're both dirty. We could use a little water

to clean up.'' With that, he turned on the hose, and Amanda ran, shrieking.

The water arced up and sprinkled the back of her shirt and her hair before she could dart out of reach. She turned on her heel. ''You've asked for it now, buddy.''

''What're you going to do about it, huh?'' Ian teased. With jerky motions, he flipped the hose nozzle up and down, and sent droplets of water flying in the air to land on her again.

Cold well water.

She gasped as a huge splat of it hit the front of her T-shirt. Ducking her head, she rushed Ian with the gusto of a linebacker. Like children playing in a sprinkler, they scuffled over possession of the garden hose. Water swirled everywhere, soaking them, and Ian's cap came off in the process. By the time Amanda managed to reach the faucet and turn it off, both of them were dripping wet, laughing, breathless.

''No fair.'' Ian dived at her, and easily wrestled her to the ground. ''You're not allowed to disarm the enemy by taking away the ammunition.''

''Says who?'' Flat on her back, she looked up at him.

''Says me.'' He leaned over her, his chest across hers, one leg hooked over her own.

Amanda's breath caught in her throat. She felt mesmerized by Ian's dark eyes, his touch, his very presence. ''Who says you're the enemy?'' She'd meant the question to sound light—a continuation of their banter. Instead, it came out on a choked whisper that was closer to suggestive. Like it came from a woman who hadn't been held in a while. At least not until Ian had come along.

She thought about the kisses she'd shared with him on their buggy ride. And the kisses she'd wanted to share with him the day he'd pushed her on the swing. She'd pulled back then, and she knew she should do so again. But, heaven help her, she didn't want to. She wanted Ian, and she wanted him now.

"Kiss me," she said.

"Amanda." Her name came out on a soft moan as Ian willingly obliged her.

He slid his body all the way onto hers, their wet clothes pressed together. Her heart hammered beneath his. Not even their chilled clothing could block out the warmth of his skin, and she sighed with pleasure as he parted her lips with his tongue. He kissed her, running his hands over her shoulders, slipping them beneath her to cradle her neck.

Amanda responded with a hunger she hadn't known in a long time. Something about Ian felt so right, so good. Her sensibility fled in the wake of his kisses, his touch, as she wrapped her arms around him and let her tongue rove his mouth—first playful, then demanding.

No, no. Stop.

But she refused to listen to her own voice of reason, or to think about the fact she was likely setting herself up for a heartache. If nothing else, she shouldn't be doing this to Ian. Kissing him like a woman gone mad, a woman who had no reservations. No hang-ups. No problems.

It wasn't fair. She couldn't give him what he wanted, and even though at this moment all he seemed to want was her—physically—she knew he was a better man than that. If Ian Bonner hadn't already given her his heart, he was at least dangerously close to doing so. If she didn't stop now, she might be in grave danger herself. Because it would be so simple, so very, very easy to fall in love with this man. If she didn't put an end to the hot kisses he now sprinkled down her neck, and across her chest, the two of them were bound to end up clawing away each other's clothes right here on her lawn.

Ian nibbled a path over her wet T-shirt, where her nipples stood obligingly beneath the thin material. He took one in his mouth and suckled, and Amanda moaned. Hot moisture instantly dampened her already water-soaked underwear, and the ground beneath her seemed to spin. "Ian." She breathed his name, making an effort to grasp his shoulders and shove. But instead, she found herself rubbing circles on the taut muscles of his back, urging him closer. Encouraging him not to stop. His mouth felt warm and wonderful and all she could think about was how it would be even better if no material separated her flesh from his tongue.

She wriggled beneath him, and he hardened against her, his blue jeans pressed to her shorts. It took a moment for the fact to register that something else hard was pressing against her, on her back just below her right shoulder. Something that felt like a rock.

"Mmm." Amanda murmured against Ian's mouth, the sound half longing, half pain. "Wait, Ian, wait. Something's poking me."

An impish grin curved his lips, and she couldn't help but chuckle. "No, not that. Here." She struggled to sit up, and with a groan of frustration, Ian moved to let her. Amanda twisted around to look for the object on the ground beneath her. With a puzzled frown, she lifted it from where it had become embedded in the grass.

A class ring on a broken chain. A man's ring, it would appear, with a black onyx stone. Something about it seemed familiar, and she wracked her lust-fogged brain in an attempt to make sense of it.

But before she could, Ian grasped her wrist firmly in his hand. She looked at him, and was stunned by what she saw. His face had gone pale, and as he sat up and reached for the ring and chain, he began to shake. Violently.

"Ian. What's the matter?"

"My God," he whispered. His eyes locked on hers. "Where did this come from? Amanda, how did this ring get in your yard?"

Dumbfounded, it took a moment for her thoughts to swirl into some semblance of order. But Ian didn't give her a chance to answer. Instead, he grabbed her by the shoulders and gave her a little shake. "Amanda, tell me!" The shake wasn't rough, but it startled her all the same.

Irritated by his odd behavior, she shrugged out of his grasp. "Why are you getting so upset?" Was he jealous? Did he think she'd been rolling around on the lawn with someone else? Someone who owned the ring?

And just that fast, her thoughts shifted. Her eyes locked on the piece of jewelry, and she noted the graduation year, engraved on the gold, antique-finished surface. She'd watched as Ian tilted it to expose the inscription on the inside. Now, she leaned closer for a better look.

Ian Bonner.

The name inside was his. Amanda's hands began to tremble, and she clamped one briefly over her mouth.

"Oh, my God." She stared at Ian. "That ring belongs to Gavin," she said. "The boy who mows my lawn."

CHAPTER TEN

A ROARING SOUND RUSHED through Ian's ears and his vision blurred. *His son.* Right here in Boone's Crossing. *It couldn't be that easy.*

He'd given his class ring to Jolene shortly after they'd started going together, and she'd worn it on a chain around her neck because it was too big for her finger. Surely she hadn't given it up with their baby. There had to be another explanation, but even as he rose to his feet, eyes still locked on the ring, he knew there was not. Amanda's voice blurred to the background as memories washed over him. He'd given the ring to Jolene all right, but it had cost a pretty penny, and he'd wanted it back when they broke up.

I'm not giving it back, Ian.

Why? What possible reason could you have for wanting to keep it, other than to piss me off?

But she hadn't budged. Could she really have given it to their son—to the people who adopted him? Was it likely they would have then held on to it? It seemed doubtful. He was grasping at straws, letting his imagination run wild. The odds that the kid who mowed Amanda's lawn—*Gavin*—was his son, were even more slim than the possibilities he'd conjured up.

"Ian?" Amanda's voice penetrated his mental fog.

He stared at her, standing there in her wet clothes

with grass stuck to her skin, her T-shirt. "I'm sorry," he said. He'd shaken her, for God's sake. "Amanda, I didn't mean to be so rough—so short with you."

"It's all right." She folded her arms in front of her. "Just tell me what's going on." She swallowed. "Why would…" She looked at the ring as though it might suddenly burst into flames. "If that belongs to Gavin, then…is he…your son?"

Hearing the words spoken out loud, Ian realized how ridiculous they sounded. Things like this only happened in movies. "I doubt it." He let his breath out on a long sigh. "I gave this ring to Jolene a long time ago. She wouldn't give it back to me when we broke up, and I couldn't figure out why. But I think I know now."

Lord, he wanted it to be true. He wanted to think she'd passed the ring down to his son, but that couldn't be. He was sure. "She might have pawned it. She sometimes looked for ways to get money without having to work." His tone sounded bitter even to his own ears. Jolene had been a kid, too. He supposed he was being hard on her. But it hurt so much, not knowing how to reach his son.

Amanda frowned. "But that still doesn't explain why Gavin would have it. Why would a teenage boy want someone else's class ring, unless it meant something special to him? And if Jolene pawned it… Well, it could and should be anywhere by now."

Hope fluttered once more in his chest. "Maybe."

"No, really. What are the chances that the ring would still be here—in this area?" Amanda shook her head. "That would be too coincidental."

"And finding out Gavin is my son and he's right

here in Boone's Crossing wouldn't?'' Ian's head
swam. ''I—my gosh, I don't know what to think.
What do I do?'' He took her by the arms once more,
but this time his touch was gentle. He smoothed her
skin. ''You're soaked. I'm soaked. How about we dry
off and then mull this over a little more sensibly?''

But he couldn't imagine being sensible right now.
He continued to tremble, and eagerness rose inside of
him. He had to get in touch with this boy—this
Gavin—and see for himself. See if there was any
chance at all….

Ian shook the thought off. It was best not to get his
hopes up. Not after all this time. He'd hit so many
dead ends in the last umpteen years. He'd nearly given
up.

''I've got plenty of towels,'' Amanda said. ''Come
on.'' She motioned as she headed for the porch steps.
''I'll make us some coffee, too.''

A short time later they sat at her table, mugs of
black coffee in front of them. Ian barely tasted his.
Amanda had changed to dry clothes, and he'd mopped
what he could of the water from his skin, hair and
shirt. His jeans stuck to his legs, but he didn't care.
He couldn't take his eyes off the ring. He held it in
the fingers of both hands, almost reverently, tilting it
this way and that. The faceted stone winked up at him
like a knowing eye. Other than having a bit of moist
grass clippings stuck to the antiqued gold, the ring was
clean and shiny. As if it had been well cared for.
Which blew his second theory—that it had somehow
become embedded in the dirt years ago in the yard of
Olivia Satterfield's log cabin, only to resurface now.

''Can you call him?'' he heard himself ask. He

looked at Amanda. She studied him, concern lining her face. He could tell she wanted this to be so. Wanted it nearly as much as he did.

"Gavin?" She shook her head. "I don't have his number."

"Then how did you reach him to mow your lawn?"

She pursed her lips and gave a little shrug. "He happened by one day shortly after I'd moved here. Asked me if I'd like to have my grass mowed. It was knee deep, and I jumped at the chance."

"And after that?"

"We made arrangements for him to drop by every week and mow. He'd usually come on Tuesdays."

Yesterday.

He'd missed him by one day. Ian's stomach rolled. Pocketing the chain, he slipped the ring onto his own finger, but it stopped above the knuckle. He'd filled out from the boy he'd been in his sophomore year, to the man he now was. Was Gavin skinny and gangly? Or were his fingers too big for the ring? "Guess this doesn't fit him."

"Guess not," Amanda said. "I noticed he always wore a chain around his neck, but I never really paid a lot of attention to the ring on it." A troubled frown creased her brow. "Surely he's realized by now that it's gone."

Ian's hopes rose. "Probably so. Maybe he'll come looking for it." Or maybe the kid would have no idea where he'd dropped the ring, if he mowed a lot of lawns, went to hang out at the mall with his friends....

Ian's thoughts shifted abruptly. "I can't believe I wouldn't have seen this kid at some point, if he lives here in Boone's Crossing."

"He doesn't live here," Amanda said. "That much I know." She snapped her fingers. "Remember when I told you Gavin and his cousin, Delbert, got a kick out of feeding Skippy—my little squirrel?" He nodded and she hurried on. "It's Delbert who lives here— Delbert Brock. Gavin's visiting for the summer. He told me he was mowing lawns to earn some spending money."

Ian soaked up the information like a sponge. "Okay. So, all we need to do is look up Brock in the phone book." He rose, impatient. "Do you have one?"

"I'll get it." Amanda shoved her chair away from the table and disappeared into the living room. Back a moment later, she handed him the phone book.

It covered Boone's Crossing and the surrounding area. His hands still not steady, Ian sat down once more and thumbed through the *B*s, looking for Brock. But there was no listing. Frustrated, he flipped to the pages of the other little towns in the directory. *Come on, come on...*

Nothing.

"It's not here," he said.

"Try information." Amanda had already retrieved her cordless phone, and she thrust the handset at him.

Ian dialed. A recorded voice informed him the number he wanted was a nonpublished one. He clicked off the phone and set it down. "Unlisted," he said. Then he brightened. "What am I thinking? You said he comes by on Tuesdays. I'll just wait." He rose to replace the phone on its base. "He'll come to mow, you'll call me and I'll be here." Impulsively, he leaned over and kissed her on the lips. "Amanda, I love you!'' The words slipped out like a fawn skidding on the ice.

Do you? His inner voice taunted.

He thought he might. He didn't know. Right now, his emotions were on overload.

Amanda's face flushed, and she grimaced, obviously not taking the words literally. ''Don't be too quick to say that, because you won't love me when I tell you what I said to Gavin yesterday.''

His smile slipped. ''Which is…?''

''I told him not to come back.''

''What?'' Without meaning to, he raised his voice.

She cringed. ''I told him that I was going to start doing my own yard. I thought it might be a constructive way to spend my time…that I might even plant a small flower or vegetable garden. That's why the roses you brought are so perfect.'' Her whole body sagged as she slumped in her chair. ''Oh, Ian, if I'd had any idea…''

''It's okay. You couldn't have known.'' Ian raked his hand through his hair and realized he'd left his ball cap outside. He looked into his coffee cup as if to find an answer to all that had happened in the last few minutes.

Amanda reached over and curled her hand over his. ''Promise me you'll be careful.'' Her eyes held a look of concern. ''I wouldn't want you to get your hopes up only to find that Gavin's not…not who you think he is.''

He knew she was right. But he didn't want to believe anything else. ''I know.'' He squeezed her hand. ''It seems so unreal.'' He stood. ''I need to get my hat.'' He glanced at his watch. ''Heck, I've taken up most of your evening, and here it's a work day. You probably want to get your supper and rest a bit.''

''You don't have to rush off,'' she said.

''That's all right.'' The sudden need to be alone with his thoughts overwhelmed him. ''I've got to get the animals fed.'' He slipped the ring into his pocket, then pushed the screen door open and stepped out onto the porch, Amanda close behind.

''Well, if you're sure.'' She stood on the steps while he retrieved his cap and put it on, then came down into the yard to help him gather and stack the disposable containers the roses had been in.

Had they really only planted them this evening? Finding the ring made him feel as though he'd slipped through time. Maybe he'd go see Papaw before he went home. Tell him all about it.

Ian carried the containers to the trash barrel he'd spotted out behind the shed, glancing down at the ground as he walked. Even in the short, mowed grass, he could make out the impressions where he'd lain with Amanda, and the way she'd felt beneath him, all warm and soft, came back to him in a rush. Her wet T-shirt had left little to the imagination, and he'd let himself get carried away.

He walked back to where she stood. ''I'll stop by the nursing home tomorrow,'' he said. ''I've got to pick up Papaw's laundry.''

''Okay.'' She gave a little wave as he headed for his truck. ''Thanks again for the roses. I really do love them.''

''You're welcome.'' Ian climbed behind the wheel of his truck and started the engine. Once more, Amanda waved as he backed out of the driveway.

He waved back, then headed down the road, a thousand thoughts whirling through his mind.

"UNBELIEVABLE." Papaw stared at the ring Ian had placed in his palm, and shook his head. "Lord works in funny ways, doesn't He, son?" His blue eyes studied Ian's.

"I'd say so. But I'm still not sure the ring really means anything."

"Only one way to find out. You've gotta find the boy—see who he is. What he has to say about this." He shook his closed fist as if getting ready to roll a set of dice. Holding his hand out, he dropped the ring into Ian's palm.

"Papaw, do you remember Lily Crenshaw?"

"Sure do. She's here, you know. Came in a couple of days ago."

"Amanda said she heard Lily call Jolene by a different last name than Bradford—Kennedy is what she said."

Papaw's toothless smile stretched his features until he looked like a jack-o'-lantern. "You know, she and I were an item once, before I met your grandma. Me and Lily, I mean." He gestured with one hand. "She's still a pretty woman, too, with her long blond hair."

"I'd guess it's more like white, isn't it?" Ian said, feeling obliged to tease Papaw, even though he didn't feel much like being funny at the moment.

"Platinum, son, platinum. Like Marilyn Monroe. Now there was a woman. Mm-mmm!" He smacked his lips. "When she walked, it looked like a pair of bobcats was scufflin' 'round in a burlap bag."

Ian chuckled. It was hard to stay in a dark mood in

Papaw's presence. "So Lily was your Marilyn Monroe, is that it?"

"Naw." Zeb waved both hands in dismissal. "She was just a bit of a sidetrack before I found Opal. But anyway, I hadn't seen Lily in a while. She'd moved away from Boone's Crossing…oh…I'd say along about 1989, '90, something like that. Moved back a short while ago after her husband died. I'd pert near forgot she was Jolene's great aunt until you mentioned her."

Hope darted through Ian all over again. "Amanda said Lily told her she was Jolene's kin."

Zeb grew serious. "Son, I told you to sign over your baby boy because I thought it was the best thing at the time. And I still think it was. But if you want to find him, then do it. I'll help if I can. I can talk to Lily, see what she knows."

"I appreciate that, Papaw." Ian patted his hand, always glad to find a way to make his grandpa feel useful. "Listen, I'm going to go home and try looking on the Internet."

"Might find something there," Zeb agreed. "They say the Web's a big place."

Ian hid a smile. "That they do, Papaw. I'll bring you some doughnuts tomorrow, how's that?"

"Chocolate?"

"You bet."

"You've got a deal." Zeb reached up and hugged him. "Take care of yourself, son. Don't let the past cloud your future."

"I won't." Ian returned the hug and left.

But Papaw's words haunted him as he drove homeward. Was he letting the past get in the way of what was in the here and now?

Amanda's face came clearly to mind. The woman sure could kiss. And she sure could mess with a man's mind, not to mention other parts of his body. She'd told him she was the wrong woman for him. And from what she'd said about not wanting kids, he'd been hard pressed not to agree. Yet he couldn't get over his feelings for her. Maybe if he could find Gavin—if Gavin was indeed his son—he could lay the past to rest and move on toward the future.

Papaw would surely agree with that.

AMANDA SAT in front of her computer, the headache she'd developed shortly after Ian drove away thumping in her temple. On her desk, her coffee sat cold and forgotten.

Apart from directly asking Gavin if he was adopted, there was only one other way Amanda could come up with to help Ian. Clicking the mouse on a search box for the local telephone company's pages, she punched in Jolene Kennedy. The search engine also asked for a city and state—the city being optional.

Amanda tried Tennessee. *Sorry. We are unable to find the person you're searching for.*

Okay. She tried Kentucky. And Virginia. She began to realize how hopeless her search was as she went through the entire list of states. Jolene could be anywhere. And her telephone number might be under her husband's name, or maybe not even listed at all. Just as the Brocks hadn't been. Putting in "Kennedy" with no first name pulled up a hoard of choices. If she called every one of them in the fifty states…

Sighing, Amanda looked up at the clock and was surprised to see how the time had flown by. She shut her computer down and made her way to the bathroom. She could use a long, hot soak in the tub. Maybe it would take away her headache and help clear her mind.

As she sat in the water, letting the fragrance of rainforest-scented bath oil surround her, thoughts of Ian invaded her head. She remembered how his mouth had felt, hot and demanding, and how the hardness of him had pressed against her. Making her go all soft and wet with longing. She'd promised herself not to step over the line with him. And she'd told herself she wasn't ready for anything in the way of a serious relationship.

So why was it that her headache had suddenly disappeared? And that some hope of happiness in her future had begun to creep in and whisper suggestively in her ear? Whenever Ian was around, she felt better. Less sad. Less fearful.

It was damned hard to stick to her previous determination to keep her distance from him when her heart told her she'd already fallen for Ian Bonner.

TRUE TO HIS WORD, Ian came to see Zeb the next morning. Amanda was in her office, the door propped open, when he stuck his head inside the room. "Morning."

He looked as if he hadn't gotten much sleep. She could relate. She'd tossed and turned all night, her thoughts flitting from one thing to the next. Ian… Gavin…her past. She motioned for Ian to come in.

"Close the door, please."

He raised one eyebrow, his sense of humor intact as he shut the door. "Are you planning to take advantage of me?" he drawled. "Or do you want to wait and take another shot at it on your back lawn?"

"Not today," she quipped.

Ian sobered. "I couldn't quit thinking about you last night. Or the ring."

"Me, neither." Amanda slid her chair out from her desk and swiveled around to face him. He sat on the desk's corner, holding a box of doughnuts. "I took the liberty of looking up Jolene Kennedy on the Internet," she said. The hopeful look he gave her was enough to break her heart. "I'm afraid I came up empty-handed."

Ian sighed. "I started to search, too, but I was too tired to handle anything more." He rubbed his eyes. "I laid awake half the night, thinking about everything." He stared intently at her. "What does he look like—Gavin?"

The underlying meaning behind his question was obvious. "Not like you, I'm afraid," she said gently. "He's a cute kid, though. He's got light-brown hair— almost blond—and he's tall. Maybe six-two or -three. I have no idea what color his eyes are." She shook her head. "Isn't it strange, that we look into someone's eyes when we're talking to them—yet how often do we really pay attention to what color they are?" She ignored the churning in her stomach that said she'd noticed Ian's eyes from day one.

No way could she forget that.

Ian moved his thumb across the doughnut box in absentminded circles. "I'm probably getting all fired up over nothing. Chances are, there's some other explanation as to how he ended up with my class ring."

"Well, like you said, he might come back looking for it."

"Yeah." Ian nodded. Then he gave a dry laugh. "You know, I thought about it, and what exactly would I say to him, even if I had his phone number? Even if he would've showed up on your front porch yesterday. 'Hi. I'm your dad?'"

She reached out and took his hand, and gave it a little shake of encouragement. Touching Ian made her long to feel his arms around her once again. "You'd think of something. If you'd like, you can talk to Lily and see if she really does know anything about Jolene or where she is."

"Jolene's kinfolk never wanted anything to do with me. Maybe Lily won't either."

"And maybe she will." She let go of his hand, knowing it wasn't appropriate to be thinking about touching and kissing Ian when she was at work.

"Papaw said he was going to talk to her. Guess it might be better that way." Suddenly, his eyes lit up. "The other day, I was trying to remember the name of the attorney who handled the adoption. I kept thinking it was something like Beck or Breck. Maybe it was Brock."

She hated to dash his hopes. "But he didn't adopt your son himself, did he?"

"No." His enthusiasm faded. "You're right. Guess it's just a coincidence."

"Well, they say fact is stranger than fiction."

A knock sounded on her office door, and Amanda stood and opened it.

"Sorry to bother you," Roberta said. "Hi, Ian." She waved, then continued. "Dr. Tompkins is on the phone for you, line one."

"Thank you, Roberta." Amanda left the door open and moved to the phone on her desk.

"Hey, I'll catch up with you in a minute," Ian said. "I'll go see what Papaw's up to, and pick up his laundry." He stood and held up the box of doughnuts, mouthing the words "Want one?" as she pressed the button with the blinking light on her phone.

This time she nodded, unable to resist the temptation of chocolate. It was even harder to resist the temptation to give in to her heart, and let herself truly love Ian.

She turned her attention to her conversation with Dr. Tompkins. Something he said, just before he ended their call, left her mind turning back to Ian as she hung up the phone. *The hospital's having a blood drive next week. I'd like to see all my nurses be first in line.*

Blood types. Blood kin. She hoped with all her heart Gavin truly was Ian's son, and that one way or another, he would know soon.

Providing, of course, they could find Gavin.

CHAPTER ELEVEN

IAN LEFT the nursing home and went straight to work, glad to have something to do to keep busy. He hadn't been exaggerating when he'd told Amanda he had tossed and turned all night. He hoped Papaw could get some information out of Lily Crenshaw. If he could at least track Jolene down, maybe she'd finally be willing to answer his questions, providing of course, she had any answers.

As Ian stopped to take a late lunch break and put a load of Zeb's clothes into the washer, the phone rang. He rushed to answer it, hoping it might be Amanda. Maybe she'd talked to Lily or found out something through Papaw.

"Bonner Welding."

"Hey, Ian," Neil said. "We still on for Saturday?" He and Neil planned to take the Cumberland Cubs camping near a local historical landmark. Public land surrounded the area, and arrowheads could often be found along the riverbank. The Cubs were excited beyond words.

"You bet. I can't wait." Getting out for a weekend of hiking and fresh air might give him a chance to sort out his thoughts in regards to what had happened between him and Amanda yesterday. "How's Troy, by the way? I haven't stopped to see him lately."

"Doing good. He wanted to come along, but Patricia wouldn't hear of it. She's afraid he might fall with his crutches or something."

"Well, maybe next time." He and Neil went over a few last-minute details, then hung up. He really had meant to go visit Troy this week. The kid was pretty bummed to already be missing out on scout activities, with summer officially just around the corner. Maybe Amanda would like to visit him, too.

He dialed the nursing home and waited for her to come to the phone. While on hold, he pictured the way she'd looked in her office this morning, all professional in her nurse's uniform. He wouldn't mind the chance to play doctor with her.

Her voice startled him from his daydreams. "Hi, Ian. What's up?"

He explained about the camping trip, and how Troy was going to miss it. "I thought I might go cheer him up later. Want to come along?"

"I'd love to. Shall I meet you at your place?"

"That'd be fine." He gave her directions and they decided upon a time. He hated to hang up the phone, loving the way Amanda's voice sounded, soft and sweet in his ear. Remembering the way she'd felt beneath him, when he'd kissed her as they lay in the grass. "I'm looking forward to it."

"Me, too. See you later."

Ian closed the shop early, so he'd have time to clean up the house a little, as well as shower and change clothes, and finish up Papaw's laundry. When Amanda showed up at six-thirty, dressed in a cute floral-patterned sundress and sandals, her hair flowing around her shoulders, he couldn't stop himself from sweeping her into his arms for a kiss. "You look beautiful," he said.

"Thank you." She blushed and took a step backward. He sensed her hesitation, as though she wasn't quite sure what to do with him.

Should he apologize for practically stripping her clothes off her yesterday, or should he pretend it hadn't happened? "Come on in." He held the door for her, and she stepped inside, Cuddles close on her heels.

Amanda reached to scratch the dog's ears, then stood looking around the living room. Ian immediately thought back to the time he'd imagined her coming here, to his house. He hoped he'd made it presentable enough.

"This is a nice place," Amanda said. "I love old farmhouses. They don't build them like this anymore."

"No, they don't." He could tell her compliment was genuine, and it made him feel good. He loved the old farmhouse as well. It wasn't fancy, but it was comfortable, and held a lot of memories. He tried not to imagine making new ones with Amanda. "Would you like something to drink before we go?"

"I'm fine, thanks."

"What have you got there?" He indicated a plastic shopping bag she held in one hand.

"It's a model of a classic car I picked up for Troy. I thought it might give him something to do to pass the time."

"Good idea." Her thoughtfulness didn't surprise him in the least. It was one of many things he admired her for. He should've thought of taking Troy a gift himself. But it wasn't like his mind hadn't been a little preoccupied lately, and not just with Amanda. "You didn't happen to find out if Papaw talked to Lily, did you?"

She lifted her shoulders. "I don't think he did. Lily felt a little weak today, and wasn't up to sitting in the day room. I'd thought I might talk to her, but the poor thing needed her rest and I hated to bother her with a bunch of questions."

"That's all right. I wouldn't want you to pester her if she's feeling poorly. It'll just have to wait." But it was hard to hide his disappointment. As much as he looked forward to spending time with Amanda, he was also nearly out of his mind with wanting to get more information that might help him locate Gavin, or at least find some answers.

"How are you doing?" he asked. "I've been worried about you, too, you know."

"Me?" A shadow crossed Amanda's face, but was quickly gone. "There's no reason to worry about me."

"You know that's not true." He took hold of her once more. "You're going through a rough time. And I'm afraid I've acted selfishly in putting my efforts to find Gavin ahead of thinking about your feelings."

"Don't be silly." She shrugged out of his grasp. "I want you to find him, especially if he's your son."

He might've known she'd be unselfish in her way of thinking. "I know that. But I was afraid that what I'm doing—asking you to help me look for Gavin— might stir up things from your past."

"You didn't ask, I offered. Remember?" She reached to cup his jaw, her touch firm, her hand soft and warm. "I'm working on healing. But that doesn't mean I'd ever resent you for finding what you're looking for.''

He ran his hand across her wrist, down her arm. Amanda was what he'd been looking for—if only she would feel the same way he did about having a family. He'd give anything to turn the clock back and have her not lose the baby she'd carried. But then he never would have met her. Maybe something good could come out of what she'd been through. "I've never known a woman like you." He took hold of her hand and kissed it before letting go.

"Is that good or bad?"

He laughed and she smiled at him, then stepped back as though to put some distance between them once more. As she did, her gaze found the wall near the front door, and she turned to study the family photos that hung there. She paused in front of the one taken on Mamaw and Papaw's wedding day.

"Is this Zeb and Opal?"

"Yep. That's their wedding photo, taken nearly seventy years ago."

"Oh, my gosh." She put a hand to her throat, and at first he thought her comment was in regards to the length of time his grandparents had been married. "Zeb's eyes." She gestured toward the photo, then looked at him, excited. "And the shape of his mouth."

"Yeah?" Ian frowned, not sure where she was headed.

"Ian." Amanda stared at the photo once more. "How old was Zeb when this was taken?"

"Seventeen. Why?"

She faced him once more. "Gavin has eyes like that," she said. "And his mouth is shaped the exact same way. He looks so much like that picture when he smiles…'' She rubbed her arms. ''My God, it gives me goose bumps.''

She wasn't the only one. A shiver raced up Ian's back. ''Are you sure?'' he asked.

Amanda nodded. ''Positive. As far as I can see, anyway. I guess I didn't notice it sooner because Zeb looks so youthful, so different in the photograph. And even though that's a black-and-white, I remember now that Gavin's eyes are blue, like your grandpa's.''

Ian let out a breath he'd barely been aware of holding. ''Age changes us all, doesn't it?'' He wanted so much for it to be true, that Gavin looked like Zeb. But then, a lot of people had blue eyes.

''I can imagine how anxious you are to find Gavin,'' she went on. ''If you'd like, we can go back to Shade Tree after we visit Troy. Maybe Zeb will have talked to Lily by then. She might feel better after napping all afternoon.''

''It's worth a try. I was going to drop Papaw's clothes off anyway.'' He picked up the duffle bag that contained his grandpa's things, then slipped his arm around Amanda as they headed outside.

TROY WAS EXCITED to see them and even more excited over the model car Amanda brought him. ''These are so cool to build,'' he said. ''I do them all the time, but I don't have this one.''

''Well you do now,'' Amanda said. She glanced around the living room. ''Is your mom here?''

''She'll be back in about fifteen minutes. She had to run Tara over to her best friend's house. They're selling Girl Scout cookies.''

"Will she mind if we wait for her to get home?" Ian asked. "I hate to see you here all by yourself, buddy."

His words echoed Amanda's thoughts. At nine years of age, Troy was old enough to stay alone for a short while. Still, with him being on crutches, anything could happen.

"She won't mind," Troy said. "Have a seat." He moved his crutches to make room for them on the couch. "Wanna sign my cast?"

"You'd better believe it." Amanda scrawled a cheerful message along with her name, then handed the pen to Ian.

He soon had Troy laughing as he pondered what to write, making up a silly limerick. The two drifted into conversation about their favorite basketball team, leaving Amanda with her thoughts. Not for the first time, she wondered, where was Troy's father? She looked around the room and saw nothing in the way of family photos, outside of school pictures of Troy and Tara. No sign of a man's presence in the house. The only shoes resting on a mat near the front door were some child-sized, lime-green flip-flops and a pair of tennis shoes that looked as though they belonged to Troy.

The living room was cluttered with normal everyday things, newspapers and magazines scattered on the coffee table. A *Harry Potter* paperback, displaying well-read, curled-edge pages, lay next to a Barbie doll whose hair had been sprayed purple to match her glittery outfit. Four chairs surrounded a circular table between the kitchen and living room, and draped across the back of one was a pink smock with Patricia's name embroidered on the pocket.

Patricia arrived minutes later, juggling a box of canning jars as she elbowed the screen door open. "Well hey there, Amanda…Ian. How are y'all doing?" Her warm smile made Amanda feel genuinely welcome.

Ian quickly moved to take the box from Patricia. "Still growing your own vegetables?" he asked.

"I sure am." She kicked her shoes off and indicated the kitchen table. "You can set those jars there. I picked them up at the flea market the other day and forgot to bring them in from the trunk of the car. I want to make sure I have plenty when I start canning this fall."

She chatted away, and Amanda couldn't help but admire her as she learned more about the woman. Patricia was indeed a single mother, and worked fulltime as a hairdresser at The Last Tangle. Still, she made time for her children's activities that included their respective scout troops and soccer teams. The fact that she also managed to tend a garden and can her own fruits, jams and vegetables, left Amanda's head spinning. The woman deserved a merit badge.

Longing stirred within her, and Amanda tried to brush it aside. She told herself she wasn't envious of Patricia's role as a mother. Why would she be, when she didn't plan to have kids? After she and Ian had said their goodbyes to Troy and Patricia, and headed for his truck, Amanda fell quiet.

"Is something wrong?" Ian asked as he drove toward Shade Tree.

"Not at all. I was just thinking about what a terrific mother Patricia seems to be."

"That she is." He smiled.

Amanda smiled back, but deep down inside, she no

longer felt cheerful. A familiar, dark, empty feeling gripped her. The one that haunted her every time she thought about Nikki, Cody and little Anna. "My sister would've made a wonderful mother." She struggled with the thick, choked feeling that clamped around her throat. "And Cody was so excited to be a dad."

Ian's gaze held hers as they halted at a stop sign at a four-way intersection. "You'd make a good mother, too, Amanda. Maybe you shouldn't be so quick to sell yourself short." Before she could protest, he went on. "Your life is your own business, and I know what you've told me. But I think you need to let more time pass before you decide you don't ever want to have another baby."

"I don't need more time." Irritated, knowing he meant well, she bit the words off anyway.

He gave her a look that said he didn't agree, then pulled through the intersection. "Did your sister and brother-in-law ever think about adopting a child?" he asked.

Again, his words riled her. "Adopting a child isn't like going out and getting a puppy. You can't replace one baby with another."

"I didn't mean it that way." Ian's frown covered the hurt look on his face, and immediately Amanda felt bad for snapping at him.

She knew he hadn't meant anything snide in his comment, and she also knew he cared about her. The thought left her heart fluttering in her chest, partially with fear—that she was letting herself become emotionally close to Ian—and partly with excitement for the same reason. A thousand times, she'd told herself not to get involved with him, that anything could happen. And a thousand times, she hadn't been able to listen to her sensible voice. Maybe she should listen now. The best way to set things right was to distance herself from him, and that would be hard.

"I'm sorry," she said in answer to his comment. "I know you didn't." Pursing her lips, she faced forward and stared through the windshield.

If Gavin turned out to be Ian's son, maybe the two of them could form a relationship. She'd love to see that happen for both their sakes, and for her own as well, since it might give her and Ian a little breathing room. Maybe spending time with Gavin would make Ian think all the more about what he'd lost in giving up his son. It might make him see that she was right.

She was the wrong woman for him. And nothing could change that.

Zeb was sitting in front of the television when they arrived, eating a container of applesauce and watching country music videos. He gave them a toothless smile. "That Shania Twain sure is something. She could take me riding on her motorcycle any day."

"Papaw." Ian gave his grandpa's shoulder a squeeze. "No off-color comments in the presence of ladies."

Zeb jabbed Ian in the arm. "Get your mind out of the gutter, boy." He gestured toward the TV screen. "See there, she's riding a motorcycle. What did you think I meant?"

No longer able to contain herself, Amanda burst out laughing. "Oh, Zeb." She wiped a tear of humor from one eye. "You're too much. I wish I had a grandpa like you."

He patted her hand as she laid it on his shoulder.

"I'd be proud to be your grandpappy, honey. What are you kids doing running around here at this time of evening?"

"We were hoping you'd talked to Lily," Ian said as he took Zeb's neatly folded laundry from the duffel bag and began to put it away.

"As a matter of fact, I did." Zeb laid his spoon down on the nightstand and tossed his empty applesauce container into the trash. "But I don't know how much help it'll be. She said Jolene married a Joshua Kennedy some years ago and was living in Strawberry Plains last she knew." He shook his head. "Only trouble is, Lily was listening to the radio when we talked." He circled his ear with one hand. "She can't hear, and she had the music on so loud, I could hear it through her headphones when she put 'em in her lap. Dolly Parton was singing that song about a mountain man named Joshua, and I'm thinking that might be what made Lily say the name. Might not be Jolene's husband's name at all."

"Well, Papaw, it's worth a try, and I sure appreciate your help." Ian gave Zeb a quick hug. "I'll look it up and let you know if it amounts to anything."

"You do that. And thanks for doing my wash. Miss Kelly, you have a good evening. Don't let this boy keep you out too late."

"I won't." Amanda smiled. "See you in the morning, Zeb." She walked with Ian out to his truck. "If this doesn't work," she said, "I have another idea. We can ask around and see if any of our neighbors…any of your customers or any of my residents' relatives…have Gavin mow their lawns. Maybe one of them took down his number."

Ian gave her a wry grin. "Now why didn't I think of that? You're not only beautiful, but smart." His eyes twinkled.

Minutes later, he pulled into his driveway and parked next to her Honda Civic. As usual, he hurried around to help Amanda from the pickup. When he'd done so on their first date, she'd thought he had only been trying to impress her with old-fashioned charm. But now she realized that his chivalry was genuine— a result of being raised with the same down-to-earth manners Zeb seemed to hold dear.

"Thank you," she said, taking his hand as she stepped out of the truck. "And thanks for inviting me to see Troy. He's a cute kid."

"You're welcome, but you're not planning to leave are you?"

"I really should." She hesitated. "It's almost nine, and I thought you'd like some privacy. You know, to call Jolene before it gets any later."

"Are you kidding? You've been with me on this the whole time. There's no way I'm letting you go now."

She had to admit she was curious as to whether or not he would reach Jolene and get any useful information. But curiosity aside, she truly felt excited and anxious for Ian. He'd waited a long time to find his son. What if she was wrong about Gavin having Zeb's eyes and smile? Maybe she'd wanted so badly to help Ian, she'd imagined the resemblance. She couldn't bear the thought of him facing further disappointment. Then again, if he needed a shoulder to lean on, the least she could do was give him one.

"All right," she said. "If you're sure."

"Come on." He slipped his arm around her shoulders and steered her toward the porch. Cuddles bounded up to greet them as though she hadn't seen them in weeks, and Amanda laughed. She found herself imagining how it would be to come home with Ian to this house. To have Cuddles greeting her as part of Ian's family. She knew that thinking this way could get her in trouble. It wasn't fair to Ian to even begin to contemplate a fantasy she knew she'd never be able to turn into reality.

Once inside the house, Ian fired up the computer. Amanda held her breath as he searched for a Joshua Kennedy in Strawberry Plains, Tennessee.

"Bingo!" Ian slammed his fist down on the desk, a wide grin spreading across his face. "Guess Lily knew what she was talking about after all." He jotted the number on a piece of paper.

"I guess so." Amanda smiled. "Would you mind if I get a glass of water?" She gestured toward the kitchen, not really thirsty, but wanting to give him some amount of privacy to make his call. Even though he'd made it clear he enjoyed having her take part in searching for information on his son, she still didn't feel comfortable eavesdropping on his conversation.

"Help yourself." Ian shut off the computer and picked up the phone. "The glasses are in the cupboard to the left of the sink."

Amanda headed for the kitchen, Cuddles on her heels. She glanced over her shoulder and saw Ian dial the phone. As he paced in front of the couch with the cordless to his ear, she held her breath; hoping, praying for a miracle.

One that would bring Ian happiness.

And another that would rescue her from loving him.

CHAPTER TWELVE

IAN'S HEART RACED as he waited for someone to pick up the other end of the phone line. He'd waited and wondered for so long. What if this proved to be yet another dead end?

Jolene hadn't been forthcoming with any facts all those years ago, but maybe time had given her a change of heart. He prayed she would give him the information he so desperately needed to know. While he might be able to track Gavin down in another way, he supposed he simply wanted to hear it from Jolene herself—that Gavin was indeed their son.

Braced for her voice, wondering if he'd even recognize it after so many years, he was taken aback when a little girl answered the phone.

"Hello?"

"Uh—hi. May I please speak to Jolene Kennedy?"

"Yeah. I'll get her." The phone clunked down on a hard surface with a sharp rap in Ian's ear. "Mo-om! Telephone."

A chill danced up the back of his neck. *Jolene had a daughter.* For years, he'd done little else but think about the son they'd given up, hoping and praying that he'd have a chance to do things better the next time around. That he'd one day have a family of his own. Apparently, Jolene had one, and for some reason the possibility hadn't occurred to him. Knowing she'd moved on with her life and probably found happiness gave him a good feeling in a way, but in a way it made him sad, too. Was he the only one who'd been looking for their son?

A shuffling noise on the line told him someone had come to the phone. A woman's voice sounded in his ear. "Hello?"

His own voice wouldn't work, and he cleared his throat. "Jolene?"

"Yes?"

He paused, not really knowing how to begin, now that he'd found her. "I'm not sure I've reached the right party. My name is Ian Bonner, and I'm looking for Jolene Bradford."

For a split second, he thought she'd hung up. "Ohmigod—how did you get this number?" She spoke in a low, panicked tone. "Why are you calling?"

He hadn't expected her to react quite this way, but then, he supposed it was a shock, him contacting her out of the clear blue. "Jolene, I know it's been a long time since we've talked. I didn't call to upset you or cause any problems. But, I have reason to believe our son might be in Boone's Crossing. I'm calling to see if you have any information that would help me get in touch with him."

"I asked him not to call anymore," she said, her voice still barely above a whisper.

"What do you mean?"

"Galen—that's his name, right? He phoned here a couple of weeks ago, and I asked him not to do it again." She paused, and Ian thought he detected a note of pain in her voice when she continued. "My past is just that—my past. My girls and my husband don't know anything about my life in Boone's Crossing. I can't let them know. Please try to understand. Goodbye, Ian."

With that, she hung up, leaving the dial tone humming loudly in his ear. For a moment, he stood there, trying to absorb what she'd said.

Gavin had called her, and she'd turned him away. How could she do that? As though he meant absolutely nothing to her.

Galen—that's his name, right?

She hadn't even bothered to get his name right. Their son, who'd come looking for his birth mother, had been abruptly turned away over the telephone. The son he'd give anything to find. The son he'd do anything for.

The son he'd never stopped loving.

"Damn it!" Ian slammed the cordless phone onto its base, hands shaking, anger rising inside of him. At that precise moment, he caught a glimpse of Amanda from the corner of his eye. He'd nearly forgotten she was in his kitchen.

"What happened?" she asked. She set the glass down and walked toward him, concern etched in her features. She hesitated, her hand poised to touch him. "Maybe you need some privacy after all."

"No." He moved forward, needing to hold her, wanting to have someone who cared listen to him. "Don't go." He raked a hand through his hair as frustration overtook his anger.

Amanda stood quietly for a moment, waiting. "I take it things didn't go well."

"No." Ian shook his head, then slumped onto the couch. She sat down beside him. "Do you know what she told me?" He couldn't even bring himself to say Jolene's name.

"What?" Amanda asked softly.

He tried, unsuccessfully, to battle down his emotions. "She told me that Gavin phoned her, and she asked him not to call anymore. She said she has a new life, and her past is not part of it." A lump wedged its way from his chest to his throat, and he swallowed in an attempt to dislodge it. But it sat there, like a hunk of lead. "She hung up on me. She's got a little girl, who answered the phone." He shook his head, still stunned by it all, trying to absorb the information heaped upon him in a matter of seconds. "Guess she's got more than one daughter, from what she said." His stomach churned.

Amanda reached out and touched him. Her hand lay firm on his arm. "I'm sorry."

He looked into her eyes and knew she meant it. He covered her hand with his and squeezed, wanting to hold her there forever. Wanting to absorb the warmth and love he felt in Amanda's touch. "I don't know what I expected," he said. "But not that."

"Well, don't be too quick to judge Jolene," she said quietly. She pursed her lips in a gesture of compassion. "You haven't seen her in a long while. Maybe she has her reasons for feeling the way she does."

He sighed. "I suppose you've got a point. Jolene has every right to live her life the way she wants." To get on with it. But he could not do the same, couldn't turn his back on the son they'd had together.

"Well, at least now you know Gavin must truly be your son, since he called Jolene."

The fact hit him hard. She was right. His addled mind hadn't completely added two and two. He'd dialed Jolene, hoping for a phone number that might lead him somewhere, hoping for a clue that might be a final piece to the puzzle he'd struggled to solve for so long now. In the back of his mind, he'd been afraid to find out that Gavin wasn't his after all; that he was no closer to finding his son than he'd ever been.

He hadn't expected Jolene to tell him she'd actually talked to their son. His boy. He still couldn't believe she'd turned Gavin away like some stranger on the street. But then, that was basically what Gavin was to her. A stranger. A young man who'd grown from a baby she'd given up to a boy she'd never seen, to the young man he now was.

Funny, he'd never thought of his son that way at all. Not as a stranger. In his heart, he'd held his child close all these years, even before he'd known his name. His son had always been someone to him. Someone of importance. Someone he still desperately wanted to see, to meet, to talk to.

Ian stared into Amanda's eyes. "I'm so close. So close to reaching him. To seeing him again." Overcome by emotion, he took her in his arms. He needed to hold her. "Why didn't he call *me?*" he whispered against her neck. "How could Jolene tell him to leave her alone like that? How could she?"

"I don't know." Amanda massaged his shoulders and his back, her hands soft and loving. Caring. "But she obviously loved your son enough at one time to pass your ring to him. She can't be completely hard-hearted. Maybe she let him down gently.''

"What if I can't find Gavin?'' Sudden desperation gripped him. "What if the fact that Jolene turned him away makes him think I will, too?''

"You don't know that.'' Her gaze softened further. "Don't give up now. We'll find him somehow.''

"I sure hope you're right.'' Ian caught hold of her hands and grasped them gently between his. She'd become more and more a part of his life as time passed, and it felt so right to have her here to lean on. He caressed her wrists, her arms. "You're so special to me,'' he said. "Here I am, furious with Jolene for giving up a chance I've tried to come by for twelve years now. Losing hope that I'll be lucky enough to see my son.'' He brought one hand up to caress her chin, her throat. "And you have this way of pulling me back down to earth, back to my senses. Of making me see things in a whole new light.''

She licked her lips, and what he saw in her eyes made his world cave in. How was it he'd never noticed how empty his life had been before Amanda had come into the picture? "Come here.''

He wrapped his arms around her and held her against him, wanting to lose himself in the feelings she evoked in him. He desperately needed to let go of the pain that held him captive, and simply slide into a world where hurt did not exist. Where children did not lose their parents; where daddies never gave up their sons, and mothers never had to face the heartbreak of an empty cradle.

His lips found Amanda's almost automatically. And as she kissed him back, he knew without a doubt she'd been mistaken. She wasn't the wrong woman for him at all.

She was the only woman. But how to convince her?

"Amanda," he whispered. "I want you so much. I need you."

She trembled in his embrace. "Ian—"

He silenced her protest with another kiss. "Don't talk," he said. "Don't even think. Just feel…feel how much I care about you. How much you mean to me."

This time, she stiffened. "I can't, Ian. We can't."

"We can." He sprinkled kisses over her cheeks, her temple. "You're wrong about us. Let me show you." His lips found hers once more. She kissed him back, and slowly, gradually, began to relax.

And when he scooped her up and carried her to the bedroom, nothing had ever felt so right in his life.

AMANDA SANK AGAINST the quilted mattress of Ian's four-poster bed. Every fiber of her being told her this was not what she should be doing. She didn't belong in Ian's bed or in anyone's for that matter. But her heart ached with an emptiness she couldn't seem to fill, and Ian's arms were so warm, strong and inviting. She felt safe and secure tucked inside his embrace, as though nothing could reach her or harm her.

More than that, a hunger—an arousing desire—consumed her, washing away all sensibility. It had been far too long since she'd been held in a man's arms, and Ian's embrace felt better than any she remembered.

"Ian." She spoke his name on a hoarse whisper as she tried for one last save, one last grasp at resistance.

"Shh." He kissed away her words of protest.

"Don't talk. Don't think. Just let yourself go, Amanda." He smoothed her hair back. "You make me feel so good, so happy. I want to do the same for you. I want to make love to you." He lowered his mouth to hers again, and his kisses grew more fervent, more hungry, with each stroke of his tongue.

For a moment she found it easy to experience the same things Ian spoke about—happiness, warmth, desire. *Would* it hurt to let herself go this once? Would it damage her heart to let him into it for a short time, to love and be loved if only now and not forever? She knew she couldn't promise him forever, and that it wasn't fair to let him think otherwise. Still, her inner voice cried out to give in to the temptation he offered, and blocking all further thoughts from her mind, Amanda wrapped her arms around Ian. She kissed him back with an urgency that let him know she wanted him every bit as much as he wanted her.

His hands found her shoulders, and he slid the front of her sundress down to expose the strapless bra she wore. He kissed his way down her neck, her chest, and with his teeth, maneuvered her bra out of the way. Hungrily, he reached for her breast, cupping it in one hand, softly kneading her flesh. She moaned and arched her back as he tongued her nipple, then closed his mouth over the peak of her breast and suckled.

This time there was no clothing to act as a barrier between his mouth and the pure pleasure he gave her. Amanda found herself lost in Ian's touch as he continued to stroke and explore her body. He kissed his way down her leg and cradled her foot in his palm as he removed first one shoe, then the other. He kissed the arch of her foot and her toes, then worked his way back up. She reached to undo the buttons on his shirt, all the while indulging in the taste of his warm skin.

She peeled the shirt away from his broad shoulders and sighed with bliss as she ran her hands along tanned, muscular biceps. With no effort at all, she lost herself in the pure ecstasy of the touch of his hands, forgetting everything save the here and now, and the way Ian's body felt pressed against hers. Her sundress soon lay in a heap on the floor beside the bed, along with Ian's clothes and boots.

Deftly, his fingers found the clasp on her bra, and he slipped it off of her, tracing a trail with his tongue from her breasts to her belly button and back up again. Purposely tormenting her. She moaned, longing for him to move lower. Instead, he rolled onto his back and encouraged her to shed the last of her inhibitions, guiding her hand to the front of his briefs. Amanda shivered with pleasure as she stroked him, then rid him of his underwear. He slid her panties off and tossed them onto the floor as well, then grasped her arms and coaxed her into mounting him, deliberately keeping her from the actual joining of their bodies. She growled her protest, then brazenly sat astride him. Her gaze locked on his, inviting him to explore her body. He'd left the bedside lamp on, and she felt warm and deliciously wicked as she watched him watching her.

"You're gorgeous, Amanda," he said, his voice hoarse with longing. He ran his hands from her breasts down her sides to her hips. His rough palms skimmed her flesh with the lightest of touches. He slowly explored the curls between her legs, his fingers seeking her most intimate place. His thumb rubbed the nub of her flesh as he reached inside of her.

Amanda gasped and moved in rhythm as he stroked her. "Ian. I want you." Hot and moist, she rubbed against him, then lowered herself onto his hardened flesh. He let her stroke and tease with purposeful movements of her hips, then rolled her onto her back. He kissed her, then slid down her body, this time using his tongue as she'd longed for him to do. By the time he worked his way back up to her breasts, Amanda didn't think she could take any more of his delicious torment. He slid inside of her, then back out, teasing her, drawing out her ecstasy.

She cried out as he sent her tumbling over the edge. And as she trembled with the aftermaths of her climax, Ian began all over again, touching, teasing, stroking her. Selfishly, she indulged in wave after wave of pleasure, knowing she should've stopped him long before now, not caring. She was at a safe time of the month in her cycle, but still...

"Ian," she finally gasped. "I'm not on birth control. I—"

But he stopped her by covering her mouth with yet another kiss. He licked her neck, her earlobe, sending hot shivers across her damp body as he whispered. "It's okay. I'll be careful." With that, he drew her fully against him, moving inside of her, first slowly, then more rapidly as his excitement reached a peak. Encouraging her to wrap her legs around him, he drove himself into her with near desperation, then quickly pulled away, shuddering, his head laid on her shoulder, the warmth of his body spilling forth between their thighs.

Amanda shook, this time with fear at knowing how close they'd come to making a baby. Emotions swept over her, confusing, demanding. She wanted more of Ian. The hot, intimate way their bodies pressed together made her mad with longing, and tears of pent-up emotions brimmed and threatened to spill down her face. She fought them back, along with the overpowering desire that stormed its way through her. It wasn't only physical, though that was most definitely a major part of what she felt right this minute. Something inside of her blocked out her voice of reason, instead whispering in her mind.

You could love this man so easily... Let go...let go...

But she couldn't, and she knew suddenly that what she'd done was all wrong. Not in a sinful way, though she'd always hoped marriage would find her with one single partner to share her life with. But because she had no business playing with Ian's heart and mind the way she'd just done. Heated emotions had led them both to let desire overrule good sense. Allowing herself to cross the line wasn't right, and it wasn't fair. She couldn't—wouldn't—give Ian what he wanted most. Children. So what was she doing in his bed?

"Ian." She bit her lip, holding back the words that threatened to surface. Words of love and promises she couldn't keep. Instead, she struggled to find a way to be honest with him. She ran one hand over his shoulder, still loving the way he felt, all hard and muscular against her. "Ian?"

His only reply was a contented "M-mm," as he burrowed his head more deeply into her shoulder. One hand found her breast, and he nuzzled against her as though she were a downy pillow. His even breathing told her he'd fallen asleep.

She didn't know whether to laugh or cry. It was such a typically male thing, yet somehow it felt more like a compliment than an insult. She craned her neck to peer at Ian's face in the soft glow of light from the bedside lamp. His features had relaxed into a near-boyish innocence. Worry lines she'd noticed as of late had completely vanished, and he slept with the comfort of a man who had not a care in the world.

And here, he'd torn her world in two.

Because she hadn't simply given Ian her body. She'd given him her heart. It was the last thing she'd wanted, and the first thing she finally realized as she quietly slid from his bed. He stirred, but otherwise did not move as Amanda found her clothes scattered among his. She flicked off the lamp and made her way down the hall in search of the bathroom.

Feeling shy about helping herself to Ian's linen closet seemed silly in light of what had occurred between the two of them. Yet she did. She cleaned herself up, and as she dressed, thought about the final moments of their lovemaking. They'd been careful.

But had they been careful enough?

Pushing the thought to the back of her mind, Amanda went once more down the hall, unable to resist one last look at Ian before she left. He still slept soundly in the shadows cast through the window by the yard light. Cuddles had come into the room and curled up next to the bed, and she wagged her stubby tail. Amanda murmured to the dog, then bent to place a kiss on Ian's temple. Carefully, she smoothed his hair, hating to leave, knowing she must. Someday,

some lucky woman would love this man for all
eternity.

As she slipped quietly from the bedroom, from the
house, closing the door behind her, Amanda wished
with all her might that someone could've been her.

CHAPTER THIRTEEN

AMANDA WAS GLAD the next day was Friday and a busy one at that. It gave her less time to dwell on what had happened between her and Ian, though she admittedly felt more than a little disappointed when he didn't come by to see his grandpa. She'd chatted with Zeb in the day room that morning, and he'd asked if Ian had been able to locate Jolene.

"He did find her," she replied, unable to hide a grimace, "but maybe I ought to let him tell you about it."

"Not good, huh?" Zeb grimaced as well.

Not good at all. The phone call had led to heightened emotions, resulting in her falling into bed with Ian. She'd mumbled a reply to Zeb's question, and could have sworn he watched her with knowing eyes as she left the room. Though it was silly, she couldn't stop feeling like a teenager caught necking in the car. No doubt Zeb would approve of her relationship with Ian, but he would surely resent any woman who might hurt his grandson. Doing so was the last thing Amanda had in mind. Ian was a good man, and he deserved better than a woman who would lead him on.

Torn between hoping to see him and wanting to avoid him until she could somehow get her emotions under control, Amanda made her way outside on her lunch break. She couldn't stop thinking about the love-making they'd shared, nor could she shake the fear inside of her. Fear of the commitment it implied, and fear of what might have happened if she'd become pregnant. She'd let her feelings for Ian overwhelm her and make her do something she normally would not have done. Let herself climb into his bed and give in to her heart without looking back.

Her stomach churned. She had no appetite but a cold drink sounded good, and she'd noticed on her drive to work that morning that her gas gauge was near empty.

With her purse tucked under her arm, she headed for her car. The convenience store down the street had monster-sized fountain drinks and the lowest per-gallon price in town. Still daydreaming about the evening she'd spent with Ian, Amanda pulled up at the pumps, filled her tank, then moved her car to the parking area in front of the store. The temperature had climbed into the eighties, and the humid heat struck her with full force as she climbed from the air-conditioned haven of her Honda and slammed the door shut.

It wasn't until she'd paid for her gas and soft drink, and returned to the car that she realized she'd retrieved her purse from the seat upon exiting the Honda, but had locked her keys in. Amazing how easy it was to become immune to the warning tone the car offered to prevent keys being left in the ignition. She'd tuned it out, along with everything else, her mind cluttered with thoughts of Ian.

"Confound it!" She slapped her purse onto the roof of the car, jerking reflexively as the hot metal punished her. With a sigh, she stared into the Honda's interior. The cartoon cat dangling from her key ring mocked her with a cheeky grin. *Wonderful.*

She turned around, her focus on the pay phone near the end of the building, and from the corner of her eye, caught a glimpse of two boys on bikes as they rode across the parking lot—Gavin and Delbert. Standing on one pedal, Gavin jammed his foot on top of the front forks of his bright orange bike. With a maneuver too quick to follow, he sent the tail end of it spinning around in a circle, then halted the motion with a touch of his foot before landing on both pedals once more. With a pull on the handlebars, he lifted the front tire from the ground and rode toward Amanda, wearing a grin. Delbert followed. Amanda's breath caught in her throat. Keys forgotten, she called out a greeting.

"Hey, Miss Kelly." Gavin halted in front of her while Delbert simply waved, then continued to ride in circles around the parking lot. Gavin slouched on his seat, tennis shoe-clad feet balancing the bike in place.

"Gavin. I'm so glad to see you." Amanda laid her hand on his shoulder, then brought it back to her throat. Good Lord, what should she say to him? *I know your father and he's looking for you?* "Um…" Feeling foolish, she gestured toward her car, suddenly thanking the heavens above that she'd locked her keys in. Gavin might not be able to do anything to assist her, but it would give her a reason to stall and talk to him while she gathered her wits. "I locked my keys in the car. I was just about to call for help."

"There's no need for that." He gave her a cute but cocky smile, and goose bumps pricked her arms the same way they had the day before, as she saw Zeb in that smile. "I can get them out," Gavin assured her with boyish confidence. "I've done it a million times."

"You have?" Amanda let herself relax and tease the kid. "Don't tell me you mow lawns by day, and you're a car thief by night."

He chuckled, and the sound curled around her as she realized he had Ian's laugh. Why hadn't she noticed sooner? "Naw. But I've locked my keys in my truck more than once, and my buddies have, too. I always get them out. Hang on—I'll be right back." With that, he spun the bike around, called out to Delbert, then headed across the parking lot to the strip mall next door, where a coin laundry and dry cleaners were located.

Moments later, he returned, a wire coat hanger in hand. Amanda and Delbert watched as he laid his bike down, then proceeded to straighten the coat hanger. With patience, he threaded it between the rubber seal separating the door from the window and maneuvered it around until he was able to pop the lock.

"I knew it." Delbert shot his cousin an admiring grin. "He gets them out every time."

"It's not that hard." Gavin lifted up on the handle to make sure the latch came free, then extracted the wire, opened the Honda's door, and leaned in to retrieve Amanda's keys. With a mock bow, he placed them in her hand.

She shook her head and laughed. "I can't thank you enough. You just saved me the cost of a locksmith."

"No charge." He gave her a crooked smile, and Amanda was overcome by a motherly urge to reach

out and ruffle his hair. To pull him into a hug and tell
him that while he'd been given up, he'd never been
forgotten by his birth father. To reunite him with Ian
and watch a smile spread over Ian's face as well.

With near panic, she realized he was about to get
on his bike and leave. "Gavin." She put a hand on
his arm. "Hold up a second." Should she ask him
about the ring? Make up a story about needing him to
mow her lawn after all? Deciding the truth was easiest
and best, and actually wouldn't give away anything
anyway, she asked, "You didn't happen to lose a ring
the last time you mowed my lawn, did you? On a
chain?" She gestured as though indicating one around
her neck.

To her delight, his features shifted from surprised
to overjoyed. "I sure did. You found it?"

She nodded. "Mm-hmm. It was in my yard. I
thought maybe you'd miss it and come looking. I
didn't know how to get in touch with you."

"I did look," he said. "Man, I've been going crazy
trying to find that ring." His features softened. "It
belonged to my—my dad. I came over to your house
yesterday, but you weren't home and I didn't see it
anywhere."

"My mom took us to Pigeon Forge the other day,"
Delbert offered, "to Dolly's Splash World and Dol-
lywood. We just got back yesterday."

Amanda mentally shook her head at the irony that
Gavin had been at her house when she and Ian were
busy hunting down clues to find him. "Well, look no
more," she said. "I have to go back to work right
now, but can you meet me at my house later this evening? Say about five-thirty?"

"Sure." He nodded vigorously.

"Thanks again, for getting my keys out."

"You bet. I'd do it a hundred times to get that ring back." The glow in his eyes moved her. And she wondered how much he knew about the ring, and his birth father.

A sudden thought struck her as she drove back toward Shade Tree. Gavin had said the ring belonged to his dad. But did he realize his dad lived right here in Boone's Crossing? Surely not.

Believing for once that fate had turned a kind hand toward someone, Amanda parked her car and hurried to her office, anxious to phone Ian.

IAN HAD BEEN DISAPPOINTED to wake up the previous night to an empty bed. Embarrassed that he'd fallen asleep on Amanda, he'd debated calling her. But the clock had said it was well past midnight, and he hadn't wanted to scare her with a middle-of-the-night phone call. He hoped she didn't think he'd fallen asleep because he'd used her as an outlet for his physical needs. Or because he hadn't treasured her company beyond a physical aspect.

On the contrary, Amanda had made him feel so wonderful, so fulfilled, that he'd fallen asleep due to pure relaxation. She'd felt so right and natural in his arms, he could have held her all night. Every night. Forever.

He'd thought about going to the nursing home again this morning, to see Amanda and take Zeb some sweets. But things had gotten busy at the shop and had stayed that way right up until noon. He supposed it was for the best. He'd much rather see her in private, not at work, since he wanted to talk to her about what had happened between them.

He was about to return to his task of welding a fifth wheel hitch into the bed of a customer's truck when the phone rang. He answered, pleasantly surprised to find it was Amanda.

"Ian, I've got some wonderful news. I found Gavin!"

"You did?" He sat down on the pickup's dropped tailgate. "Where? Did you tell him anything? Did you get his phone number?"

She laughed. "Whoa, slow down. All I told him was that I'd found his ring. He's coming to my house tonight at five-thirty to get it. Can you be here?"

Could he! "You'd better know it." He'd take off early—anything for the chance to meet Gavin. He listened as Amanda explained how she'd run into him. "Papaw was right. The Lord does work in mysterious ways. I can't thank you enough, Amanda."

"There's no need to thank me. See you at five-thirty."

Ian hung up, feeling more excitement and anxiety than he ever had before. He was finally going to see his son.

His thoughts shifted to Amanda. She hadn't said a word about last night. But then, she was at her office, so that was likely the reason. He hoped she didn't regret what had happened between them. He sure didn't. The only reservation he felt about the entire situation, about being involved with her, was the fact that she didn't want kids. What if she never changed her mind? What if he'd fallen in love with her only to discover the two of them couldn't come to an agreement on that issue? Telling himself it was both too late and too soon to worry about it, Ian focused on work, anxious to finish his day and meet Gavin.

AMANDA GOT OFF AT FOUR and hurried home. She changed her clothes, brushed her hair, and stared anxiously at the clock. It wasn't quite five. She wondered who would arrive first. Probably Ian. She knew how anxious he must be to get here.

Out on her porch, she fed croutons to Skippy and waited. To her surprise, it was Gavin who showed up almost a half hour early. He pulled his Ford pickup into the driveway and parked beside her car.

Amanda greeted him. "How's the lawn mowing business?" Now she felt bad for having let him go. He sure seemed like a good kid.

"It's keeping me busy." He sat on the porch rail. "Hey there, Skippy."

Amanda handed Gavin some croutons and watched as he fed the little squirrel. It felt odd to think of him as anything more than the kid who'd mowed her lawn. What should she say to him? How much should she tell him before Ian got here?

"Would you like something to drink?" she offered. "I've got pop and lemonade."

"Naw, but thanks anyway. I've got to get back in time for supper or my aunt will have a fit."

"Oh." Disappointment filled her. She had to find a way to stall, a way to ease Gavin into the situation she'd helped create. "Maybe you can call her."

Gavin gave her a funny look. Criminy, she was blowing it already. He obviously thought she was weird, asking him to call his aunt so he could stay for a glass of lemonade.

"Call her?" He shrugged. "Why? I won't be late if I get my ring now and leave."

Oh, brother. Amanda took a deep breath. "You told me the ring belonged to your father."

Gavin nodded. "It did. My birth father, that is." He gave her a little half smile. "My folks adopted me when I was a baby, and they've always been up-front about that. But I'd been wondering about my birth parents, so my dad helped me track them down. That's why I'm here. I came to stay with Delbert and my aunt Betty, not just to visit, but so I could meet my father. I've been trying to work up the nerve to go see him, but so far I haven't done it." Again, he shrugged. "My birth mother didn't exactly welcome me when I found her. I guess I've been afraid that the same will happen with him."

"So, you know your father's name, then?"

"Oh yeah. It's Ian Bonner. He owns a welding shop here in Boone's Crossing. I think I'm finally going to do it—go see him, maybe tomorrow..." He let the words trail away as Ian's truck pulled into the drive, and came to a halt behind Amanda's Honda.

The big black Ford, with Bonner Welding painted on the doors. Amanda's mouth went dry, and she looked at Gavin.

He was staring at the truck. "Oh my God," he said. He glanced briefly at her, then back at Ian. "Is that—that's him, isn't it? My dad?"

IAN STEPPED OUT of the truck and walked toward Amanda's porch, feeling as though he were in a dream-world. He'd hoped to arrive before Gavin, but he'd gotten waylaid by a customer at the last minute and couldn't get the guy to stop talking long enough to get a word in, to say he needed to go. He barely noticed the look of anticipation on Amanda's face, because he couldn't tear his eyes away from the boy who was his son.

He tried to speak, but his mouth refused to cooperate, his voice refused to function. Even as he walked, he did so automatically, without conscious effort. He could not believe how nervous he was, half-frozen with something between fear and the biggest case of joy he'd ever known. He prayed he wouldn't choke up and cry. Not in front of Amanda, not in front of his son.

"Hi, Ian." Amanda must have sensed his awkwardness, for she stood and moved toward the steps. As casually as she could manage, hands trembling, she leaned against a support post, and glanced from him to Gavin.

Ian felt every bit as shaky.

"Hi, there." His greeting included Gavin. Instinctively, he held his hand out. But the words *I'm Ian Bonner* stuck in his throat. Amanda had said she'd told Gavin nothing. How to begin?

Gavin's hand closed around his in a firm shake, not quite the grip of a boy and somehow not yet a man's. His palm was clammy, and Ian noted the anxious look in his eyes. He, too, could not seem to tear his gaze away. Had Amanda told him after all?

"Gavin Brock. Nice to meet you, sir."

His polite greeting struck Ian hard, making him proud his son had been raised with manners, and at the same time, tearing him up inside. To hear this boy he'd grown to love—even without knowing him—call him sir.

"Ian Bonner," he said. "I'm sure glad to meet you, too."

Gavin raised his chin in a gesture that indicated Ian's truck. "Nice Ford." He grinned, shy, yet obviously attempting to find a way into this awkward situation.

"Thank you." Ian glanced at Gavin's pickup. "I see you're a Ford man, too." As soon as the words left his mouth, he wondered if he'd put too much emphasis on "too." *Like me. And your great-grandpa Zeb. You're a Ford man, son.*

"Yeah." Gavin seemed to falter for what to say next, his eyes still locked on Ian's.

He couldn't stop staring at the boy, mesmerized, as though seeing a movie star up close for the first time. Only this was so much better than meeting a famous stranger. This stranger—this bright young man with light, neatly cut brown hair, and eyes that were indeed blue and so hauntingly like Zeb's—was no stranger at all. He was the child of Ian's heart, a child who'd grown up without him.

Overcome by the longing to pull Gavin into a fatherly hug, to pound him on the back in camaraderie and take him away somewhere where they could make up for all the lost years, Ian scrambled for something more to say. Amanda obviously understood exactly what this moment meant—what it had caused him to feel—for she spoke up without hesitation.

"He knows, Ian."

Those three little words took a moment to sink in.

He glanced at her, then focused on Gavin. "Amanda told you?"

"Who you are? No sir. I already knew."

He hadn't expected such an answer, and he nearly sagged against the porch rail, both with relief and surprise. "You did? How?"

"My dad hired a private detective to help me find my birth parents."

The word *dad* hit home, and sudden resentment that another man had been there to watch his boy grow up, rose within Ian. *You made the choice....* The words echoed in his mind. He knew he should be grateful that his son had been raised, from all appearances, by a decent man.

He listened as Gavin went on.

"I've been staying here in Boone's Crossing with my aunt Betty and my cousin Delbert. Mowing lawns for spending money, trying to work up the nerve to go see you." He gave a little shrug. "Miss Kelly found the ring you gave me, and she told me to meet her here."

That Gavin thought he had given the ring to him was enough to make Ian ache with regret. He reached into his shirt pocket and pulled out the ring and chain. He may not have been the one to give him the class ring before, but he could give it to him now. Gavin took it, obviously glad to have it back, and Ian found enormous pleasure in that small observation.

"Thank you," Gavin said. Briefly, he studied the ring and broken chain, then slipped them into the pocket of his jeans.

"Listen," Amanda said, moving away from the porch rail. "I'm going into the house to give you two some privacy. If you want something to drink, just holler.''

Ian started to protest, to tell her not to leave. He wanted her to be a part of this, yet at the same time, he relished the idea of having time alone with his son. He could also sense that Gavin felt awkward. Maybe he'd feel better talking with only Ian present. He waited until Amanda went inside and closed the door. Then he gestured toward the chairs on the porch. ''Want to sit down?''

''Sure.'' Gavin sat, and Ian took the chair beside him, a thousand questions running through his mind. He truly didn't know where to start.

Deciding that open honesty was best, he plunged right in. ''I'm sure you've got a million questions. I know I do.''

''Yes, sir.'' Gavin nodded.

''You don't have to call me 'sir.' Ian will do fine.''

''All right.'' Gavin laced his fingers together and leaned his forearms on his long legs. ''Who goes first?'' Again, he grinned in a way that so very much reminded Ian of Papaw.

It sent a thrilling shiver throughout his body, and without even thinking about it, he laughed out loud. ''I'm glad you're okay with this, because to tell you the truth, I'm as nervous as a long-tailed cat in a room full of rocking chairs.''

''That makes two of us.''

Ian crossed one booted foot over his ankle. ''Would you like to tell me how you came here—to find me?''

Gavin took a deep breath. ''My parents are great people.'' Ian's heart gave a twinge. Again, he felt both sad and indebted. ''They were real understanding when I came to them and asked about you and my birth mother. Like I said, my dad hired a detective, but finding you was easy, since you still live here in Boone's Crossing.'' He glanced down at his black tennis shoes. "I called her first—just because I'd already planned to come spend the summer here. She didn't want to talk to me." He shook his head, and the hurt Jolene had caused was apparent in the look on his face.

Anger claimed Ian all over again. "I'm sorry to hear that."

"Yeah." Gavin looked back up at him. "It made me lose my confidence for a while. Made me sort of afraid to contact you. But I'd already come here to stay with Delbert, so I borrowed Aunt Betty's mower, and started doing lawns while I worked up the nerve to come to your shop. I was truly thinking about going there tomorrow, but then I ran into Miss Kelly at the Quick Fill and she told me she had my ring, and here I am."

It sounded so simple. Ian wanted more. To spend hours and days and weeks with this young man, getting to know him. To learn all about his life…his interests, his dislikes…his other family. Ian tapped his fingers against his ankle. "I've got so much to tell you," he said. "I really don't know where to start. I looked for you." And with that, he went into the details of what had happened. "I couldn't remember the name of the attorney who handled the adoption."

"Joe Brock," Gavin said. "He's my dad's brother. He moved his practice to Knoxville when I was a kid. Then a couple of years ago he and Aunt Betty got a divorce, and she moved back here to Boone's Crossing with Delbert."

"I knew it was something that sounded like Breck." Ian shook his head. "Unbelievable." He went on, filling Gavin in on more details, explaining how his search seemed to grow more and more cold as time passed. Until Amanda found the ring.

"So, if you gave the ring to my birth mother, then it was her who gave it to my parents, right?"

"She must have." As Amanda had pointed out, at least Jolene had done that much.

Gavin sat straight in the chair. "My folks never said. They just told me it belonged to my birth father, so I assumed you gave it to them for me. I've worn it on my neck ever since I was about eleven. They wouldn't let me have it when I was little, because they thought I'd lose it. Mom kept it in her jewelry box, and sometimes when she wasn't looking, I'd go in there and take it out and sit on her bed with it." He gave Ian a sheepish grin. "I'd put it on my finger, even though it was way too big, and make up stories in my mind—about you. You were an FBI special agent, forced into hiding by a group of spies. Or maybe you were an astronaut, and you were so busy exploring space, you didn't have time to come see me."

Ian's heart nearly ripped in half. Gavin's words were not bitter...they were only the recollection of a child's active imagination. Yet they cut like a knife. He tried to hide his heartache. "I wish I could have come to see you." He grinned, attempting to lighten the mood. "I hope you're not disappointed that I'm a welder instead of an FBI agent."

Gavin laughed. "Not at all. I'm pretty interested in

welding myself. I've taken classes in school. I want to learn to build my own bike frames.''

''Really?'' Ian noted the T-shirt Gavin wore, with a picture of a kid jumping high on a BMX bike.

He listened as Gavin talked about his sport. ''That's really why it took me so long to come back here to look for my ring. The day I mowed Miss Kelly's yard, me and Delbert went to the bike park in Knoxville and rode. Then we did some street riding, and I didn't notice the ring was gone until later. I called the bike park, but they hadn't seen it, and Delbert and I tried our best to retrace all the places we'd ridden in town, but I couldn't find it.'' He leaned forward in the chair once more. ''Then Aunt Betty took us up to Pigeon Forge for a few days, and I didn't have time to look anymore before we left. When I got back, I went to every single house where I'd mowed, including this one.''

''You came here? When?''

''Yesterday, when Miss Kelly was at work. It's so funny how it turned out with her locking her keys in her car, then telling me about finding the ring.'' He shook his head as though relieved. ''Man, I was so glad to hear that.'' He sobered and met Ian's gaze. ''That ring means a lot to me, si—Ian. It's all I have from my birth parents...from you I mean.''

Ian took a deep breath. His head felt light. ''I'm sure glad she found it, too. Like I said, I've been going crazy trying to figure a way to get a hold of you. To make sure...to see if you really were my son.''

Gavin shifted uncomfortably. ''I reckon I am, but it does feel strange. It'll take some getting used to.''

Ian folded his arms and leaned back in the chair. ''I

know what you mean. But I've got all the time in the world."

Sudden panic raced across Gavin's face. "Oh, man—speaking of time." He glanced at his watch. "I'm supposed to be headed home for supper." He hesitated. "But I'd sure like to talk to you some more. Do you think I could use the phone?"

Ian stood and, unable to resist, clapped Gavin on the shoulder as he stood as well, head for head as tall as he was. "You bet." Ian rapped on the door and Amanda appeared.

She showed Gavin where the phone was, then stepped out onto the porch. "How are things going?" The anxious look in her eyes filled him with gratitude. After all, he would never have found Gavin without her.

"They're going fine." He shook his head. "This still seems unreal."

"I'll bet." She crossed her arms in front of her chest and looked at him, and his thoughts rapidly shifted from Gavin to the previous night.

Unable to keep from doing so, he slipped his arms around her and stared directly into her eyes. "How are things with you?" he asked quietly. "I was disappointed to find you weren't in my—" He glanced toward the open door that led into the kitchen where Gavin was using the phone. "Weren't with me this morning."

Amanda briefly tucked her teeth over her bottom lip. "I thought it might be better if I left. Besides—" her tone lightened "—you fell asleep."

"And I am truly sorry about that," he said. He wanted to kiss her, but somehow felt awkward with

Gavin nearby. His son didn't even know him. Ian didn't want to give the impression of being all over Amanda. "I felt so relaxed, I guess I couldn't help myself."

To his surprise, she chuckled. She started to say something, but the screen door creaked open and Gavin came outside once more.

"Aunt Betty said I can stay as long as I want—within reason."

Ian smiled and let go of Amanda. "That sounds like a fair deal." He looked at the two of them, and suddenly found himself fantasizing much the way Gavin had done years ago. Only in his daydream, his idea of a perfect world, the three of them would be a family. "How would you two like to go for a chocolate shake?"

"Fine by me," Gavin said.

"You guys go ahead." Amanda gestured, her body language telling him she was once more backing off, to give him time alone with his son. "I've had a long day, and I have to work tomorrow."

Tomorrow.

Saturday.

The Cumberland Cubs.

Ian tamped down the selfish thoughts that rose within him. He'd so much rather spend the weekend with Gavin than act as co-scoutmaster, which wasn't fair. But it was a gut-honest reaction. Now that he'd found his son, he felt a need to not let go. To not let him out of his sight. And he wished with all his might Amanda would join them for a milkshake. "Are you sure?" he prodded.

She nodded. "Gavin, it was nice to see you again.

Please don't be a stranger.'' She gestured toward the tree where Skippy the squirrel had disappeared some time ago. ''Skippy enjoys your company and so do I.''

''Thanks.''

''See you later, then,'' Ian said, still hating to leave her. He hoped his eyes conveyed his thoughts. *I loved last night.* And I love you, Amanda.

''Bye.'' She gave him a little smile.

''So, my truck or yours?'' Gavin asked.

Ian grinned, and caught the genuine look of happiness Amanda gave him as he and Gavin descended the porch steps. ''Let's take yours.''

After all, he'd waited a lifetime to share something with his son. He'd missed his first tooth, his first steps, and probably his first date. And he wasn't the one who'd taught Gavin to drive.

But somehow, pride swelled in his chest as he climbed into the dark-blue Ford pickup and rode away with his son behind the wheel.

CHAPTER FOURTEEN

THE YARD SEEMED QUIET—too quiet—once Gavin and
Ian were gone. Amanda turned on the garden hose and
watered her roses, recalling the way she and Ian had
chased one another when they'd planted the flowers.
The way they'd lain on the ground and kissed, and
how it had felt to make love to Ian last night. She
knew she couldn't avoid the subject forever, and that
she needed to have a talk with him soon. Maybe it
would be best to get things out of the way once he
returned to her house, providing Gavin didn't stay, or
that he and Ian didn't have further plans for the evening.

The feeling of seeing father and son reunite had
been an experience she'd never forget. She'd found it
hard to keep back the tears as she'd watched the two
of them drive away, so happy, so alike in many ways.
Surely now that Ian had found his son, he would understand what he stood to lose if he were to continue
to be involved with her. He'd missed out on raising
Gavin, and now that he'd seen what it was like to
spend time with him, surely Ian would want children
all the more. Children he could be with from day one,
to love and watch grow. He needed a woman who
could and would give him that.

Ignoring the way her stomach churned at picturing

him with another woman in his life, Amanda finished watering the rosebushes, then coiled the garden hose into a neat roll. She sat on the porch, lost in thought, and didn't realize how much time had passed until she saw Gavin's Ford pull back into her driveway. She watched with a smile as he and Ian exchanged a manly hug, pounding each other on the back before separating. Gavin called out a goodbye to her and drove away.

Ian stood at the edge of the yard, watching the truck out of sight. "He's a good driver," he said, grinning proudly as he approached the porch, a takeout cup in his hand. "I won't stay, but we brought you a chocolate shake, too."

"Why, thank you." She took it from him, her fingers brushing against his. Her heart gave a sad little blip at knowing what she had to tell him, even though it was for the best. "You don't have to leave so quickly. I'm not *that* tired." She took a sip from the fat red straw, not really tasting the ice cream, but touched by Ian's gesture. Why did he have to be so nice? It made what she had to do all the harder.

Before she could say anything further, Ian sat down in the chair next to hers. "Gavin's really something," he said. "We sure had a good time."

A smile tugged at Amanda's lips. It felt good to see him happy. "Yeah? Tell me about him."

Ian went into details…what sports Gavin liked— primarily BMX. Where he lived, what classes he took at school. "Can you believe all this time I've been looking, and he's been just a two-hour drive away in Johnson City?" He shook his head. "I still can't get over it. Oh, and he's going camping with me and Neil and the Cubs tomorrow, providing his aunt approves. We're going to have a blast.''

"That's wonderful." She laid a hand on his arm. "I truly am happy for you, Ian. For both of you."

"It never would've happened without you," he said. He laid his hand over hers. "I owe you a debt of gratitude."

"You don't owe me anything," she said. "Fate would've brought the two of you together sooner or later. I was merely a catalyst."

"Don't sell yourself short."

Amanda looked down at the cup in her hand, then back at Ian. "I want you to know that making love to you last night meant something special to me. You're the most wonderful, kindest, most generous man I've ever met."

He narrowed his eyes. "Why do I sense a 'but' in there somewhere?"

Amanda sighed. "I'm that transparent, huh?"

"That's not the word I'd use to describe you." Ian grew serious. "Amanda, I hadn't been with a woman in a long while. I hope you know that I didn't just take you to bed for a quick tumble. Being with you meant way more to me than that."

She gave his hand a squeeze, ignoring the way her insides twisted at his words. "You're making this even harder for me." She took a deep breath. "Ian, we have to stop this. We have to step back from what's happening between us."

A genuine look of hurt crossed his face, and she hated having been the one to put it there. "Why?" He didn't give her a chance to answer. "Amanda, you mean more to me than any woman I've ever known.

I thought we had a good thing going here. Why in the world would you want to back away from that?''

"You know why," she said, sudden exasperation overwhelming her. "You told me you were looking for a woman to have children with. And you also said that you and I were responsible enough to know where to draw the line. Last night, we stepped over that line, and we shouldn't have."

He moved to the edge of his chair, turning to face her. "Why are you so determined to make such a hasty decision?"

"Hasty?" Hurt turned to annoyance as she struggled to maintain control of her emotions. Her grief counselor had helped her through the first few months after Anna's death, and told her to expect mood swings. As a nurse, she knew it was normal to experience such mood swings after a tragedy, especially the loss of a child.

Yet as someone who cared about Ian, she hated the way her feelings kept her on edge. Still, she couldn't stop the words from tumbling out. "There was nothing hasty in anything that has happened to me over the last few months. I lost a baby—a baby that wasn't even my own." She gestured emphatically. "I can't tell you the hours I've suffered going over and over what happened in my mind…blaming myself…seeing my sister's face every time I close my eyes at night. Being afraid to have a child of my own, worrying that something might happen to that baby, too.

"I don't know if I'll ever get over feeling the way I do, and right now, I can't even begin to see myself carrying another child. So please don't accuse me of making a snap decision." She fought to soften her tone. "Ian, I care about you. I don't want to see you get hurt— I don't want to be responsible for hurting you. I can't give you what you want, so please…can't you just see that and let it go?"

A mixture of emotions washed over his face. Sadness, sympathy, but most of all he looked at her with love in his eyes. Quickly, she turned away, not wanting to know how he felt, denying that he could really have come to love her so quickly.

"Amanda." Gently, Ian touched her face. "Look at me. Please." Reluctantly, she complied. "Don't you think you're being a little too hard on yourself—actually, way too hard on yourself, if you want to know my opinion?"

"What do you mean?"

"You didn't go out and purposely try to lose your sister's baby. It was an accident." His dark eyes pleaded with her. "Things like that happen in life. Things that are in no way fair. But that doesn't mean it will happen again. And you can't lay the blame where it doesn't belong. Blame the scumbag who hit you, but stop carrying this burden of guilt on your shoulders."

Amanda swallowed over a hard knot in her throat. In her hand, the cup felt every bit as cold as the pain and sorrow that lay deep within her. A pain that would not leave. "It still wouldn't change anything," she said. "Even if I could stop feeling horrible about the accident, it wouldn't bring Nikki's little girl back. And it sure won't make me feel any better knowing that I can still carry a baby and my sister can't. Especially since I'm too afraid to even go there." She swiped at a single tear that squeezed from the corner of her eye, furious with herself for letting things come this far with Ian. She never, ever should have slept with him. Not because she didn't care, but because she did.

He made her feel things she'd never felt for anyone, not even Mark, and for that she was doubly sorry. She couldn't love this man…couldn't love anyone. Not until her wounds had a chance to heal. And in light of the way she now felt, that could take months, years…possibly forever. There was no way she'd put another person through that anguish along with her. No way she'd let Ian love her, only to wind up with a broken heart she was totally responsible for.

"I truly don't believe anything will ever change for me." She gestured with one hand for emphasis, her fingers curled against her palm. "Please. Try to understand. I can't gamble on that, and I can't let you gamble on it either. All I know now is, I need some space. I need for you to give me some time alone, some room, to think." She knew she was stalling, grasping at loose straws. Fighting her own heart, the one that threatened to betray her and let her love Ian, no matter the cost. "That's why I came to Boone's Crossing in the first place."

"All right," he said quietly. He stood, then reached out to caress her cheek. "I'll give you some time and some space. But I'm not giving up on us." Briefly, he kissed her, and she found herself unable to resist him. It was not a goodbye, but a "see you later" sort of kiss. "I'm going to go visit Papaw and tell him about Gavin. Take care of yourself, Amanda. I'm a phone call away if you need me."

Touching her fingers to her lips, she watched him drive away. She could feel his kiss, lingering. The same way the longing inside her stayed, even after she could no longer hear his pickup's engine in the distance.

THE OVERCAST SKY Saturday morning matched Amanda's mood as she drove to work. She hoped it wouldn't rain on Ian's camping trip with Gavin and the Cumberland Cubs. She truly wanted to see him happy and hoped the time he spent getting to know his son this weekend would be the beginning of a lifelong relationship between the two of them. But sorrow weighed her down, now that she'd taken the first step in breaking things off with Ian. She wished, somehow, things could be different. As she parked her car in the nursing home's lot, she made an effort to put on a cheerful air. She looked forward to seeing Zeb, knowing Ian had already shared his good news with his grandpa the night before.

Zeb greeted her from his usual place in the day room, where he sat alone playing chess, his patchwork quilt draped across his lap. "Guess you heard the news," he said, a proud grin plastered across his face. "Ian found his boy."

"Yes, I did." Amanda smiled. "I'm so happy for him."

"You and me both." Zeb pondered a chess piece, made a move, then said, "You know he's bringing Gavin to see me as soon as they get back from their camping trip."

"That'll be nice."

"Maybe now Ian will finally settle down and raise up a bunch of young'uns of his own."

Somehow, she managed a smile. "That's exactly

what I'm hoping, too." She wanted Ian to have his family, but not with her. Quickly, she excused herself and headed for her office, eager to start her day, to lose herself in her job. Maybe working to block out your sorrows wasn't such a bad thing after all.

But when her shift came to an end, and Amanda made her way to the car, she was disappointed to realize that even a busy day hadn't kept thoughts of Ian from her mind. She wondered what he was doing this very minute. Was he hiking with his scouts and Gavin? Maybe teaching them some wilderness survival trick?

Was he thinking of her?

Amanda climbed behind the wheel of her Honda and headed for home, tired yet restless. Maybe she'd finally get started on cleaning out the shed. But both her plans and her mood took an abrupt swing as she pulled into the driveway. A familiar car was parked there, and on her porch, Nikki sat in one of the chairs.

Amanda turned off her engine and rushed to greet her. "Nikki! Oh my gosh, why didn't you call and tell me you were coming?"

Nikki hurried down the steps and across the yard. She wore khaki shorts and a red blouse, her once long, honey-brown hair now cut to shoulder-length and dyed a pale blond. Amanda threw her arms around her sister and held her tight, loving the familiar scent of her citrus perfume, and the welcome sight of her smile as Nikki pulled back and held her at arm's length.

"I wanted to surprise you." Her gaze swept Amanda from head to toe. "You look good, sis." She tucked her elbow through Amanda's, and they headed for the porch in matched strides. "Tennessee must agree with you."

The sudden thought that it was likely Ian, and not just Boone's Crossing, that had her looking and feeling better than the last time Nikki had seen her, danced across Amanda's mind. She pushed it aside, confused. How was it Ian made her feel so much better whenever he was around, yet her own inner feelings and fears still managed to block her happiness?

"Thanks," she said. "You look pretty darned good yourself." Nikki had lost so much weight due to the stress of the accident and Anna's death. It was nice to see her back to her normal body size. "And your hair—I love it!"

"Thanks." Nikki scanned the room as they entered the kitchen. "Gosh, it feels strange to be back at Granny's cabin—but good."

Amanda laid her purse and keys on the countertop. "This place sure takes me back to our childhood."

"It does." Nikki smiled. "I can't wait to catch up on everything with you. It's been a while since we've talked."

"I know." Amanda sighed as she slipped out of her uniform jacket and draped it over the back of a chair. In spite of her intentions to stay in touch, she hadn't phoned Nikki since her shopping trip with Sami Jo. So much had happened since their last phone call, and oftentimes, Amanda didn't know what to say to Nikki. Even now, her enthusiasm wilted as she noticed the hidden pain in her sister's eyes, and the haggard shadows above her cheekbones that makeup and a new hair color couldn't quite disguise. "I can't believe you drove all this way by yourself. Why didn't you fly?"

"I thought the drive would be good therapy. Fifteen hundred miles alone with my thoughts, if you don't count the billion-and-one times Cody checked up on me by cell phone." She gave a wry grin. "Actually, the drive was pretty long. Kansas goes on forever!"

"Tell me about it," Amanda said, recalling her own difficulties in forcing herself to make the trip alone. "But I do love the prairie, and watching the sun rise on the open horizon." Passing through eastern Colorado and Kansas had been one of the few stretches of her drive that she'd felt relaxed. For quite some time following the accident, she'd been terrified to climb behind the wheel of a car. Even then, driving on a two-lane highway had left her sweating, and the freeway made things even worse. She'd gripped the steering wheel so hard on her way to Tennessee, that her hands had cramped up, aching fiercely every time she stopped for a rest break.

"Where's your luggage?" she asked, breaking away from the negative memories. "I'll help you with it."

"I already got it."

Amanda gestured toward the fridge. "Want something to drink?"

"Sure. And I'm starving!"

"I can fix that." Again, she was glad to see Nikki's appetite had returned. It had been a long while before she herself had managed to eat regularly, and therefore the weight from the pregnancy had come off quickly. "Just let me change my clothes, and I'll whip us up something tasty."

A short time later, she sat beside Nikki at one end of the kitchen table while they enjoyed their meal of grilled chicken, French green beans and a salad of tossed greens with mandarin oranges.

"So, how is Cody?"

Nikki sighed. "He's doing okay."

"And?"

"You always could read me too well," she grumbled, stabbing a piece of lettuce with her fork. "Actually, we've decided to give each other a little space. Hopefully, it'll help us get our marriage back on track."

The words so closely echoed what she'd said to Ian, that Amanda had to give herself a mental shake. "You mean by taking a trip out here?"

Nikki was silent a moment. "That, and the fact that Cody's thinking about moving out for a while."

"Oh, Nikki." She laid her fork down, her appetite gone.

"No, now don't do that to yourself," Nikki scolded. "That's why I didn't want to tell you. I knew you'd take the blame when it's not your fault. You know things were shaky with me and Cody even before the accident."

"Yes, but not once you decided to have me act as your surrogate." They'd been so happy—finally— their woes of not having a child behind them. A baby of their own on the way. Tears welled in Amanda's eyes, and she cupped a hand to her mouth. "I'm sorry. I told myself I wouldn't cry in front of you anymore."

Nikki reached over and took her other hand. "It's okay, sweetie." Her eyes swam with tears as well. "Of course we were overjoyed about getting pregnant, but really, there's so much more to what was happening with our marriage." She gave Amanda's hand a squeeze. "Stop beating yourself up, sis. Please. It hurts me so much to see you in pain."

"Same here." Amanda sniffed and reached for a paper napkin. "I want so much for things to be better for you and Cody."

"They will," Nikki said. "Somehow." She let go of Amanda's hand, and poked her green beans with her fork. "I think this trip is a good thing—for both of us. I get to see my sister, and Cody and I get a chance to step back and take a look at ourselves from a distance."

"Then what?" Amanda asked quietly.

Nikki lifted a shoulder. "I'm really not sure. Cody's thinking about staying at Jordan's for a while. But he did agree to wait until I come back to make a definite decision. Maybe he'll change his mind."

Jordan Blake was Cody's partner on the Deer Creek police force. He was single, and dated a lot of women. Amanda cringed at the thought that Cody might move in with someone whose lifestyle could appear to be appealing to a man with marital troubles.

"So, how long can you stay?" she asked.

"A couple of weeks? Maybe a little longer, if you can put up with me."

Though she hated to see Nikki and Cody having problems, Amanda was thrilled to have her sister here. Maybe Nikki's absence *would* change Cody's mind about moving out. And her visit might also be just the thing Amanda needed to finally set things straight between her and Ian. He could spend time with Gavin, she could do so with Nikki, and with a little luck, they'd be able to ease out of their relationship without complications.

"You'd better believe I can put up with you," Amanda said with a grin. "I may not let you leave."

Nikki chuckled. "Be careful what you wish for. Cody might call and tell you to keep me."

They laughed, leaning close together, the way they had when they were kids. Amanda's heart warmed. It felt so good to laugh with Nikki.

It sure beat all the crying they'd done lately.

IAN WATCHED WITH PRIDE as Gavin led some of the Cumberland Cubs along the riverbank in search of arrowheads. The boys had taken to Gavin like a row of lost ducklings, dogging his every step, looking up to him in awe. He'd regaled them with tales of BMX competition, and the tricks he'd learned in hopes of competing himself. A lot of boys his age would've thought a group of nine- and ten-year-olds beneath them, not worth their bother. But not Gavin.

"Ian! Look at this." Jacob hurried toward him, flushed with excitement. He held out a near-perfect arrowhead, flint-colored, about two inches long. "I found it right there by that tree."

"Wow." Ian examined the arrowhead with proper reverence. "That's awesome." Over Jacob's shoulder, he winked at Gavin. He knew for a fact that Gavin had found the arrowhead earlier that day. But when he'd noticed Jacob wasn't finding anything, he'd purposely planted the arrowhead for the boy to discover. Pride swelled in Ian's chest as Gavin returned his conspiratorial wink.

The group continued their search, but by late afternoon, thunderclouds gathered, and rain pelted down. The boys took it all in stride, taking temporary cover before continuing with the day's activities once the rain had let up. Just before nightfall, he and Neil supervised the Cubs as they built a campfire, then performed the time-honored rituals of making s'mores and telling spooky stories. Once everyone had crawled into their tents for the night, Ian rolled out his sleeping bag, not minding the semidamp ground, taking in the night sounds around him. Overhead, the clouds had broken up, revealing handfuls of stars tossed against a canopy of charcoal-colored sky.

"Mind if I stretch out here, too?" Gavin stood next to him, sleeping bag in hand.

"Not at all. Be my guest." Ian traded a smile with his son, and basked in the pleasure of Gavin's company as he unrolled his sleeping bag a few feet away. Together, they lay quietly watching the sky.

Gavin folded his arms behind his head, using them as a pillow. "The stars sure are bright out here in the country, aren't they?"

"Mm-hmm." Ian looked at the expanse of speckled darkness with new appreciation. He'd always been fortunate enough to live on a farm, to experience on a daily basis things that children raised in town didn't necessarily get to see. "You know, I used to look up at the stars and wonder if you were watching them, too." He glanced over at Gavin, silhouetted in the dying embers of the fire. "I'd think about where you might be... What you might be doing at that very minute. And I'd ask myself—did you have parents who loved you? Were you happy?"

Gavin looked at him, his expression serious. "I guess I was lucky to get adopted by someone like my mom and dad." He proceeded to tell Ian all about his adoptive parents, and rather than resent the years they'd spent raising his boy, Ian felt all the more indebted to the couple who had claimed Gavin as their own.

Nathan Brock was a pediatrician, his wife Sandy a day-care provider. It was easy to see the two had spent a lot of time with Gavin throughout his childhood, and still did. They supported his sport of BMX and took a family vacation every year at a mutually-decided-upon locale. They seemed to live a well-rounded existence, right down to the proverbial family dog—a malamute named Klondike.

"Your folks sound like great people."

"They are. You know, I never really thought too much about how you might feel, giving me up." Gavin pressed his lips into a firm line. "I hope you know that I don't hold it against you. Heck, I'm the same age you were then, and I can't even begin to imagine being somebody's daddy." He shook his head in wonderment.

"Well, you just keep thinking that way." Ian spoke with a teasing growl and Gavin returned his grin.

"No worries there. I'm too busy with my bike right now to give serious thought to a girlfriend." His grin widened. "Did your Grandpa Zeb really get married when he was seventeen?"

"Yep. Really and truly."

"I can't wait to meet him tomorrow."

"He can't wait to meet you either."

Silence lay comfortably between them. "I'm sure glad I found you, Ian."

Ian looked into his son's eyes, and thanked the heavens above for the second chance he'd been given, to be a part of Gavin's life. *Finally.* "I'm sure glad you did, too, son."

And as he lay watching the night sky with the young man who was his flesh and blood, the only thing that would have made the moment better was if Amanda were there, too.

CHAPTER FIFTEEN

AMANDA AWOKE EARLY Sunday morning, and leaving Nikki to sleep in, tiptoed into the kitchen to make coffee. She hoped today's date would not register in her sister's mind. She'd tried to block it from her own consciousness with no luck. June twentieth. Her due date. If not for the accident, today would have been one of anticipation, with Anna's arrival imminent.

An empty ache gripped Amanda and refused to let go as she took her cup of coffee to the porch and sat down. All around, birds sang cheerily from the trees, and the creek bubbled and whispered in tranquil motion. She wished for that same tranquility.

"You're up early."

Snapped from her musings, Amanda turned as the screen creaked open and Nikki stepped outside. "I thought you were still sleeping."

"Are you kidding? And miss this beautiful morning?"

Amanda smiled at Nikki's enthusiasm. Her sister had always possessed a strong spirit and a way of looking at things in a positive light. It was part of the reason that seeing her so depressed for the last few months had hurt so deeply. Nikki slid onto the chair next to Amanda's, cradling her mug of coffee. For a moment, the two of them sat, simply enjoying the soothing nature sounds and the presence of one another's company.

"So, what do you want to do today?" Amanda asked.

"I don't know. What did you have planned before I showed up?"

She shrugged. "Nothing exciting, I'm afraid. I was thinking about cleaning out the toolshed. Granny's stuff is still in there."

Nikki shook her head. "I can't believe Mom just left it there. Have you heard from her lately?"

Bridget had flown in from Montana for Anna's funeral, but she hadn't stayed. As usual, she'd felt confident that her daughters could lean on each other and didn't find it necessary to stick around. "Not a word since I spoke to her about coming here. You?"

"She sent me a postcard a couple of weeks ago. From Alaska."

"Alaska? Good grief, what's she doing there?"

"She's decided raising sled dogs might be profitable." Nikki quirked a brow. "She answered an ad in a magazine for a 'live-in companion,' placed by some guy who's a musher."

"Oh, Nikki. She did not!" Amanda gaped at her sister. Though Bridget had always been flighty, she'd shied away from any type of commitment when it came to men. As far as Amanda knew, her mother had maintained only a handful of relationships over the years, all of them very short-term.

"She did. I'm serious." Nikki chuckled. "She says he's finally 'The One.' I hope she's right."

"Well, maybe he'll slow her down some." Amanda sighed, wishing her mother could truly find happiness.

Bridget might have a chance, if she'd stay in one place long enough for it to catch up with her.

She finished her coffee. "You never answered my question. What would you like to do today?"

"Help you clean out the shed."

"You don't have to. That's no way to spend a vacation."

Nikki waved one hand in dismissal. "Oh, come on. It'll be fun going through Granny's stuff. Remember how much we used to love dressing up in her high heels and jewelry when we were kids?"

Amanda forced a smile, her mind on other things besides playing dress-up. Instead, thoughts of the last time she'd been in the shed with Ian flooded her mind. Nikki didn't need to go through what she'd felt upon finding the cherry-wood cradle. Especially not today.

"I remember. But really, Nik, wouldn't you rather do something else?"

"I came here to be with you," Nikki said, her hazel eyes serious. "I can sightsee while you're at work, so come on. Finish up your coffee and let's get busy." She stood and moved to the porch rail as she sipped from her mug. "Those roses are gorgeous." She indicated the freshly turned soil around them. "You must've planted them recently."

"I did." Amanda hesitated. She hadn't yet told Nikki about Ian, primarily because she didn't want her sister nagging her to give things a chance with him, which she knew Nikki would do.

As though reading her mind, Nikki studied her intently. "You started to say something else, didn't you? What was it?"

"Nothing." Amanda did her best to look nonchalant.

But Nikki stared her down. "Come on. Give. What aren't you telling me? You look like a kid caught sneaking out of the bedroom window."

Amanda sighed. "The roses were a gift. From...a friend."

Nikki's eyebrows raised. "A friend, huh? A male friend?"

"Yes." She gave her sister a mock glare. "Satisfied?"

"No." Nikki sat down in the chair once more, cradling her mug in both hands. "Tell me more. Who is he? Are you dating? Is it serious?"

The flat denial on the tip of Amanda's tongue would not come out. She lifted a shoulder. "I don't know if I'd really call it serious...." *Liar,* her inner voice accused. Things had gone farther between her and Ian than she'd ever intended. But she refused to dwell on thoughts of the lovemaking they'd shared. And she certainly couldn't let herself focus on how happy she felt whenever he was around, or on how nice it would be to have such a good man in her life on a permanent basis. She explained to Nikki how she'd met Ian, and without going into a lot of detail, told her they'd decided to slow things down a little. Give it some time.

"Well, I guess there's nothing wrong with that," Nikki said, her tone indicating she suspected there was more to the situation than Amanda was telling her. "I want to meet him."

"Why?" Before Nikki could argue, she hurried on. "Nothing's going to come of our relationship."

"How can you say that? Ian sounds like a really

nice guy.'' Nikki narrowed her eyes. ''Have you slept with him?''

''Nikki!''

''Well, have you?''

Amanda sighed. Decided there was no point in trying to fool her sister. ''Yes. But it shouldn't have happened. That's why we're backing off from each other for a while.''

Nikki looked at her with genuine sadness. ''Amanda, why are you doing this to yourself?''

''Doing what?'' She squirmed in her chair.

''You know perfectly well what.'' Nikki reached out and gave her arm a little shake. ''You're punishing yourself, and that's not right. I told you, I don't want you to do that.''

''I'm not.'' Amanda hid behind the sudden need to sip her coffee. For a moment, she thought Nikki would keep up the argument. She'd always been like a dog worrying a bone when it came to persistence.

''Okay,'' Nikki said. ''So, let's get busy.'' She stood and set her mug on the porch railing beside a support beam.

Amanda eyed her with suspicion at her sudden willingness to drop the subject. And at the same time, realized Nikki had managed to sidetrack her from the subject of cleaning out the toolshed. Now, thoughts of the cradle came to mind once more. Unable to think of any more excuses for leaving the task to another day, yet not wanting Nikki to go through what she herself had in finding the cradle without warning, Amanda stood but made no move to walk toward the shed. ''Hang on a second.'' Nikki halted halfway down the steps and looked back at her expectantly.

"I've been putting off cleaning the shed because of something I found in there...something that upset me."

Nikki's puzzled frown shifted, and Amanda could tell by the look on her face that she knew exactly what that something was. "The cradle." Nikki sighed and clamped her hand against her forehead. "For some reason, I thought it was in the loft." Granny's cabin had a small, atticlike loft that still held a full-length antique mirror and a cedar chest filled with some of Granny's hand-crocheted doilies and embroidered linens.

"Let's just leave it. Really, I can deal with the cradle, and cleaning out the shed, another time." She'd have a yard sale after Nikki went home.

"No." Vehemently, Nikki shook her head. "Why should you have to be the one to do it?" Retracing her steps, she came back to stand on the porch, and took Amanda's hand. "I know what today is. That's part of the reason I came out here to be with you. So you wouldn't have to face today alone." Her voice quivered. "Sometimes I wish I'd never asked you to be my surrogate. There is no way I would have ever purposely put you in a position to suffer so much pain—physically, emotionally." She pressed her fingers to her mouth, and Amanda pulled her into a hug.

"Don't," she said, rubbing Nikki's back in a gesture of comfort. "Don't do that to yourself. We've been over this before. I love you, and I wanted to help you."

Sniffing, Nikki pulled back and nodded. "Okay... okay." She gripped Amanda's hand once more. "Come on. We'll do this together. Like we've always done things.'' Her lips curved with obvious effort, and the fact that her sister was willing to face seeing the heirloom cradle, even though it would likely be even harder on Nikki than it had been on herself, gave Amanda renewed inner strength.

Her resistance melted. ''All right. Hang on while I get the key.'' She retrieved it from its place near the back door, then rejoined Nikki in the yard. She hadn't been inside the shed since Ian had repaired her window, except to shove the cradle back under the bench where she'd found it. As she unlocked the door and pushed it open, hot, stale air washed over her, making her feel claustrophobic all over again. But outside, the morning was still fairly cool and mild, and she could always duck outside for a minute or two as needed.

''Whew, we're going to have to get some air in here.'' Nikki fanned her hand in front of her face. Purposely ignoring the cradle, though Amanda knew she'd spotted it, she strode over and opened the window above the workbench, then moved through an obstacle of clutter to the far side of the shed to open the window there as well. Dusting her hands on the legs of her shorts, she gave the double doors that led to the driveway a hopeless look. ''There's no way we're going to get those doors open with all that junk stacked against them. Have you got a fan?''

Amanda nodded. ''I'll get it.'' She stole a glance at the cradle. If Nikki could handle this, so could she. After retrieving a circular fan from her bedroom, she returned to the shed. Nikki was already busy, digging through an open box. Amanda set the fan on the workbench, plugged it in, and turned the switch on high.

''Oh, look what's in here.''

She turned to see what Nikki had found, and immediately, her mood brightened. "Popcorn's bridle." Smiling, she moved to stand beside her sister, fond memories of days spent riding the little brown-and-white pony coming back to her with clarity.

"Remember how we used to trot him through the apple orchard?" Lovingly, Nikki kneaded the worn, stiff leather between her fingers, then held it to her nose. "I loved the way his coat smelled. All warm and sweet."

"Me, too," Amanda said. "I never could figure out why some people think horses smell bad." Nikki and Cody had horses, but Amanda hadn't been riding in a long while, since they'd wanted to make sure nothing jeopardized the pregnancy—an ironic twist of fate. The closest she'd been to a horse lately was Banjo, Zeb's mule. She thought about his well-groomed buckskin-colored coat. And the way his shod hooves had clacked against the road as she and Ian moved along in the buggy, Cuddles between them.

She snapped out of her musings to find Nikki watching her. "Where would we be without our memories?" Nikki spoke almost reverently.

If only all memories were good, Amanda thought. Involuntarily, her gaze fell once more on the cradle. Nikki followed her line of sight, then laid the pony bridle down and moved over to the workbench. Kneeling, she took hold of the cradle.

"Nikki." Amanda started to protest.

"It's all right." Firmly, Nikki gave it a tug, and Amanda moved to help her, dislodging the cradle from between a toolbox and an old trunk.

"I should have gotten this out of here sooner,"

Amanda said, unable to stop the feelings of sorrow and regret that flooded through her. "As a matter of fact, I was planning to clear out most of this stuff and have a big yard sale. Someone can put this cradle to good use, I'm sure."

Nikki looked at her as though Amanda had slapped her. "How can you say that?" Pain laced her words.

Amanda stared at her, perplexed. "What? Nikki—" The words stuck in her throat. Everything had changed since they'd shared memories of the cradle with their friends at the baby shower. All had been right and wonderful then, Anna alive and well, safely tucked inside her womb. But now, everything was not all right.

Nikki's gaze softened, and so did her voice as she reached out and touched Amanda's shoulder. "I told you—stop beating yourself up, Amanda." She pursed her lips together, her eyes swimming with unshed tears. "This cradle isn't going anywhere...not until it's needed. And not by some stranger." She slipped her arm around Amanda's waist, and stared into her eyes. "I want you to rock your babies in this cradle, sis. I want you to be happy."

Cupping her hands over her nose and mouth, Amanda shook her head, trying not to cry. "I can't," she whispered. But how could she stand here and tell her sister she didn't want any children, when children were the one thing Nikki wanted most in life? Suddenly, she felt selfish. She returned Nikki's hug, her head spinning with confusion. There were no easy answers.

"Yes, you can." Nikki spoke firmly. "And you will." She held her at arm's length. "You need time, honey, just like I do. Just like Cody does. But please—don't get rid of the cradle.''

That Nikki could be so strong affected her more than words could say. And even though she knew Nikki was wrong, that she would never be able to bring herself to have children when the sister she loved with all her heart and soul could not; when her own fears stood in the way like a brick wall, she nodded. ''Okay.''

''Now come on,'' Nikki said, taking hold of the cradle once more. ''We've got a lot of work ahead if we're going to make any headway at all on this stuff.'' Amanda helped her move it across the room where they set it in the corner. ''We can put everything you plan to keep in this area,'' Nikki said, forever the organizer.

Together, they set about the task of sorting through items ranging from a set of a dozen old canning jars, to some of Grandpa Satterfield's tools that Granny had never been able to part with. The tools made Amanda think of Ian once again. He'd been so sweet to her that day in the shed, his touch gentle, his words caring as he'd guided her outside for fresh air. He was a good man, and he deserved everything equally as good in life, including a wife and as many kids as his heart desired.

She would keep the cradle, since it meant so much to Nikki, and was a memento of their own childhood.

But it would have to continue to gather dust in the shed.

THE WEEK PASSED QUICKLY, between work and the pleasure of having Nikki around. They took flowers to Granny Satterfield's grave on Tuesday, even though Amanda worried it would upset her sister to go to the cemetery. Lord knew, they'd both seen enough of death to last a lifetime. But Nikki had wanted to pay her respects to Granny, and Amanda had to admit she'd been thinking about taking some roses to the grave for quite some time now. She felt better, going there with Nikki rather than alone, the two of them holding hands like they'd done when they were small. They'd said a prayer after placing red roses at the base of the marble headstone, and as they walked away from the graveyard, Amanda let a picture form in her mind of Granny rocking little Anna while the angels gathered around to sing a lullaby.

For the rest of the week, Amanda did her best to make sure her sister's stay in Boone's Crossing was a pleasant one. Since her shift at the nursing home usually ended at four, there'd been plenty of time each evening for them to do something fun. Nikki had insisted on keeping busy when Amanda wasn't home, and she'd sorted through what items they hadn't yet gotten to in the toolshed, making it easier to separate what was to go in the yard sale and what was to stay.

Amanda had seen Ian twice—once on Monday when he'd brought Gavin to Shade Tree to meet and spend time with Zeb, and again, when he'd stopped by her house on Thursday. Nikki had been completely charmed by his old-fashioned southern manners and his sense of humor, and Amanda had found it difficult to keep her hands to herself. She'd ached to hold Ian, and feel his kisses.

When he said his goodbyes, he'd slipped his arm around her, coaxing her to walk him to his truck. He'd kissed her, and she hadn't protested, unwilling to cause a scene with Nikki nearby. Ian had left with a promise to see her soon, and the look in his eyes told her he'd meant what he'd previously said. That he wasn't about to give up on the two of them.

When she'd returned to the house, Nikki gave her the third degree all over again about her relationship with Ian. Amanda did her best to dance around the subject, all the while fighting her own feelings. Nikki's arguments in Ian's favor made it all the harder for Amanda to hang on to her determination—to keep her and Ian's relationship on hold.

As the weekend dawned, the weather took a turn for the worse, and a rainy Saturday provided the perfect excuse to spend a day at the mall. Amanda called Sami Jo and invited her to go with her and Nikki. They decided to see a movie, and chose a romantic comedy. Afterward, they wandered through the mall, eating caramel apples and window-shopping, like three old friends.

Amanda couldn't help stealing a glance at Sami's still-flat stomach. It wouldn't stay that way for long, and she wondered how she would handle being around her once Sami started to show. She told herself she'd handle it like any good friend would. She *was* truly happy for Sami, and babies were a reality of life, one she could not continue to avoid. Everywhere she looked, it seemed she saw pregnant women or babies in strollers.

She noticed Nikki staring at one particularly cute toddler in a yellow sundress and bonnet, and immediately her protective instincts for her sister flared anew. She tucked her elbow through Nikki's and addressed her and Sami Jo. "What say we go for pizza, ladies?"

"Oh." Sami clapped a hand against her chest. "Be still my heart. Hugh Grant and pizza, all in one day."

Nikki laughed and the sound instantly boosted Amanda's spirits. So much so, that she overindulged in pepperoni with extra cheese, onions, green peppers and black olives, and woke up the following morning with a queasy stomach.

"You look a little green around the gills," Nikki said when Amanda came into the kitchen to make breakfast. "Too much junk food, huh?"

Amanda groaned at the mere memory of all the goodies they'd consumed. "Remind me not to mix popcorn, candy apples and super-supreme pizza ever again." She brewed some peppermint tea, and it helped ease the whirling of her stomach a bit.

By the next day, she felt fine, but as the Fourth of July weekend approached she began to feel nauseous once more, and a warning bell went off inside her mind. Could what she'd feared most have already happened? Was she pregnant? Panic tried to push its way inside of her, but this time she fought back with more than just relaxation techniques. She thought about keeping calm for Nikki, and about the way Ian made her feel. Good, warm and happy.

She hadn't seen much of him lately, outside his visits to Shade Tree, and when he'd invited her and Nikki to a family barbecue, she'd been unable to resist saying yes. What could it hurt, with so many people around? It wasn't as if they were going someplace intimate, and after all, she'd never intended to turn her back on Ian altogether. Though it would be difficult to try to think of him as only a friend, the way she'd originally meant for him to be, Amanda knew she had to make the effort.

Nikki planned to stay for the Fourth, then head home once the holiday weekend was over. Amanda hated to think of her leaving, and hoped her time spent in Tennessee would prove to be exactly what she and Cody needed, to miss each other enough to work on their marriage.

On the Friday before the Fourth, Amanda found herself making more than one hurried trip to the bathroom at work, and now she was scared. Roberta scolded her, accusing her of being a typical nurse…taking care of others but not herself. She said a summer flu bug was going round, and Amanda was more than happy to let her co-workers think that was the cause of her illness.

But she knew better. A sense of dread overtook her by the time she headed home after her shift. Her breasts were tender, and even though she didn't think her period was overdue, she had to admit that the stress of losing Anna had put her off the regularity her body normally followed. Dear God, had she miscalculated what she'd thought was a "safe time" in her cycle on the night she'd slept with Ian? No time of the month was completely guaranteed, and she'd known that. But her feelings for him had allowed her to get caught up in the moment rather than insisting on stopping unless one of them had a condom, which they hadn't.

She hoped to heaven she could keep Nikki from noticing how queasy she was. There was no way she'd burden her sister with her suspicions. Especially not until she was certain, and even then, she had no idea how she'd break the news to her. Lord, for that matter, how on earth would she tell Ian? Her head began to spin, and she prayed her suspicions were wrong.

The barbecue was to be held at Ian's, since Sami Jo's yard was too small, and their other relatives lived in Kentucky and Virginia—a bit too far for Zeb to travel. He'd been making progress with his gradually healing hip, and had recently been able to take a few steps using a walker. Ian's father, Matthew, would come from Virginia to pick Zeb up in a car he could manage to get into. Amanda felt some amount of trepidation at meeting Ian's dad and the rest of his family. They'd likely end up hating her for breaking Ian's heart, which made her all the more determined to get Ian to see their relationship for what it was and back off.

But if she were indeed pregnant, what then?

She drove with Nikki to Ian's, hoping she'd be able to regain her appetite enough to keep him from noticing anything out of the ordinary. But the mere thought of hot dogs and ketchup was enough to send her stomach whirling anew. "Morning sickness" was a term used far too loosely, since her stomach had a mind of its own no matter what the hour.

She hadn't experienced this much queasiness when she'd been pregnant with Anna. Maybe it was all in her mind. It could be she was experiencing hysterical symptoms, brought on by the continual aftereffects of the accident, complicated by being around Nikki once more.

But the nurse in her knew that wasn't so.

CHAPTER SIXTEEN

IAN WATCHED AMANDA interact with his family. He'd been proud to introduce her to his father and his aunts, uncles and cousins. Just as he'd been proud to have his family get to know Gavin. He'd met Gavin's aunt Betty the Monday after his camping trip with the Cumberland Cubs, before he'd taken his son to meet Papaw. Betty agreed that Gavin needed time to get to know his newfound family, and after a phone call to confer with Nathan and Sandy Brock, had accepted Ian's invitation to the barbecue.

He felt like he had the world by the tail. His son was here, laughing and talking to Papaw and to Ian's dad—the grandfather who'd once turned his back on him, but who was now overjoyed to meet Gavin, anxious to get to know him better. And best of all, Amanda was here with her sister, whom Ian had liked immediately upon their first meeting. The bond between the two women was obvious, and he could see firsthand how Amanda had come to act as surrogate for her sister, and why the loss of the baby had so greatly affected both of them. Not that he'd ever thought otherwise. It was just that seeing Amanda's closeness to Nikki made it all the more real, all the more tragic.

Ian strolled over to where Amanda sat beneath a

shade tree with Nikki and Sami Jo, rubbing the toes of one sandaled foot against Cuddles's upturned belly. The Rottie sighed with pleasure, making the three women laugh. But beneath her smile, Amanda looked somewhat pale. There was a hint of shadows beneath her eyes, and worried, Ian sat down in a lawn chair next to her and took her hand. "Are you feeling okay?" he asked. "You look a little peaked."

Her face blanched further. "I'm fine."

Frowning, Ian reached over and touched her forehead. "You don't feel feverish," he said, somewhat relieved.

Amanda brushed his hand away with a tolerant smile. "I told you, it's nothing. Just the heat."

He nodded at the paper plate she'd set on the circular, wrought-iron table between her chair and Nikki's. It held a half-eaten hot dog and an unfinished portion of potato salad. "You didn't eat much."

"I've already scolded her," Nikki said. "I'm afraid I've kept her too busy for the past couple of weeks. She's not getting enough rest."

"Are you sure it's not still the aftereffects of our pizza night?" Sami Jo kidded. "Seriously, Amanda, you need to take care of yourself. There is a summer bug going around."

"So I've heard." She looked at him. "I'm fine, thank you. I am a nurse, you know."

"Yeah, and you probably make a horrible patient." He swiped his finger against the tip of her nose in a playful gesture. "Don't get too big for your nurse's cap, or we'll have to hog-tie you, throw you in bed and feed you chicken soup and weak tea."

Amanda wrinkled her nose. "I don't wear a nurse's

cap.'' Abruptly, she changed the subject. ''So what have you and Gavin been up to?''

''This and that.'' Ian looked across the yard to where Gavin was deep into a competitive game of horseshoes with Delbert, Zeb and Matthew, Zeb pitching the shoes from the seat of his wheelchair. ''I've been showing him a thing or two about welding, and we're planning to go horseback riding sometime next week. There's a rental stable outside of town that's got some pretty nice trails. You and Nikki are welcome to join us.''

''Thanks, but Nikki's leaving on Monday, and I've still got to get my yard sale going. The rain last weekend messed me up.''

''Oh, come on. Go riding with us. It'll be fun, and I promise I'll help you with the yard sale later.''

This time, he saw a definite shift in the expression on her face. She glanced away as though seeking another excuse to say no. Ian fought back irritation. Why was she so all-fired stubborn about the two of them getting together? Surely she would move past the pain she felt one day, and decide she did want children after all.

But what if she didn't?

The same inner voice that had been taunting him for quite some time now, intruded on his positive thoughts. It scared him, for he knew it was possible Amanda might never change her mind. He needed to be prepared for that. She'd vehemently told him, more than once, that there were to be no babies in her future. Maybe he'd made a mistake in letting himself fall for her in spite of this fact. But how was he supposed to turn his back on her at this point, when he cared so much?

Purposely, he focused on the here and now. "So, what do you say? Wanna go?"

"I don't know. I really have been feeling pretty tired, and it's been a while since I've ridden. Maybe another time."

"All right then." He let it drop. But as the afternoon waned, and his cousins' kids began to excitedly clamor for an answer as to when the fireworks would be lit, Ian soberly recalled Papaw's comment some weeks ago.

I bet the two of you will be going steady by the Fourth of July. Maybe you'll make some fireworks of your own.

Was Amanda really so determined not to have children that she'd turn her back on him because of that? Or was there more to it? Maybe she just didn't feel the same way about him as he did about her.

But memories of their lovemaking nixed his theory as quickly as water doused flames. He and Amanda had been more like fire fueled by gasoline, igniting with a hot, fierce intensity that had overwhelmed him, sending him completely out of control. He very nearly hadn't been able to restrain himself when the crucial moment came—to pull out in light of the fact that they had no other means of protection. And he knew exactly what had caused his desire to rage out of control. It wasn't just the fact that he'd had the hots for Amanda from the moment he'd laid eyes on her. It was because he'd fallen in love with her.

Knowing she didn't feel the same way about him made things difficult, but not impossible. Oh, no. He was far from being ready to give up yet. And as Sami Jo's husband, John, and his fellow bluegrass players set up a makeshift stage where their band could perform, Ian made his way back over to the lawn chair where Amanda still sat.

"Got a minute?" he asked.

She looked up at him, her expression slightly apprehensive. "Sure." She took the hand he offered and rose from the chair. He led her from the backyard, up a footpath that came out on a level area where he'd thought to one day make a garden. Earlier, Ian had laid a blanket out, hoping to spend some time alone with Amanda, cuddling and listening to the music. He'd also made a little something for her in the shop earlier that day, and had left it by the blanket. He now coaxed her to sit with him, relishing the moment.

"I was thinking of you today," he said.

"You were?"

"Uh-huh. That's why I put the blanket here. I thought it might give us a chance to be alone while John and his Bluegrass Boys keep everyone distracted." He gave her a teasing smile, and to his satisfaction, she returned it. Though not without some amount of reservation.

"Don't you suppose being alone might lead to trouble?" she quipped. The tall grass surrounding the blanket kept them from view. "Besides, I shouldn't have run off and left Nikki."

Banjo and guitar music stirred the night air, as John's clear voice rang out in song.

"Nikki's a big girl," Ian said. He reached into the grass beside the blanket and pulled out the present he'd made. "Here." He'd wrapped it in plain white freezer paper.

"For me?" Her lips curved, and she tore open the wrapping and laughed. "It's Skippy." He'd welded the twelve-inch-high squirrel out of scrap iron.

"Yep. I got the idea from that 'tacky' goat in your granny's yard." His lips quivered as he suppressed a grin.

Amanda turned three shades of red. "Oh my gosh— you made that for her?"

"I did."

"I'm so embarrassed."

"Don't be." Now he laughed. "It is sort of tacky. But your granny sure liked it."

They sat together for a moment in a somewhat awkward silence, Amanda cradling the iron squirrel on her lap. He could feel her tension, and decided he might as well clear the air.

"Amanda, I've sort of noticed you've been giving me a bit of a cold shoulder lately, and I'm pretty sure I know why." She started to protest, but he raised a hand. "Hear me out, please." He took a breath. "I want you to know how I feel about you. But I don't want you to say anything—just listen, okay?"

She nodded. "Okay."

But her mouth thinned into a line, and she looked as dejected as a wet kitten. He felt like a heel, but he had to tell her. Otherwise, she might push him away forever. "I love you, Amanda. And I meant what I said about not giving up on us. Any fool can see you're doing your best to put some distance between us, and I'm here to tell you, that's not going to work. Hell, I'd thought about doing the same thing at one time, but I can't stay away from you. And if you think I'm going to be tricked into being around you less and less, until my feelings sort of slip back into some kind of casual thing like we had in the beginning, you're wrong.''

She opened her mouth, and he held up a warning finger. ''Uh-uh.''

Glaring, she clamped her mouth shut.

He nearly smiled. He'd never seen her mad, but the expression on her face gave him an idea of how cute and fiery she must look when her dander was up. ''I'm not going to pressure you, but I also don't aim to settle for anything less than what I want. For me, there's no halfway—it's all or nothin'. Now, I've said my piece, and you know how I feel. What you do with it is up to you.''

''That's it?'' Puzzled, she stared at him.

''Yep.''

''You're giving me an ultimatum?''

''Not at all. There's no penalty involved here, Amanda. Either you love me enough to be with me, or you don't. I'll wait for your decision, but I'm not going to keep seeing you on a casual basis, stringing things along. That is what you were planning to do, wasn't it?''

''Did Nikki talk to you?''

He laughed without humor. ''No. But I'm glad to see I read you right.''

His heart leaped with panic as she gave him a look of genuine annoyance. Maybe he'd pushed her too far. But it was too late to backpedal.

''I still see that as an ultimatum. Either I fall into

your arms, spouting words of love, or I stay away from you completely.''

''No.'' He shook his head. ''You can be around me all you want—at Shade Tree. Or here, at my place. But if you come to me, Amanda, I'm going to assume it's with your heart in your hand, same way I'm facing you now. I won't come to you anymore. I won't pressure you in any way.'' He loved her too much to do that, to make her uncomfortable. The way he saw it, this was an easy out if she chose to take it. And though his heart was breaking at that thought, getting things out in the open beat the hell out of slowly peeling the bandage away from his emotional wounds.

He had only himself to blame. Amanda had been up-front about her feelings from day one, and he knew what he was doing right now therefore wasn't fair. But he couldn't help it. He was desperate. Desperate and in love, and he needed to either have her in his life completely, or let her walk away. There was no sense in chasing after her like a lovesick fool.

''I appreciate your honesty,'' she said. ''Are you sure you want me to stay for the fireworks?'' A note of pain laced her voice.

He hadn't set out to hurt her, and Ian very nearly weakened and took her into his arms. A part of him longed to grovel at her feet, like a grateful puppy, accepting any tidbit of affection she cared to give. But if he did that, he'd never get over her if she didn't love him back. And too much time had already passed in his life—time spent alone—for him to let that happen. Being around Gavin had awakened him to harsh reality. It was time for him to get married and have the kids he'd always wanted.

He could not be with a woman who didn't want a family.

He had no idea how he'd cope if Amanda chose to turn her back on him, but he'd have to find a way. Somehow.

"Of course I want you to stay," he said, softly. Unable to resist, he reached out and rubbed a silky lock of her hair between his thumb and forefinger, remembering the way it had spilled against the pillows when he'd made love to her. "I wish you'd stay forever."

Amanda held his gaze, her bottom lip tucked beneath her teeth, as though fighting back words she needed to say. Her eyes glistened, and he wasn't sure if it was with tears or with some other emotion. Maybe even anger. But her touch was gentle when she reached out and closed her hand over his wrist. She held on to him for a moment, then carefully disengaged his fingers from her hair and stood.

"Maybe it would be better if we listen to the music with the rest of your family." Still clutching the squirrel he'd given her, she turned and walked back down the path toward the yard.

Leaving him to feel exactly like the man in the song George Clooney had made famous.

The song his cousin John now crooned into the microphone, the words spilling through the air, out into the woods beyond.

Without Amanda, he would indeed be in constant sorrow.

ON THE DRIVE HOME, Amanda kept telling herself things had worked out for the best. Ian had given her a far easier out than she'd ever hoped for. She'd wanted him to go find happiness elsewhere, and now he could. But what if she was carrying his baby? What then?

"You're awfully quiet." Nikki spoke from the passenger seat. "Are you still feeling sick?"

"A little," Amanda lied. She was sick all right—heartsick. How had she managed to make such a mess of things?

"Want to talk about it?" Nikki watched her knowingly.

She sighed. "There's nothing to talk about."

"I noticed you slipped away with Ian, but you weren't gone long. And why did you not sit with him during the fireworks?"

How could she tell her sister that fireworks of her own were already going off inside her mind, inside her heart? What could have been more romantic than watching fireworks with the man of your dreams? But her dreams were shattered, knowing she couldn't have a future with Ian. She had no right to love him, feeling the way she did. Still harboring the pain from the accident that continued to rule her life.

"What's wrong with me wanting to watch fireworks with my sister and my friend?"

"Nothing," Nikki said. "Except when the alternative is to watch them with a man who makes any bad-boy movie star you care to name look like chopped liver."

"Ian's not a bad boy."

"No, he's certainly not." Nikki quirked her mouth in a way that reminded Amanda of Granny. She'd always gotten that same expression on her face when she meant to give her girls a lecture. "He's sweet and kind and thoughtful." She glanced pointedly at the image of Skippy sitting on the console between them. "And I'd like to know what in the world is wrong with you, sis? You're not stupid, so the only other explanation I can find is that this is a form of self-punishment."

Amanda took her eyes off the road long enough to glare at her sister. "Nikki, please don't start in on that again. You don't know what all is going on."

"No, I don't. And it's admittedly none of my business. But I love you, Amanda." Nikki reached over and touched her. "I want to see you happy. It's so hard for me, having you fifteen hundred long, hard miles away." With a gesture of exasperation, she let her hand fall to her lap. "It would be nice if I could at least know you'd finally found a good man."

"So my life isn't complete without a man, is that it?" Amanda knew she was being unreasonable, but her feelings for Ian had her frightened enough to become defensive against a truth she wanted to deny.

"You know that's not what I mean." Nikki's voice softened. "Any fool can see you're crazy for the guy. So why don't you let him know?"

A hot, gravelly sensation clogged the back of Amanda's throat. She had loved Ian all right—right into his bed. Right into a situation she wasn't ready for, one that she could not talk about with Nikki. Not yet, until she knew for sure.

"I can't, hon. Now can we please leave it at that?" She could tell she'd hurt Nikki, and it made her feel like dirt. Never in a million years would she want to cause her sister further pain. That they'd always shared their deepest, most personal feelings had to leave Nikki wondering why Amanda was clamming up on her, especially in light of the fact that she was leaving to go back to Colorado tomorrow morning.

"Nikki."

"What?"

"When I'm ready to talk about this, you know you'll be the first person I call, don't you?" From the corner of her eye, she saw Nikki smile. But her heart wasn't in it.

"I'd better be. If I have to find out anything secondhand through Sami Jo, I'll come back here and kick your butt."

They laughed, and Amanda felt somewhat better.

But only for a while. She stayed up late that night with Nikki, and they popped corn and reminisced once more about old times, but avoided any talk of the future. Nikki seemed no more willing to go into detail about her problems with Cody than Amanda was to spill her guts about all that had happened between her and Ian.

Funny, how each of them sought to protect the other; Nikki thinking Amanda would blame herself for her near breakup with Cody, Amanda worried that Nikki might feel empty and lost if she found out Amanda might be pregnant. One way or the other, she planned to find out, as soon as Nikki left. Knowing how quickly gossip flared in a small town, she'd driven to Kentucky the other day on her lunch break and purchased a home pregnancy test, which she'd hidden, first in her purse, and then in her room. She prayed it would prove her suspicions were wrong, her symptoms were caused by something else. Maybe it *was* the flu, and her cycle was messed up due to stress.

Amanda clung to such thin threads of reasoning.

God forgive her, she could not bear the thought of being responsible for another precious life. And she could not imagine how she would cope if the test came up positive.

"YOU DRIVE CAREFUL, you hear?" Clad in her bathrobe and nightgown, Amanda set Nikki's suitcase in the trunk and closed the lid. She'd gotten up extra early to be with Nikki before she left, and hadn't wanted to waste even the few minutes it would take to shower. Instead, she'd cooked Nikki a big breakfast while her sister showered, dressed, and packed her last-minute items. She herself hadn't eaten more than a few bites of fruit and toast, and had blamed her lack of appetite on feeling down over Nikki's departure. "And call me when you get to Nashville." Nikki had opted to take the route home that would lead her through the country music capital, and allow her to stop and see the sights before continuing on.

"You sound like Cody." Nikki chuckled, then gave Amanda a sad look and held her arms out.

Amanda pulled her sister into a hug, prolonging the moment, not wanting to let go. "I'm going to miss you so much," she said.

"Well, you know the way home if the wind blows you out of Tennessee," Nikki said, holding her at arm's length. Then she grew serious. "Amanda, please give Ian a chance. Promise?"

Guilt had her stomach roiling, threatening to dislodge what little food she'd consumed a short time ago. "You do the same with Cody," she said, avoiding a direct answer.

Nikki gave her a look that said she knew Amanda wasn't being straight with her. "I really love Cody." Nikki pursed her lips. "All I can hope is that our marriage is strong enough to get us through this rough patch."

And if it wasn't, Amanda would always feel she was to blame. No matter what had happened prior to the pregnancy to put a strain on Nikki and Cody's relationship, losing their precious daughter had been the final blow. "It will be," she said, hoping with all her might her words would prove to be true. "So long, sweetie."

"See you later, mashed po-tater."

"After a while, Gomer Pyle."

The childhood refrain left Amanda trying not to cry, as she watched Nikki pull away and head down the road. She missed her already.

Taking a deep breath, she clenched her fists at her side. Might as well not put it off any longer. In the bathroom, she slipped out of her robe, opened the pregnancy test, and reread the instructions, even though she knew exactly what to do...what to look for. She was stalling, still clinging to one last thread of hope.

A short time later, she looked down at the wand, and her heart sank. The little blue line said it all. She was pregnant.

Pregnant and in love with Ian, and oh so scared and confused.

"No," she whispered. "Please, God, no." With a sob, she tossed the test wand into the trash can, stuffing it in the very bottom as though to erase the truth behind its results. Turning, she reached for the faucets on the tub and started the water for a shower.

A baby! Inside her womb, where sweet little Anna had once been, she carried another innocent child. A precious little life that would depend on her for nourishment and growth. A complete human being, with a heart and a mind and the need for love and guidance and protection.

Her doctor had reassured her she'd be able to have more children, even after the damage caused by the accident. She'd been lucky. Some women weren't. Women like Nikki, who couldn't carry a baby to term. Amanda knew this baby inside of her was a blessing. A child of her own that she could rock and hold and cherish, but at what expense? How would Nikki truly feel, deep down inside, when she heard the news? How could she ever expect her sister to look into the baby's face and not see Anna? Not see what Nikki and Cody had lost, and what Amanda had, when she hadn't even tried, or planned, or hoped to have a child of her own.

Throwing off her nightgown and underwear, Amanda stepped into the tub and pulled the shower curtain closed. She couldn't stop crying. She let the water pour over her, mingling with her tears, washing across her skin, her hair, but unable to slough off the pain that wracked her body.

Dark memories overtook her. A cold winter day. Anna's funeral, held in the tiny little cemetery on top of a mountain. When it was over, Amanda had walked among the headstones, trying to understand how God could let a thing like this happen. Seeing all the little brass and stone markers of the children buried there had been so difficult. So many little ones buried in the frozen ground.

And the things people put on their children's graves...

Colorful pinwheels, spinning on the chilled wind. Birthday cards that would never be read. Teddy bears, faded by weather, wet and forlorn in the falling snow. Waiting through eternity for a child's touch that would never come.

Dear God, what if something happened to this baby, too?

"No!" Clenching her fists, Amanda tilted her head back and let a wail rise from her throat. Her heart felt as though it had been torn in two. The sound of the pounding water mingled with her cries, and she willed the hurt, the confusion, to leave and never come back.

But instead, the pain only intensified.

She sank into a heap at the bottom of the tub. Lacing her hands behind her head, she brought her elbows together, and covered her face with her arms. Emotions she'd held in check for so long now, not wanting to upset Nikki further, seeped out like sand from a cracked vase. She'd always tried to keep her tears hidden, muffling them in a pillow, even when she was alone. Worried that if she were to completely let go, there would be no one for her sister to lean on. No one for Nikki to turn to, or to care for her.

She'd cried beside the stream the night Ian had found her, and his presence had thankfully forced her to pull herself together. To not let sorrow overwhelm her. But now, as she closed her eyes and felt the water rushing over her, she allowed her sobs to escape unchecked. Relished being able to finally let go and cry it all out.

Then she wrapped her arms around her stomach, cradling the unborn baby in her womb. A baby she already wanted to protect. Already wanted to love.

Scared to death the doctor was wrong, and that she'd somehow lose this child, too.

And even more frightened at knowing this baby would cause Nikki pain. This baby, that should have been not Amanda's, but hers.

CHAPTER SEVENTEEN

IAN WHISTLED as he drove toward Amanda's. He'd promised to leave the ball in her court, to stay away unless she decided differently. But this morning when he'd went to fold up the blanket he'd forgotten about last night, he'd found her driver's license and a few dollars lying beside it. She must have tucked the items into a pocket of her shorts, or in the little fanny pack she'd worn, since he hadn't noticed her carrying a purse. At any rate, it seemed that fate had given him good reason to go see her this morning.

True, he could've taken her things to the nursing home, but then that would mean Amanda would have to drive to work without her license. Probably not a big deal, given the low level of traffic in Boone's Crossing, and the short distance between Amanda's home and work. Still, he thought she might want to have it. She might even be worried, wondering where she'd lost it.

He parked his truck beside her Honda, glad to see she hadn't left yet. He'd thought not, since it was a little early. Maybe he could talk her into going out to breakfast before she went to Shade Trade. *Careful* his warning voice scolded. He'd promised not to pressure her. But it was so dang-blasted hard not to, when he loved her so much.

"Hi, Skippy." As he walked up the porch steps, he clucked to the little squirrel who was curiously sniffing his yard-ornament image, sitting near the door. Skippy stood on his hind legs, wiggled his whiskered nose, then scampered away. Chuckling, Ian rapped on the screen. The inner door was open, and Nikki had obviously left, since her car was gone, so Amanda was definitely up and about. When no answer came, he knocked again. And when he still got no response, he began to worry.

Telling himself he was being silly, Ian pulled the screen open and leaned inside. "Amanda?" He stepped into the kitchen, feeling a little out of place. But then, he'd shared his bed and his most intimate feelings with her. Why should he hesitate to walk into her house? He called her name again as he walked toward the hallway. From the bathroom, he could hear the shower running. The door was ajar, and he shook his head in self-reprimand. He was a worrywart all right, thinking she'd fallen and hit her head or something, when she was merely taking a shower.

Abruptly, his thoughts turned in a direction he most definitely had no business taking, not after his conversation with Amanda yesterday. But like it or not, he couldn't stop the image that filled his imagination. Amanda, all beautiful, wet and naked, water streaming in rivulets over her body. Her long hair hanging loose and silky, dark from being wet. Her skin warm and scented with whatever kind of soap it was that turned him on every time he got near her.

His body began to respond to his musings, and cursing himself, Ian turned to walk away.

And felt the hairs on the back of his neck stand on

end. A loud, keening wail rose from the depths of the bathroom. An animallike sound, full of sorrow and pain. *Dear God.*

"Amanda!" He rushed to the door and pushed it open. She didn't respond, and he moved quickly to the tub and thrust the shower curtain aside. His heart leaped into his throat at the sight of her. She was curled into a fetal position in the bottom of the tub, the water sluicing over her, not in the sexy image he'd imagined, but as though she willed it to drown her.

"What's wrong? Are you hurt?" She was sick— that was it. She'd been sick at the barbecue, and obviously it was far more serious than she'd let on. Maybe it was her appendix. Panicked, Ian turned off the faucets and reached for the oversized towel on the vanity. Wrapping it around Amanda, he coaxed her to stand, taking her gently into his arms, holding her as though she might break if he weren't careful. He lifted her from the tub and set her gently on the vanity chair near the sink. "Do you need a doctor?"

Without looking at him, she shook her head, her chin touching her chest, eyes closed. When she finally opened them, a blank, haunted look had taken the place of her usual upbeat spirit, and it scared him. This went beyond any type of reservation she'd shown in the past, beyond any quiet professionalism, any sadness. She looked as if someone close to her had died, and again, panic gripped him. "Amanda, I'm going to call 911. Hang on."

"No." She clamped her hand on his sleeve, and her eyes finally focused. "What are you doing here, anyway?" Sniffing, she raked one corner of the towel across her face to wipe away her tears. Tears that came to an abrupt halt as she sat in the chair, trembling.

"Never mind that." He wrapped the towel more securely around her and knelt in front of her. "What's the matter? Tell me."

She worried her lip with her teeth, then took a breath. His own left his lungs as she spoke. "I'm pregnant."

For a heartbeat, he stared at her, dumbstruck. Then joy rose within him, only to quickly fall, at seeing Amanda so unhappy over the news. "What?" Maybe, somehow, he'd misunderstood.

But there was no mistake. Still clutching his sleeve, she stared at him, her green eyes filled with dread. "I'm going to have a baby."

His thoughts moved in slow motion, comprehension belatedly dawning as his mental fog lifted. Of course she would be apprehensive, to say the least. After what she'd gone through, it was only natural for her to have a strong reaction. But was it enough to make her this upset? Ian fought the cold, hard fear that churned inside of him. It rose with a metallic taste in the back of his throat. Surely, she would never consider...

"Why were you crying?" he asked. He had to know. If she was even thinking about not having this baby... Ian blocked the thought, finding it unbearable. "My God." Gently, he held her by the shoulders and stared directly into her eyes. "I know this wasn't planned, and I swear to you, Amanda, I was careful—at least, I thought I was. Please don't cry. You've made me the happiest man on earth. Oh my God, a baby!" He wanted to whoop and shout. He was going to be a father. At last, he'd have the opportunity he had missed out on so many years ago. The chance to do things right this time, to be with his child from day one.

But Amanda's expression negated all that. She shook her head. "Ian, I can't do this again." Tears welled in her eyes, and she slumped against the back of the chair.

Fear-driven anger rose within him as he struggled to understand what she was saying. "You don't mean—" He couldn't even bring himself to say the word.

Abortion.

Over his dead body.

But before the thought could barely take root, Amanda gripped his arms and shook her head. "*No.* Heavens, no, Ian, I would never…" She let the words trail away, her eyes now dark with fury. "How could you even think that?" She shoved him away.

"Because, you said…" He felt detached from his thoughts, as if this were happening to someone else. "But you didn't mean—"

"No!"

"Well, then, what are you trying to say?" He waited, not wanting to hear what she might tell him. If she couldn't have his baby, then maybe she meant there was something wrong. Something medical. He'd never thought about any possible complications as a result of the accident that had robbed her of Nikki's baby. Fear gripped him anew.

"I don't know what I'm trying to tell you." A shudder wracked her body as Amanda took a deep breath. She looked at him, no longer angry. She looked defeated, tired. "Ian, I'm so confused."

"Come here." Gently, he eased her to her feet. "We need to talk, and you ought to put some clothes on before you catch a chill." It seemed ludicrous, that she would get chilled in the warm, steamy bathroom or the humid air of the July morning that crept through the open windows and door. But he felt the need to protect her, to do something to make her feel better. "Here." Spotting her bathrobe lying in a heap on the floor, he picked it up and replaced the damp towel with the pink robe. Amanda gathered it around herself, and moving as though on autopilot, belted it at her waist. Ian guided her down the hall to her room. She sat on the bed, and he sat beside her, waiting.

"I can't begin to tell you how privileged I felt when Nikki asked me to be her surrogate. I was thrilled to be able to help her and Cody, to see their dream of having a child of their own come true. It meant more to me than anything in the world." She stared at the wall, her eyes unfocused. "Anna belonged to Nikki and Cody biologically, but she was also a part of me, because she was growing inside of me. Inside *my* womb." Amanda wrapped her arms in a protective gesture around her middle. "She was my niece, and I knew that giving birth to her would create a special bond between the two of us, beyond what most children share with an aunt. I pictured having a baby of my own one day, and that she...he...and Anna would play together. And then, *boom.* It all ended. Just like that." Amanda shook her head, and suddenly the fact that she was no longer crying frightened Ian even more than he'd been moments ago.

He wanted to cry for her. "I know how much you

must be hurting," he said. "I hate it that you had to go through something so awful."

"It never stops." She clenched the belt of her terry-cloth robe in one hand. "It's like a weight on your chest, crushing your lungs. You feel hollow and empty, like you've somehow lost yourself, too. It's all you can do to get out of bed every morning and try to function. Try to act normal."

He put his hand on her knee, and looked into her eyes. "And on top of all that, you had to face Nikki and Cody." Lord, he wouldn't have wanted to be in her shoes.

"Yes." Amanda nodded, and a tear slid down her cheek. "Watching them suffer was even worse than the pain I'd felt. Right then and there, I made a vow I'd never go through that again. I would never carry another baby in my womb, never have to worry that something might go wrong." She swiped at her cheek with one hand. "And now, here I am, pregnant."

Ian cupped her face gently in his hands. "But you're not alone this time," he said. "You had no one to lean on when you lost Nikki's baby, did you?" He didn't wait for an answer. "You were so busy worrying over how your sister and your brother-in-law felt, that you didn't take time to worry about yourself. I imagine they fell apart, and who did you have to lean on?"

Amanda looked at him, her expression shifting from confusion to abrupt realization. "You're right," she whispered. "I never thought of it that way."

"That's because you're such a giving person." He wanted to pull her into his arms and hold her, kiss her, tell her how much he loved her. "Amanda, you will never be alone again. I'll be here for you, every step of the way.'' He couldn't stop the grin that spread across his face. ''A baby! We're going to have a *baby*. We'll get married. Gavin can be my best man, and Sami Jo can be your maid of honor. Or maybe Nikki can come back. I know she'll be happy for us—you've got to believe that. Wait until Papaw hears the news. Why he'll—''

''Ian!''

He clamped his mouth shut and blinked. Amanda stared at him as if he'd lost his mind. Scowling, she pushed him away and stood. ''Would you please stop for a minute? I haven't even had a chance to process the fact that I'm pregnant, and here you're going on about weddings and matrons of honor.'' She shook her head, then her eyes widened as her gaze fell on the bedside clock. ''Oh, my gosh, look what time it is! I have to get to work.'' She moved toward the closet, and he stopped her by gently taking hold of her shoulders.

''Whoa, wait a minute. You're in no shape to go anywhere. Why don't you call in sick? Or let me do it for you. Where's the phone?''

She shrugged away from his grasp. ''I can't do that. My residents need me, and besides, I need to keep busy.'' The look she gave him was so forlorn, it just about killed him. ''I don't know what to think or feel right now. Things are moving way too fast.'' She clamped her hands to her head as if staving off a monstrous headache, then moved to the closet. She yanked a pair of white uniform pants and a light blue blouse off their hangers and tossed them on the bed.

''I wish you'd reconsider,'' Ian said.

Her mouth set in a firm line, she faced him. "Ian, please. I know you mean well, but I'm feeling more than a little overwhelmed right now. Can we talk later?"

But her tone said that the argument had already been settled. What on earth would he do if she didn't want to raise this baby—his *baby*—with him? What did she plan to do—give it to her sister?

Telling himself the thought was ridiculous, refusing to panic, he pressed a kiss to her forehead. "All right." He reached into his pocket and pulled out her driver's license and money. "You dropped these in my yard." She took the items, still looking dejected. "I'll come over after you get off work." He knew he was pushing things, breaking his promise, but he didn't dare give her too much time alone to think.

He couldn't bear the notion of her making some drastic decision on her own.

AMANDA DID HER BEST to pull herself together once Ian left. But her head was spinning as she drove to the nursing home. Marriage! She couldn't believe he had even suggested it. She was sure he'd only done so as a knee-jerk reaction. Once he calmed down and thought things over, he'd realize there was no way the two of them could get married.

Why not? Amanda's inner self taunted.

It would never work. She tried to deny her own fears by telling herself Ian only thought he loved her, because she'd helped him find his son and because she now carried his child. She refused to think about how much she'd grown to care for him, and that deep down, she knew how much he cared about her, too.

Refused to acknowledge the fact that if she were to reach inside herself, she'd have to admit she loved him. What she had to focus on now was this baby, and how she was going to break the news to Nikki. Though her sister had told her to move on, to have children and be happy, she had a feeling that once the reality of her pregnancy became known, Nikki would find the situation harder to face than she'd presumed.

Amanda got busy right away once she'd reached Shade Tree, focusing on her morning duties, looking after her residents. Her stomach rebelled against the blueberry bagel she ate at her desk, and she found herself walking briskly to the rest room as usual. She passed Zeb in the hall on his way to physical therapy, and spoke a hurried greeting to him and the orderly who pushed his wheelchair. Minutes later, she made her way back to her office, wishing for the hundredth time that she'd stop thinking about Ian every time she laid eyes on Zeb. But she might as well wish for the sky to turn green.

How on earth would she be able to face Zeb once Ian told him about the baby? What would Zeb say when he learned that she and Ian had made a baby without benefit of marriage? He was such an old-fashioned gentleman. She didn't want to upset him.

Trying not to dwell on anything negative, hoping Ian wouldn't show up at the nursing home, Amanda turned her attention to her duties. Nikki called a short time later to let her know she'd arrived in Nashville. Afterward, Amanda hung up the phone, feeling more awful by the minute for not coming right out and telling Nikki about the baby. She supposed in the back of her mind, she'd hoped the pregnancy test would prove negative, that her symptoms would all be hysterical ones, and she would spare her sister the stress of a false alarm.

But now that she knew for certain, she wished she'd never let Nikki leave. Picking up the phone book, she thumbed through the listing of gynecologists. She knew home tests rarely failed, but she needed to be one hundred percent sure. If only Ian wouldn't have burst into her house this morning. She hadn't planned on blurting the news to him that way, and was embarrassed that he'd caught her in such a state—naked and crying in the shower!

After scheduling a doctor's appointment for later that week, Amanda forced herself to get busy once again.

When she spotted Zeb in the day room after lunch, she did her best to act casual. "How'd your physical therapy go this morning?"

"Right well, I expect." He grinned at her. "I'll be up out of this chair on a permanent basis in no time, chasing women down the hall."

Amanda managed a chuckle. "Guess I'd better give everyone forewarning."

"Now don't do that," Zeb said. "You'll spoil the fun." Then he leaned close and lowered his voice. "Have you told the boy yet?"

She frowned, making an effort to follow his train of thought. Knowing he often referred to Ian in such a way, she still wasn't sure what he meant. "Told him what?"

"About the baby."

Amanda froze in place.

"Close your mouth, honey, you don't want to catch

any flies.'' Zeb grinned. ''I might be old, but I'm no
fool, and I've seen enough of morning sickness to recognize the symptoms. Opal had it right bad with every
one of our young'uns.'' She started to protest, but it
was no use. ''Today's not the first time I saw you
looking green around the gills,'' Zeb said.

Amanda sighed. ''I told Ian this morning.''

He grinned again. ''So, when's the wedding?''

''Shh.'' She waved her hand at him, casting a
glance around the room, but the only people within
earshot were residents whose hearing wasn't at its
sharpest anyway. How did she tell this sweet old man
that there wasn't going to be any wedding? That she
wasn't exactly celebrating the news? Suddenly, the
knowledge that the baby she carried not only connected her to Ian, but to Zeb as well, overwhelmed
her. Zeb would be the baby's great-grandfather, just
as he was Gavin's. And while having Zeb as family
was a welcome thought, knowing that she couldn't
marry Ian purely for the sake of the pregnancy left her
feeling upset all over again.

''We're going to have to talk about this later,'' she
said. ''And in the meantime, can you please keep it a
secret?''

''Who am I gonna tell?'' He raised his eyebrows
and his shoulders in a gesture of innocence. Then he
patted her arm. ''Don't be fretting, you hear? Ian will
do right by you, or I'll tan his hide.''

Amanda gave him a weak smile, then headed back
to her office. How had things gotten so out of hand so
quickly? Sitting at her desk, she again thought of
Nikki. She couldn't tell her about the baby over the
phone. This was something they needed to talk about

in person. She'd really botched things, and somehow, she had to straighten them out. She picked up the phone and dialed the number to Nikki's cellular.

"That was fast," Nikki quipped, without so much as a hello. "I didn't expect you to check up on me for, oh, at least another five minutes."

"Very funny. Where are you?"

"I'm strolling down Music Row. I'd forgotten how awesome it is here. No wonder Mom had dreams of being a country star. You should've come with me."

"You know, that's not a bad idea," Amanda said, grasping the easy opening. "How about I join you when I get off work?"

Nikki laughed. "Missing me already, huh?"

Amanda swallowed over the lump in her throat. "You'd better believe it."

"You know, I was thinking about getting a motel room anyway," Nikki said. "That way I can take my time seeing the sights, and head on out again tomorrow. I'll call you when I check in and let you know where to meet me."

"Sounds like a plan." Amanda hung up, feeling both relief and nervous anticipation. A part of her also still worried about Nikki's failing marriage. She knew her sister well enough to easily see that Nikki's side trip to Nashville and impulsive decision to spend yet another night away from home was simply a means to further delay facing Cody.

And now, she was about to deliver news that might cause the situation to plummet further downhill. With a sigh, Amanda moved away from her desk, both dreading and looking forward to getting it all over with.

BEFORE HER SHIFT ENDED, Amanda made arrangements with the Director of Nursing to take the next day off. Nashville was a good three-and-a-half-hour drive from Boone's Crossing, and she didn't want her time with Nikki to be rushed. She would work Wednesday instead, and go to her doctor's appointment on Thursday during her lunch break. As she prepared to leave for home, she looked out over the day room and did a double take. Zeb sat once more at his usual place in the corner, his chessboard set up on the card table. And sitting across from him as his opponent, was Lily.

For the first time that day, Amanda's spirits lifted. Smiling, she walked toward them. "Do my eyes deceive me, or have you finally found a chess partner, Zeb?"

The old man gave her a crooked grin, dentures in place. "I reckon Lily's a worthy adversary." Unobtrusively, he tossed Amanda a wink.

"You'd better know it." Lily cackled, moving a piece on the board before throwing her hands up in a triumphant gesture. "Checkmate!"

"I'll be hornswoggled!" Zeb raised his own arms in a gesture of surrender, then cast Amanda a sly look.

What a guy. She gave his arm an affectionate pat. "You've met your match, Zeb." She turned to Lily. The poor little woman had had a tough time kicking the flu that had plagued her. "I'm so glad you're feeling better, hon. You two have fun, and I'll see you tomorrow."

At home, Amanda quickly changed clothes, wondering all the while if Ian was about to pull up in her driveway. She couldn't avoid him forever, but for the

moment, she had no choice. She couldn't begin to resolve anything with Ian until she talked to Nikki. Yet
she couldn't just leave him hanging either. He'd said
he planned to stop by this evening.

With decisiveness, she reached for the phone and
dialed Bonner Welding.

IAN GLANCED at the clock, and with a sigh, laid his
hood on top of the welder. He usually tried to keep
the shop open during regular business hours. Often, he
stayed much later than that, taking pride in keeping
his customers happy with dependability and top service. But today he was antsy, unable to think of anything but Amanda and their baby.

Their baby. He wanted to shout it from the rooftop,
and sweep Amanda off her feet to the nearest church.
He wanted to help her pick out little booties, and spoil
her with ice cream and pickles. He could not believe
that his dreams of having a child with the woman he
loved had come true.

But Amanda's reaction to the news threatened to
shatter that dream. He understood her pain—at least
he'd thought he did—and wanted nothing more than
to find a way to help her set the past aside and focus
on what they could have together as a family.

While he loved Gavin with all his heart, he'd never
truly loved Jolene. Their brief relationship had been
nothing more than teenage infatuation, and sadly
enough, they'd put an innocent child in the middle of
it all. Knowing Gavin had a good life made him feel
better now, but before finding his son, he'd punished
himself a thousand times over for the irresponsibility
he and Jolene had demonstrated.

The same way Amanda punished herself for the loss of her sister's baby. On that level, he could see where she was coming from. But how to get past it? Could *he* honestly say he'd truly gotten over his own loss, at having missed out on his son's childhood?

Finding Gavin had led Ian to believe he'd quieted the demons that had plagued him for sixteen years. But had he really? Was he truly happy about the baby Amanda now carried, or was he simply trying to replace the son he'd lost?

The ringing phone startled him from his musings, and he moved to answer it. His spirits were immediately lifted by the sound of Amanda's voice.

"Hi, Ian," she said.

"Amanda. I was just thinking about you." The words tumbled out in a rush. "Are you okay?" Lord, she'd scared him that morning, crying like her world had ended.

"I'm fine." Then she sighed. "Actually, I'm not fine. Ian, I know we need to talk, but there's something I have to take care of first. I can't even think clearly until I talk to Nikki. I have to tell her about the baby, and I can't do it over the phone."

Fear gripped him. Was she planning to return to Colorado?

"Okay. So, what are you saying?"

"I'm meeting her in Nashville. I don't know how long this will take. I'm not even sure what I'm feeling right now, or where everything is headed." Her voice dropped. "Maybe it was a mistake to leave Colorado, so soon after...after losing Anna. Sometimes, I get so homesick I can hardly stand it. I just don't know what to think anymore."

A lead weight settled in his chest, and panic gripped him and wouldn't let go. "Amanda, please don't do anything drastic. I—we need a chance to work things out."

"I know," she said, her voice barely more than a whisper. She cleared her throat, as though trying to get a grip on her emotions. "I'll call you when I get home."

"All right. Just promise me you'll take care of yourself—that you'll be careful." Now it was his turn to be haunted by her accident. That she would even have the courage to get behind the wheel of a car said a lot for her spirit and determination. He only hoped that same strength would come through for her now.

"I will. See you later."

Ian hung up the phone, feeling somewhat comforted by the fact that she wasn't going to Colorado—at least not now. But what if she changed her mind? What if Amanda decided the only way to make things right with Nikki was to go home? To raise her child close to her sister, where they could nurture the baby—his baby—together and watch the child grow. Where Nikki could at least gain some comfort in being an aunt, if not a mother.

Somehow, some way, he was going to have to convince Amanda that her place was here, with him, in Tennessee. He could not bear the thought of losing her or his baby.

He'd already lost one child. He'd be damned if he'd stand still and lose another.

CHAPTER EIGHTEEN

AMANDA DROVE HOMEWARD from Nashville Tuesday morning, a thousand thoughts running through her mind, a million emotions racing through her like a shot of adrenaline. This time, her farewell to Nikki had been easier. Probably because she felt like she'd finally made peace with her sister, and maybe even with herself.

Focused on the road, she let her mind wander back over their conversation of the night before. She'd met Nikki in the lobby of her hotel, and they'd taken a walk through the hotel's atrium where a small pond stood centered among raised rock and flower beds. A pair of black swans, elegantly beautiful in their plumage, glided across the surface of the lily-pad-filled water. A handful of people dotted the area, and Amanda wished for someplace more private to talk to Nikki. She was about to suggest they go on up to Nikki's room when her sister's soft laugh caught her attention.

Amanda turned to find Nikki focused on a little girl, who looked about two years old. Chubby cheeked, with huge blue eyes and strawberry-blond curls, the child tugged on her mother's hand, eager to move closer to the pond's edge. Excitedly, she pointed at the graceful swans. "Guckies, Momma." Her grin revealed a row of little teeth, white and perfect, and her tiny nose wrinkled in delight. "Oh, pretty guckies." She let go of her mother's hand and crouched, knees bent, to clap with delight as she shrieked and giggled over the swans. She wore a darling outfit of white shorts, sandals and a sunshine-yellow top, with a heart emblem on the front, and "I love Grandma" was printed inside.

Nikki's eyes sparkled as she looked at the little girl, and Amanda's heart skipped a beat. She saw longing in her sister's gaze, but she saw something else as well. Joy. Pleasure.

Nikki turned to face her. "Isn't she just too cute for words?" Chuckling, she glanced at the curly-haired toddler once more. "I love watching kids. They have a way of making a person see things on their level— from their perspective." She shrugged. "I guess that's why I enjoy teaching my kindergartners so much." She hooked her elbow through Amanda's. "Let's get some pellets and feed the 'guckies.'"

They'd put quarters in the dispensers next to the pond, and spent a good hour in the atrium, feeding the swans and a pair of mallard ducks that had joined the foray. Amanda's mind had drifted back to the evening she'd gone to the park with Ian, and seen the couple with three kids there, feeding the ducks. She longed to share such a moment with him, with their child.

Nikki ended up sharing her pellets with the strawberry-haired toddler and her mother, laughing with delight at the little girl's enthusiasm as she fed the ducks and swans.

Even so, Amanda's nerves were on edge when they later made their way up to Nikki's room. Not even the long drive to Nashville had helped her prepare for what she was about to say.

Perched on the edge of one of two double beds, she'd laced her hands together in her lap and faced Nikki, who sat across from her on the other bed. "Nikki, there's something I need to tell you. Something I should've told you before you left, but I was afraid to. I didn't want to upset you, and I—"

"You're pregnant, aren't you?" Nikki's gaze held hers, and Amanda tried to read the feelings behind it. She might've known she couldn't fool her sister. Amanda had simply nodded, unable to find a way to express the mixture of guilt, happiness and confusion that bounced around inside her.

"Oh, sweetie." Nikki put one hand to her mouth, and her fingers trembled. "I knew it. You were so queasy...not like the flu...I just knew it."

For one heart-stopping moment, Amanda thought Nikki was going to cry, and her gut wrenched.

"A baby. Oh, my God." Nikki pressed her palms together in front of her mouth, thumbs tucked under her chin. Behind them, a smile began to spread across her face, and tears of joy streamed down her cheeks. Shaking, she stared wide-eyed, at Amanda. "Oh, sis...oh. I am *so* happy for you. So very, very happy. Come here." She gestured, then held her arms out.

Amanda moved to sit on the bed beside her, and Nikki pulled her into a hug. With her head resting on her sister's shoulder, Amanda felt numb, still not quite able to absorb what Nikki was feeling. "Are you okay, sis?" she asked, drawing back to look into her eyes.

A little sob wracked Nikki's body. "How could you even think your news would upset me? That I would

not be happy for you?'' She clasped Amanda's wrists
with both hands, the movement emphasizing her
words. "I will never stop grieving for Anna. But I will
eventually heal enough…'' She bit her lip and looked
up at the ceiling. ''…Damn it, I will…somehow heal
enough, to learn to live with losing my little girl.''
Once more, her eyes found Amanda's. ''And I want
you to reach inside yourself and find a way to live
with it, too. I have my kids—my kindergartners—and
that's enough. I've made peace with that, and I want
you to make peace with it.'' Nikki gave her a tiny
shake. ''I told you to stop punishing yourself. You're
thinking you don't deserve a child of your own, aren't
you?''

Tears squeezed from Amanda's eyes and ran down
her cheeks. Dear God, that was exactly how she'd felt.
She nodded. ''How can I think otherwise? Nikki, I'm
so scared.''

Nikki held her tight. ''I know. But I'm here for you.
Nothing's going to happen to this baby. Nothing is
going to go wrong this time, so stop thinking negative
thoughts. Forgive yourself. What happened to Anna
was an accident, and it was horrible and so *damned*
unfair. But it *was not your fault.*'' She spoke each
word with emphasis, then pursed her lips in a sad little
smile. ''I meant it when I told you to have babies and
be happy. Ian is a prize. Don't let him get away.''

The words now echoed in Amanda's mind as she
approached Knoxville and exited onto the four-lane
highway that would take her home to Boone's
Crossing. Maybe she hadn't really been listening before when Nikki told her to move on, to be happy.
But she was listening now. Anna's life had been both

precious and fleeting. Yet it hadn't been without meaning. The suffering Amanda had been through had led her here to Tennessee, and to Ian.

Nikki's courage in giving Amanda her blessing broke her heart. But it also gave her strength. Nikki had managed to scale the walls of the emotional prison that had bound her, to rise from the pain that had held her locked in its grips. Amanda knew all too well how it felt to be in such a prison, and now she wanted to know what it would be like to break away.

Losing the baby had hurt, but watching Nikki suffer had hurt worse. Amanda had gone through her own emotional pain and fears, true enough, but she'd suffered more on behalf of her sister. She loved Nikki so much, that she'd ached inside for her when Anna had died. She would have gladly endured any amount of physical pain, if only it would've brought Nikki's little girl back. To have Anna safe, to see Nikki experience the joy she so deserved in being a mother, was all Amanda had wanted, all she'd cared about.

She'd understood all that—but what she hadn't understood was that Nikki was hurting for *her*. For Amanda to continue to cling to her sorrow, her fears, would only multiply her sister's pain.

Here she'd been afraid to let go and live life the way she'd always wanted—with hopes and dreams of motherhood, and marriage to a man she loved. Afraid that nothing in her life would ever be right again; that anything she did in the way of pursuing a normal life would only blacken the darkness that engulfed Nikki.

Now she saw things in a whole new light.

When Nikki had given Amanda her blessing…to go on with her life—to be happy with Ian and raise her child with love and joy—Nikki had given her the greatest gift of all. The gift of unselfish, unconditional love.

Their roles had been reversed.

The bond between sisters was strong. But the powerful love she'd come to share with Ian was the bond she'd been seeking all along. She'd let her fears stand in the way of that. But now, Amanda wanted more than anything to finally let go of the past, and love Ian the way he deserved to be loved.

She was partway between Knoxville and Boone's Crossing in an area where the four-lane highway narrowed to two lanes, when steam began to rise from beneath the hood of her car. Simultaneously, she noticed the sweet odor of antifreeze. Cursing, Amanda slowed.

And as she tapped the brake, the night of the accident came flashing through her mind. Oncoming cars whizzed past on her left, and she began to shake. Her breath caught in her throat, and the positive thoughts she'd experienced only moments ago fled. The thought of pulling onto the shoulder of the road had her palms turning ice-cold—had her gripping the steering wheel until her knuckles turned white. Her jaw muscles ached as, unconsciously, she clenched her teeth.

She couldn't bring herself to pull over.

But now her radiator was spewing steam, and if she kept driving, her engine would seize up. She'd be stuck in the middle of the highway.

Trembling all over, Amanda pulled the Honda to the side of the road, glancing in her rearview mirror. Praying that no car would suddenly hurl around the bend in the road and slam into her. That no crazy drunk driver would weave off the pavement and make history repeat itself in a nightmare she could not bear to even think about.

Stop it! She scolded herself even as sweat beaded her forehead—gathered at her temples and slid down her face.

Making sure she had the Honda as far off to the side as she could get without going into the ditch to the right of it, Amanda turned off the ignition and, using the utmost caution, slid over to the passenger seat. From there, she opened the door and got out, telling herself she was a safe distance from the minimal amount of passing traffic. But her mind would not turn loose of the memory of Caitlin Kramer, standing on the roadside one minute, nearly dead the next.

Please, God, she prayed, as she reached for the hood latch on the car. *Please give me strength. And protect my baby.*

IAN DROVE to the bakery and ordered two oversized cinnamon rolls, dripping with icing. He took them, along with Zeb's freshly washed quilt, to Shade Tree Manor, expecting to find him just waking up. To his surprise, Papaw sat in his wheelchair, already bathed and dressed, the spicy scent of his cologne drifting across the room.

"You're up bright and early," Ian commented, setting the box of cinnamon rolls on the nightstand. He sniffed the air with exaggeration. "And what's that smelly stuff? Heck, you're liable to curdle the frosting on these rolls, Papaw."

"Oh, go on, boy." Zeb waved one hand. "You're

just jealous 'cause you ain't got my magic touch with the ladies.'' He rubbed his hands together.

"Now that, you might be right about.'' Ian sobered as he laid Zeb's quilt on the foot of the bed. "Actually, that's sort of what I came over here for. I need to talk to you about something.'' He took a deep breath. "I guess it's no secret the way I feel about Amanda.'' He met his grandpa's gaze. "I want to marry her, Papaw.''

Zeb nodded. "I reckon it's the right thing to do under the circumstances.''

Ian raised his brows. "You know?''

"About the baby? 'Course, I do. And I'm happy to see you plan to do things right this time around.''

"But that's just it.'' Ian sat on the edge of the bed. "I can't stop thinking about my past, and the mistakes I made. Even though I was young, it still bothers me.''

"You weren't no younger than I was when I set my sights on your grandma,'' Zeb reminded.

"I know, Papaw, but things were done different back in those days. Folks were expected to get married young and have a whole mess of babies. That wasn't what I wanted with Jolene, so I went and gave Gavin away to strangers, and now that I know him…well, I wish I would've done things differently.''

"You would've married Jolene?''

"No!'' The thought made him shudder, and his heart reminded him that he'd only given it to one woman. Amanda. "But I wish I hadn't given up my son. Like I said, knowing him really makes me regret that I didn't raise him.''

"And now you've gone and gotten Amanda in the

family way." Zeb's blue eyes studied him intently. "Don't you want to raise your baby with her?"

"Of course I do, Papaw. But I want to marry her because I love her, not because she's pregnant." He shook his head. "Still, I keep asking myself, would I have proposed to her this soon if it weren't for the baby?" He sighed. "I'm afraid that deep down, I might be rushing into things because I'm so afraid of losing another child. That I might be trying to replace Gavin with my and Amanda's baby. Do you think I am, Papaw? Do you think that's what I'm doing?"

"Only you can answer that question, son." Zeb gestured toward Ian as if his mind had suddenly switched tracks. "I see you brought me my quilt."

"Yeah." Ian frowned and picked up the quilt. It wasn't like Papaw to switch subjects so quickly, or to cut him off mid-discussion. Maybe his grandpa was disappointed in him for doing the same thing as an adult that he'd done as a boy—getting a woman he wasn't married to pregnant. Maybe Papaw thought he was doomed to keep making mistakes.

But Amanda wasn't a mistake, and neither was their baby. And of course Papaw knew that. Ian partially unfolded the quilt and started to lay it across Zeb's lap, still feeling sullen over the way the old man had cut him short.

"Hang on a minute." Zeb waved him away. "You know your Mamaw made that, don't you?"

"Of course." The handcrafted quilt had been around for as long as Ian could remember, its sturdy quality withstanding the test of time. "I know it's something special."

"You bet it is, and I've kept it because it means

something to me," Zeb went on. "But now I think it's time for the quilt to mean something to you."

Maybe Papaw wasn't suddenly shifting subjects.

Ian knew the quilt had been used to cover more than one grandbaby. He looked straight into his grandpa's eyes, and Zeb nodded. "It's been a long while since that quilt swaddled a baby. Go on and take it, son. I know you love Amanda. Give it to her, for your little one."

Ian swallowed. "Are you sure?" He knew how much the quilt really did mean to Zeb. It was one of the few things he had left of Opal's.

"Sure, I'm sure." Papaw gave him a wink. "I'm about rid of this here wheelchair anyway. The only lap warmer I'm gonna need is a good-looking woman."

"You feisty old codger." Ian laughed as he refolded the quilt, then tucked it under his arm. He only hoped he had half the spirit Papaw did when he got to be his age. "Hand me one of those cinnamon rolls before I go."

"If you don't mind," Zeb said, handing over the box, "I'm gonna save mine for Lily."

Ian cracked another grin, and suddenly he had no doubts as to what to say to Amanda. He handed the box back to Zeb. "You go on and take both the rolls, then." He gave his grandpa a hug. "I've got work to do anyway." He'd have to weld nonstop today, in order to keep busy enough to pass the time until Amanda got home.

"Let me know when you set a wedding date," Zeb said.

"Don't worry, Papaw. You'll be the first to know."

AMANDA RAISED THE HOOD on the Honda, telling her-self to stay calm. She had her cell phone, and she could always call for help. She ignored the little voice inside her mind that said to call Ian. This was some-thing she needed to get through on her own. Some-thing she had to do for herself, if she were ever going to face her fears.

She looked down at the radiator, then underneath the car. Antifreeze hissed and pooled beneath, but it didn't seem to be coming from the radiator itself. There was no crack in it that she could see. Then she spotted the culprit. A hose clamp had come loose, and the sweet-smelling green liquid oozed from between it and the radiator. She let out her breath. Something easy. Something she could fix on her own, but not until the car cooled down a little.

Leaving the hood open, Amanda walked away from the Honda, away from the shoulder of the road where several cars whizzed by. A pickup truck slowed, and the man inside rolled down the window and asked her if she needed some help. With a polite smile, Amanda shook her head and waved him away. "Thank you, anyway," she said. Up ahead, she spotted a little white building in a gravel parking lot. A sign in front of it read, Best Doughnuts Sold Here.

She laughed and thought of Zeb. She'd order a dozen, and take them to him. Right now, the little doughnut shop looked like heaven. All she wanted was a quiet place to sit and wait for her engine to cool.

Some time later, Amanda returned to the Honda. She put the box of doughnuts she'd purchased on the passenger seat, then rummaged inside the trunk for a screwdriver. Returning to the front of the car, she loosened the hose clamp farther, pushed the hose up flush against the radiator, then retightened the clamp, making sure it was secure. Then she retrieved a plastic container of a mixture of antifreeze and water from her trunk, and filled the radiator. When she was finished, she closed the trunk and the hood, and wiped her hands on a rag, filled with a feeling of satisfaction.

Back behind the wheel of her car, Amanda started the engine. No steam rose from beneath the hood, and the temperature gauge read fine. She wrapped both arms around her middle, thanking God for the child that lay curled inside of her, vowing to do everything in her power to be the best mother she could be.

Then she carefully checked her mirror for a break in the sparse traffic, pulled onto the highway once more, and headed for home.

CHAPTER NINETEEN

FOR THE FIRST TIME in as long as he could remember, Ian did what he'd previously done only for emergencies—closed the shop early. Then again, he supposed this was an emergency. The urgency to go to Amanda had been with him all day after he'd left Shade Tree with the quilt tucked under his arm. He had no idea how long she would be in Nashville, and she'd said she would call. So he'd tried his best to focus on work and wait patiently. But his mind had clamored with all sorts of thoughts, and ways he might convince her to spend her life with him. How could he make her believe that he loved her, not just because she carried his child, but because he'd fallen in love with her, when doubts of his own plagued him?

He would just have to find a way.

Outside, he climbed into his truck and headed for her house. If she wasn't back yet, he would wait. What he needed to tell her was more important than time or work, and he would sit in her driveway for as long as it took. To his delight, her car was parked in front of the toolshed when he arrived. Ian tucked the quilt under his arm and walked up to her front door. She opened it before he could knock.

"Hi," she said. "I was just about to call you." She held the screen open for him to come in.

Suddenly nervous, he stepped inside. Amanda looked so sweet standing there in the kitchen. Her green eyes watched him intently, and she acted as if she had something to tell him.

Afraid of what it might be, he spoke first. "How's Nikki?"

"She's okay." Amanda's hand fluttered like a nervous butterfly in front of her throat. "Actually, she's doing a lot better than I'd thought."

"I'm glad to hear that." The words he'd come to say jumbled and tangled in his mind. "Amanda, I—"

"Ian, I'm—"

Together they spoke and laughed. "You go first," he said.

Her gaze fell on the patchwork quilt. "That's Zeb's quilt." Puzzled, she looked up at him. "Why do you have it?"

He brought it from beneath his arm and held it out to her. "Papaw gave it to me, to give to you. For our baby." Her gaze softened, and he nodded. "Go on. Take it."

Amanda gathered the quilt in both hands. She smiled at him, then began to unfold it. He took hold of one edge, and helped her spread it wide. She murmured in appreciation, her eyes focused on the rainbow of colored squares that made up the quilt's center. "This is gorgeous. I never realized—this is the first time I've seen it completely unfolded."

"Mamaw made it." Ian let his gaze rove over the quilt as he spoke. "She stitched every inch of it by hand. Each square is made from something that had a special meaning for her." He let go with one hand, raising the other so the quilt wouldn't drag on the floor, and pointed. "This piece came from her wedding gown. And this one was from Papaw's suit jacket that he wore for the ceremony." He went on, describing several of the pieces of material patched together in a beautiful rainbow to form a design that spread to the quilt's borders—a piece of his own baby blanket, a scrap from material that had once made up the ball gown Mamaw had worn when Papaw took her to the city on their fifth wedding anniversary.

"This is so sweet." Amanda stared at the hand-stitched quilt with awe and appreciation. "Are you sure Zeb wants to give it up?"

He stood there for a moment, holding the quilt, letting it connect him to Amanda, who still held her end. "I'm sure." He began to refold it, and she helped.

"I'm really touched by this," Amanda said. "I don't know what to say."

He, too, had been at a loss for words, but now he spoke. "Mamaw told me something, right before she died. She said, 'Ian, don't ever forget that love runs so deep it can often hurt. But the pain is worth it. That's why women keep having babies, even though we go through hell to bring 'em into this old world.'" He gave a soft laugh. "She told me that sometimes you have to go through a little hell in order to reach heaven. And I think she was right."

For the first time, he noticed that Amanda had brought the cherry-wood cradle in from the shed. She'd put it in one corner of the kitchen, where sunlight could fall on it from the window.

"When did you do that?" He gestured.

A smiled curved her lips. "Just a little while ago,

when I got home. It was something I needed to do before I called you.''

Heart pounding, knowing this had to be a good sign, Ian took the quilt from her and walked over to the cradle. He draped the quilt across it, then turned to face Amanda once more. ''Come here,'' he said softly. She moved into his arms and he held her, all the doubts, all the fears he'd had, making one last attempt to boil to the surface of his mind. He pushed them away. For as he held Amanda, he knew there was no mistaking the feelings he had for her. He loved her, and he wanted her to be his wife.

Ian pulled back enough to place his hand on the flat of her stomach. ''I still can't get over the fact that you're carrying my baby,'' he said. ''Our baby. It's such a miracle, everything I'd ever hoped for, that I had to ask myself a question. As I drove over here, I wondered if I'd fallen in love with you too fast, and if part of it was because of the baby. I was afraid I was simply trying to replace Gavin by wanting to raise this baby with you.''

''Are you?'' For a moment, she seemed to tense in his arms, but then she relaxed and looked at him in a way that said she had no doubts about his feelings for her, or hers for him.

''No way,'' he said. With newfound confidence, he looked into her eyes. ''I love you, Amanda, and I love this baby. You've gone through hell all right, and now it's your time to be happy. It's our turn to be happy. Will you marry me?'' He held his breath, having no idea what she'd talked about with her sister. Maybe he was too late. Maybe she did plan to go back to Colorado.

She looked back at him, her green eyes serious. "Before I answer your question, I have to tell you something. Ian, I had my doubts, too. I guess you know that. Here I was, falling head over heels for you, not wanting to, but unable to stop myself. I didn't think I'd ever be able to bring myself to carry another child, and because I knew how important children are to you, I thought I was doing the right thing in pushing you away. Then I got pregnant, and all sorts of crazy things were going through my mind. I was scared, and I didn't want to hurt you, but I didn't want to hurt my sister either. That's why I had to go to her, and tell her about the baby."

"What did she say?" He could barely get the question out.

"She told me to be happy," Amanda said. "She'd already told me to stop punishing myself. I guess that's exactly what I was doing. Some part of me felt that I'd caused Nikki's life to fall apart, and that I didn't deserve to be happy since she wasn't."

"Didn't I tell you?" Ian said. "That you were being way too hard on yourself?"

She nodded. "Yes, you did. Still, I couldn't see it that way at first. But after talking to Nikki, I realized I wasn't doing anyone any favors by clinging to Anna's death, and refusing to live life the way I truly wanted to live it." She smiled. "Nikki made me see that." She tightened her hold on his waist. "She told me to go to you and tell you how I feel."

"And how is that?" he asked.

Amanda pursed her lips. "I think you know that by now."

"Maybe. But I want to hear it from you."

"I love you, Ian. More than you'll ever know."

"Oh, I think I do know," he said, kissing her. Then he hugged her and growled. "You scared me half to death, though. I thought you were going to go back to Colorado."

She gave him a mock look of reprimand. "Now why would I want to do that when I've got everything I need right here in Tennessee?"

"Do you mean that?" He touched his forehead to hers.

"I do."

"Now, I like the sound of those words. Amanda Kelly, will you marry me?"

Her smile seemed to fill the room. "You know, I like the sound of that."

She filled his world. "Is that a yes?"

"You'd better believe it." She kissed him, wrapping her tongue around his, making him go all hot and shaky with desire.

He looked forward to feeling that way for a lifetime.

BANJO'S SHOD HOOVES clipped smartly against the shoulder of the road as Ian guided the buggy away from the church toward the park, where the wedding reception was to be held. Streamers of blue-and-white ribbon decorated both the buggy and the mule's tail, and a huge Just Married sign had been taped to the back of the antique vehicle, just above the strings of aluminum cans that trailed behind. Banjo didn't seem to mind the commotion, and this time, when traffic passed by and honked, Amanda had no fears. She smiled and waved, then laced her hands around her husband's elbow. The wedding ceremony had been a traditional one, right down to the four things a bride was supposed to carry.

Amanda leaned her head against Ian's shoulder. Her something new was growing inside of her, and the something blue she wore beneath her wedding gown was for Ian's eyes only. The old and borrowed had been Sami Jo's idea, and though Gavin had rolled his eyes like a typical teenager when Sami requested the ring and chain, he'd given them over willingly. Amanda had been proud to wear the ring around her neck beneath her wedding gown. After all, it had brought Ian and Gavin together. While Gavin already had a family who loved him, he had another one here in Boone's Crossing that loved him just as much, and Amanda was happy to know Ian's son would be a part of his life—their life—from here on out.

Just as Ian had once imagined, Gavin had stood by his side as best man, and Nikki had flown back for the wedding, to be Amanda's maid of honor. Patricia Stoakes and Sami Jo had been her bridesmaids, and Patricia had sewn all the dresses for the wedding party, including Amanda's gown. It was a bride's dream of white lace and satin, with a full skirt to disguise the little bulge of her tummy, and a long train that she'd laughingly had to gather with the help of Nikki and Sami Jo when Ian lifted her into the buggy.

Bridget hadn't made it to the wedding, but Amanda told herself it didn't matter. Nothing could spoil this day.

"You're mighty quiet, Mrs. Bonner." Ian's sexy drawl broke into her thoughts, and when she looked up at him, his chocolate-brown eyes were full of love. He looked delicious in his black western-cut tux.

"I'm enjoying the moment, Mr. Bonner." Amanda smiled. "I want to remember it forever."

"And I want to remember you the way you look right now," Ian said, "until I'm old and gray, and have to let Papaw push me around in his wheelchair."

She laughed and he kissed her, and Banjo took advantage and began to veer off to one side of the road, toward the temptation of a hayfield that held a late fall cutting.

"Better watch where you're driving," Amanda said. She titled her head to indicate the procession of pickup trucks and cars that followed slowly behind them. "The wedding guests will think you're drunk, and the sheriff might even arrest you."

"I am drunk," Ian said, his dimples creasing his cheeks. "On love."

"Now that, I can deal with." Amanda took the reins from him and let Banjo have his way. Hopefully the farmer who owned the hay wouldn't mind too much.

She let the hoots and hollers of the wedding procession fade to the background as the cars and trucks drove on by, headed for the park, horns honking.

She barely heard a thing. She was too busy kissing the man she'd vowed to share a lifetime with.

EPILOGUE

AMANDA LAY propped against the pillows of the hospital bed, her newborn daughter cradled in her arms. Around her, the room had been decorated with shamrocks, and green and pink balloons. Faith Nicole Bonner had made her entry into the world at six o'clock that morning—St. Patrick's Day—Zeb's eighty-eighth birthday, weighing in at seven pounds, four ounces.

Ian sat on the edge of the bed, unable to tear his gaze away from his little girl. A tiny miracle. He could hardly believe she was really here. Zeb perched on a chair near his walker, wearing new blue jeans, a flannel shirt that had been a birthday gift from Ian and Amanda and a party hat. Beside him, on a little table on wheels, stood a two-layer chocolate birthday cake with chocolate-fudge icing.

"Go on and light the candles," Zeb said, waving one hand at Sami Jo. "We've got a lot of celebrating to do here today."

Sami Jo obliged, lighting the pair of green number-eight candles that stood side by side next to a little pink one in the shape of a teddy bear. With the door to the room closed, everyone joined in, singing "Happy Birthday" to Zeb and Baby Faith.

When the off-key song came to an end, Amanda laughed and indicated the candles. "You'll have to do the honors, Zeb. I'm afraid Faith isn't quite up to blowing hers out yet.''

''No, but just wait until next year,'' Ian said with pride. ''Then you'll know what to do, won't you my little sweet'ums?'' He nuzzled his daughter's downy blond hair.

Faith responded with a huge yawn, and they all laughed. Zeb rose from his chair and leaned over to plant a kiss on his great-granddaughter's cheek. Then he cupped his hand to his mouth and spoke in a stage whisper to Amanda. ''Don't tell anyone there's rum in that cake.''

She laughed and gave him a hug. ''I won't. Happy birthday, Zeb.''

Sami Jo raised a glass of punch in toast. ''Hear, hear. To Zeb and Faith.'' A knock sounded at the door, and Sami Jo moved to open it. Amanda gasped as her mother stepped into the room. She wore jeans and boots and a western shirt, and her long hair had more gray in it than Amanda remembered.

''Is this a private celebration, or can anyone join in?'' Bridget smiled, then bit her lip. Tears welled in her eyes as she looked from Amanda to the tiny infant bundled in her arms. ''Oh.'' Her features softened and she stepped up beside the bed.

Amanda found her voice. ''Momma. I can't believe you're here.''

Bridget nodded, opening up her arms to embrace her daughter. ''I can't believe I am either, honey. I guess I've got a lot of making up to do.'' She drew back, and her eyes feasted on her granddaughter.

''We can always use more family,'' Zeb said. ''Cut the cake, Sami Jo.'' Then he grinned as Bridget lifted

Faith into her arms with the reverence of a proud grandmother. "She's a beauty, ain't she?" He gave Ian a wink. "May she be the first of many babies."

Ian slipped his arm around Amanda. "We'll do our best to work on that, Papaw."

Amanda looked at him, her eyes shining. "Now, that's a promise I think we can keep."

HARLEQUIN *Super*ROMANCE®

Single
FATHER

He's a man on his own, trying to raise his children.
Sometimes he gets things right. Sometimes he needs a little help....

Unfinished Business
by Inglath Cooper

(Superromance #1214) On-sale July 2004

Culley Rutherford is doing the best he can raising his young
daughter on his own. One night while on a medical conference in
New York City, Culley runs into his old friend Addy Taylor. After a
passionate night together, they go their separate ways, so Culley
is surprised to see Addy back in Harper's Mill. Now that she's
there, though, he's determined to show Addy that the three of
them can be a family.

Daddy's Little Matchmaker
by Roz Denny Fox

(Superromance #1220) On-sale August 2004

Alan Ridge is a widower and the father of nine-year-old Louemma,
who suffers from paralysis caused by the accident that killed her
mother. Laurel Ashline is a weaver who's come to the town of
Ridge City, Kentucky, to explore her family's history—a history
that includes a long-ago feud with the wealthy Ridges. Louemma
brings Alan and Laurel together, despite everything that keeps
them apart....

Available wherever Harlequin books are sold.

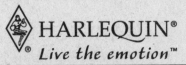

HARLEQUIN®
Live the emotion™

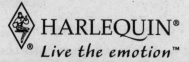

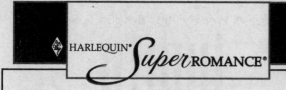

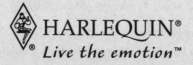